Ginny picked up our child and looked into her blank blue eyes. "Something's wrong," she said in a tight voice.

I hesitated for an instant, then stepped into the darkness where the skinturning was quick. Emerging, I went to the two female figures and drank their odors.

Then I sat on my haunches and I howled.

Ginny laid down what she had been holding. She stood motionless by the crib, looking down at it, while I skinturned again.

"That thing isn't Valerie," I heard myself say. "It isn't even human."

OPERATION CHAOS

POUL ANDERSON

A BERKLEY BOOK
published by
BERKLEY PUBLISHING CORPORATION

Parts of this novel have appeared as separate stories in *The Magazine of Fantasy and Science Fiction* as follows:

"Operation Afreet," September 1956, copyright © 1956 by Fantasy House, Inc.

"Operation Salamander," January 1957, copyright © 1956 by Fantasy House, Inc.

"Operation Incubus," October 1959, copyright © 1959 by Mercury Press, Inc.

"Operation Changeling," May-June 1969, copyright © 1969 by Mercury Press, Inc.

Doubleday Publishing Company
245 Park Avenue
New York, New York 10017

SBN 425-03750-9

*BERKLEY MEDALLION BOOKS are published by
Berkley Publishing Corporation
200 Madison Avenue
New York, N. Y. 10016*

BERKLEY MEDALLION BOOK ® TM 757,375

Printed in the United States of America

Berkley Edition, MAY, 1978

To Robert A. Heinlein—
who first incorporated magic—
and his own red-haired Virginia

OPERATION CHAOS

Hello, out there!

If you exist, hello!

We may well never find out. This is a wild experiment, test of a wilder hypothesis. But it is also a duty.

I lie dream-bound, only half-aware of my world. They are using me to call for them across the time streams because that which happened to me, so many years ago, has left its traces beneath my ordinariness; they believe a message thought by me has a better chance of finding a resonance in you than if it came from almost anyone else.

Not that the chance is good. My ordinariness quite overwhelms what little mana may still drift smokelike within. And in any case, I may well be—I probably am—radiating into nothingness.

It is only a philosophical idea, that time has more than one dimension, that any number of entire universes may coexist, some utterly alien, some whose differences from ours are perhaps too subtle to detect. . . . Why am I dreaming in this language? It isn't my normal speech. The preparations have cast me into a strange state. Damnation, I will be myself, not only myself again when I wake tomorrow but myself now and throughout the night. . . . Earths where Lee won at Gettysburg or Napoleon at Waterloo; Earths where Mithraism won over Christianity in the Roman Empire; Earths where Rome never was; Earths where another animal than man evolved toward a rational soul, or none did; Earths, whole cosmoses where the laws of nature are something else, where it is possible to do what we forever cannot, but they will never accomplish what we do with ease. . . .

Well, I am told that a little more than philosophy supports the hypothesis. There are certain indications in modern physical theory, too abstruse for me. There are anecdotes, cases of appearance or disappearance or both, which suggest that the

1

body itself can transfer between such time currents—Benjamin Bathurst, Kaspar Hauser. . . . There is what happened to me and mine, though that isn't the same thing. It is, however, the source of our duty.

You see, if parallel worlds exist, they must be linked in a very fundamental way; otherwise the hypothesis is unverifiable in principle and therefore meaningless. Deriving from the same source, embedded in the same matrix, they must in some fashion have a common destiny. Whatever manifold forms it takes, the war of Law and Chaos surely goes on in them all.

We have learned certain things. We ought to broadcast the lesson and the warning.

To you out yonder, this may appear nothing but a dream. It feels that way to me, though I recall matters which truly happened. We doubt if you—any of you whom we may reach—will be able to reply, even if willing. Otherwise we would already have gotten messages from elsewhere. But think over what you receive. Ask yourselves how you could have a simple dream that was quite like this one.

While we have no certain idea what you are like, assuming you are more than a void, we can guess. You probably do not live in worlds radically foreign to ours, or communication would be impossible. How could uncomplicated I resonate with a true alien? No, you too must be human, of technological culture at that. You too must remember Galileo, Newton, Lavoisier, Watt; the chances are that you too are an American. But we have diverged at some point. Have you had an Einstein? And if you did, what did he think about after his early papers on Brownian movement and special relativity? The questions go on without end.

You will have such questions about us, of course. So I'm going to ramble through my story. (That's hard to avoid anyway, in this drowsy twilight they've laid on me.) No doubt I'll often belabor the obvious. If you already know how electric generators work or how the First World War came out—or whatever—bear with me. Better too much information than too little. This is more than vital to you.

If you exist.

Where to begin? I suppose where the affair really began for me, during World War II, though of course the roots run much deeper and further back; the strife is older than creation. . . .

I

IT WAS SHEER bad luck, or maybe their Intelligence was better than we knew, but the last raid, breaking past our air defenses, had spattered the Weather Corps tent from here to hell. Supply problems being what they were, we couldn't get replacements for weeks, and meanwhile the enemy had control of the weather. Our only surviving Corpsman, Major Jackson, had to save what was left of his elementals to protect us against thunderbolts; so otherwise we took whatever they chose to throw at us. At the moment, it was rain.

There's nothing so discouraging as a steady week of cold rain. The ground turns liquid and runs up into your boots, which get so heavy you can barely lift them. Your uniform is a drenched rag around your shivering skin, the rations are soggy, the rifles have to have extra care, and always the rain drums down on your helmet till you hear it in dreams. You'll never forget that endless gray washing and beating; ten years later a rainstorm will make you feel depressed.

The one consolation, I thought, was that they couldn't very well attack us from the air while it went on. Doubtless they'd yank the cloud cover away when they were ready to strafe us, but our broomsticks could scramble as fast as their carpets could arrive. Meanwhile, we slogged ahead, a whole division of us with auxiliaries—the 45th, the Lightning Busters, pride of the United States Army, turned into a wet misery of men and dragons hunting through the Oregon hills for the invader.

I made a slow way through the camp. Water ran off tents and gurgled in slit trenches. Our sentries were, of course, wearing Tarnkappen, but I could see their footprints form in the mud and hear the boots squelch and the tired monotonous cursing.

I passed by the Air Force strip; they were bivouacked with us, to give support as needed. A couple of men stood on guard outside the knockdown hangar, not bothering with invisibility. Their blue uniforms were as mucked and bedraggled as my

3

OD's, but they had shaved and their insignia—the winged broomstick and the anti-Evil Eye beads—were polished. They saluted me, and I returned the gesture idly. *Esprit de corps,* wild blue yonder, nuts.

Beyond was the armor. The boys had erected portable shelters for their beasts, so I only saw steam rising out of the cracks and caught the rank reptile smell. Dragons hate rain, and their drivers were having a hell of a time controlling them.

Nearby lay Petrological Warfare, with a pen full of hooded basilisks writhing and hissing and striking out with their crowned heads at the men feeding them. Personally, I doubted the practicality of that whole corps. You have to get a basilisk quite close to a man, and looking straight at him, for petrifaction; and the aluminum-foil suit and helmet you must wear to deflect the influence of your pets is an invitation to snipers. Then, too, when human carbon is turned to silicon, you have a radioactive isotope, and maybe get such a dose of radiation yourself that the medics have to give you St. John's Wort plucked from a grave-yard in the dark of the moon.

So, in case you didn't know, cremation hasn't simply died out as a custom; it's become illegal under the National Defense Act. We have to have plenty of old-fashioned cemeteries. Thus does the age of science pare down our liberties.

I went on past the engineers, who were directing a gang of zombies carving another drainage ditch, and on to General Vanbrugh's big tent. When the guard saw my Tetragrammaton insigne, for the Intelligence Corps, and the bars on my shoulders, he saluted and let me in. I came to a halt before the desk and brought my own hand up.

"Captain Matuchek reporting, sir," I said.

Vanbrugh looked at me from beneath shaggy gray brows. He was a large man with a face like weathered rock, 103 percent Regular Army, but we liked him as well as you can like a buck general. "At ease," he said. "Sit down. This'll take a while."

I found a folding chair and lowered myself into it. Two others were already seated whom I didn't know. One was a plump man with a round red face and a fluffy white beard, a major bearing the crystal-ball emblem of the Signal Corps. The other was a young woman. In spite of my weariness, I blinked and looked twice at her. She was worth it—a tall green-eyed redhead with straight high-cheeked features and a figure too good for the WAC clothes or any other. Captain's bars, Cavalry spider . . . or Sleipnir, if you want to be official about it.

"Major Harrigan," grumfed the general. "Captain Graylock. Captain Matuchek. Let's get down to business."

He spread a map out before us. I leaned over and looked at it. Positions were indicated, ours and the enemy's. They still held the Pacific seaboard from Alaska halfway down through Oregon, though that was considerable improvement from a year ago, when the Battle of the Mississippi had turned the tide.

"Now then," said Vanbrugh, "I'll tell you the overall situation. This is a dangerous mission, you don't have to volunteer, but I want you to know how important it is."

What I knew, just then, was that I'd been told to volunteer or else. That was the Army, at least in a major war like this, and in principle I couldn't object. I'd been a reasonably contented Hollywood actor when the Saracen Caliphate attacked us. I wanted to go back to more of the same, but that meant finishing the war.

"You can see we're driving them back," said the general, "and the occupied countries are primed and cocked to revolt as soon as they get a fighting chance. The British have been organizing the underground and arming them while readying for a cross-Channel jump. The Russians are set to advance from the north. But we have to give the enemy a decisive blow, break this whole front and roll 'em up. That'll be the signal. If we succeed, the war will be over this year. Otherwise, it might drag on for another three."

I knew it. The whole Army knew it. Official word hadn't been passed yet, but somehow you feel when a big push is impending.

His stumpy finger traced along the map. "The 9th Armored Division is here, the 12th Broomborne here, the 14th Cavalry here, the Salamanders here where we know they've concentrated their fire-breathers. The Marines are ready to establish a beachhead and retake Seattle, now that the Navy's bred enough Krakens. One good goose, and we'll have 'em running."

Major Harrigan snuffled into his beard and stared gloomily at a crystal ball. It was clouded and vague; the enemy had been jamming our crystals till they were no use whatsoever, though naturally we'd retaliated. Captain Graylock tapped impatiently on the desk with a perfectly manicured nail. She was so clean and crisp and efficient, I decided I didn't like her looks after all. Not while I had three days' beard bristling from my chin.

"But apparently something's gone wrong, sir," I ventured.

"Correct, damn it," said Vanbrugh. "In Trollburg."

I nodded. The Saracens held that town: a key position, sitting as it did on U.S. Highway 20 and guarding the approach to Salem and Portland.

"I take it we're supposed to seize Trollburg, sir," I murmured.

Vanbrugh scowled. "That's the job for the 45th," he grunted. "If we muff it, the enemy can sally out against the 9th, cut them off, and throw the whole operation akilter. But now Major Harrigan and Captain Graylock come from the 14th to tell me the Trollburg garrison has an afreet."

I whistled, and a chill crawled along my spine. The Caliphate had exploited the Powers recklessly—that was one reason why the rest of the Moslem world regarded them as heretics and hated them as much as we did—but I never thought they'd go as far as breaking Solomon's seal. An afreet getting out of hand could destroy more than anybody cared to estimate.

"I hope they haven't but one," I whispered.

"No, they don't," said the Graylock woman. Her voice was low and could have been pleasant if it weren't so brisk. "They've been dredging the Red Sea in hopes of finding another Solly bottle, but this seems to be the last one left."

"Bad enough," I said. The effort to keep my tone steady helped calm me down. "How'd you find out?"

"We're with the 14th," said Graylock unnecessarily. Her Cavalry badge had surprised me, however. Normally, the only recruits the Army can dig up to ride unicorns are pickle-faced schoolteachers and the like.

"I'm simply a liaison officer," said Major Harrigan in haste. "I go by broomstick myself." I grinned at that. No American male, unless he's in holy orders, likes to admit he's qualified to control a unicorn. He saw me and flushed angrily.

Graylock went on, as if dictating. She kept her tone flat, though little else. "We had the luck to capture a bimbashi in a commando attack. I questioned him."

"They're pretty close-mouthed, those noble sons of . . . um . . . the desert," I said. I'd bent the Geneva Convention myself, occasionally, but didn't relish the idea of breaking it completely—even if the enemy had no such scruples.

"Oh, we practiced no brutality," said Graylock. "We housed him and fed him very well. But the moment a bite of food was in his throat, I'd turn it into pork. He broke pretty fast, and spilled everything he knew."

I had to laugh aloud, and Vanbrugh himself chuckled; but she sat perfectly deadpan. Organic-organic transformation, which merely shuffles molecules around without changing atoms, has no radiation hazards but naturally requires a good knowledge of chemistry. That's the real reason the average dogface hates the technical corps: pure envy of a man who can turn K rations into steak and French fries. The quartermasters have enough trouble conjuring up the rations themselves, without branching into fancy dishes.

"Okay, you learned they have an afreet in Trollburg," said the general. "What about their strength otherwise?"

"A small division, sir. You can take the place handily, if that demon can be immobilized," said Harrigan.

"Yes, I know." Vanbrugh swiveled his eyes around to me. "Well, Captain, are you game? If you can carry the stunt off, it'll mean a Silver Star at least—pardon me, a Bronze."

"Uh—" I paused, fumbling after words. I was more interested in promotion and ultimate discharge, but that might follow too. Nevertheless . . . quite apart from my own neck, there was a practical objection. "Sir, I don't know a damn thing about the job. I nearly flunked Demonology 1 in college."

"That'll be my part," said Graylock.

"You!" I picked my jaw off the floor again, but couldn't find anything else to say.

"I was head witch of the Arcane Agency in New York before the war," she said coldly. Now I knew where she got that personality: the typical big-city career girl. I can't stand them. "I know as much about handling demons as anyone on this coast. Your task will be to escort me safely to the place and back."

"Yeah," I said weakly. "Yeah, that's all."

Vanbrugh cleared his throat. He didn't like sending a woman on such a mission, but time was too short for him to have any choice. "Captain Matuchek is one of the best werewolves in the business," he complimented me.

Ave, Caesar, morituri te salutant, I thought. No, that isn't what I mean, but never mind. I can figure out a better phrasing at my leisure after I'm dead.

I wasn't afraid, exactly. Besides the spell laid on me to prevent that, I had reason to believe my personal chances were no worse than those of any infantryman headed into a firefight. Nor would Vanbrugh sacrifice personnel on a mission he himself considered hopeless. But I did feel less optimistic about the prospects than he.

"I think two adepts can get past their guards," the general

proceeded. "From then on, you'll have to improvise. If you can put that monster out of action, we attack at noon tomorrow." Grimly: "If I haven't got word to that effect by dawn, we'll have to regroup, start retreating, and save what we can. Okay, here's a geodetic survey map of the town and approaches—"

He didn't waste time asking me if I had really volunteered.

II

I GUIDED CAPTAIN GRAYLOCK back to the tent I shared with two brother officers. Darkness was creeping across the long chill slant of rain. We plodded through the muck in silence until we were under canvas. My tentmates were out on picket duty, so we had the place to ourselves. I lit the saintelmo and sat down on the sodden plank floor.

"Have a chair," I said, pointing to our one camp stool. It was an animated job we'd bought in San Francisco: not especially bright, but it would carry our duffel and come when called. It shifted uneasily at the unfamiliar weight, then went back to sleep.

Graylock took out a pack of Wings and raised her brows. I nodded my thanks, and the cigaret flapped over to my mouth. Personally, I smoke Luckies in the field: self-striking tobacco is convenient when your matches may be wet. When I was a civilian and could afford it, my brand was Philip Morris, because the little red-coated smoke sprite can also mix you a drink.

We puffed for a bit in silence, listening to the rain. "Well," I said at last, "I suppose you have transportation."

"My personal broomstick," she said. "I don't like this GI Willys. Give me a Cadillac anytime. I've souped it up, too."

"And you have your grimoires and powders and whatnot?"

"Just some chalk. No material agency is much use against a powerful demon."

"Yeah? What about the sealing wax on the Solly bottle?"

"It isn't the wax that holds an afreet in, but the seal. The spells are symbolic; in fact, it's believed their effect is purely psychosomatic." She hollowed the flat planes of her cheeks, sucking in smoke, and I saw what a good bony structure she had. "We may have a chance to test that theory tonight."

"Well, then, you'll want a light pistol loaded with silver slugs; they have weres of their own, you know. I'll take a grease gun and a forty-five and a few grenades."

9

"How about a squirter?"

I frowned. The notion of using holy water as a weapon has always struck me as blasphemous, though the chaplain said it was permissible against Low World critters. "No good to us," I said. "The Moslems don't have that ritual, so of course they don't use any beings that can be controlled by it. Let's see, I'll want my Polaroid flash too. And that's about it."

Ike Abrams stuck his big nose in the tent flap. "Would you and the lady captain like some eats, sir?" he asked.

"Why, sure," I said. Inwardly, I thought: Hate to spend my last night on Midgard standing in a chow line. When he had gone, I explained to the girl: "Ike's only a private, but we were friends in Hollywood—he was a prop man when I played in *Call of the Wild* and *Silver Chief*—and he's kind of appointed himself my orderly. He'll bring us some food here."

"You know," she remarked, "that's one good thing about the technological age. Did you know there used to be widespread anti-Semitism in this country? Not just among a few Johannine cranks; no, among ordinary respectable citizens."

"Fact?"

"Fact. Especially a false belief that Jews were cowards and never found in the front lines. Now, when religion forbids most of them to originate spells, and the Orthodox don't use goetics at all, the proportion of them who serve as dogfaces and Rangers is simply too high to ignore."

I myself had gotten tired of comic-strip supermen and pulp-magazine heroes having such monotonously Yiddish names—don't Anglo-Saxons belong to our culture too?—but she'd made a good point. And it showed she was a trifle more than a money machine. A bare trifle.

"What'd you do in civilian life?" I asked, chiefly to drown out the incessant noise of the rain.

"I told you," she snapped, irritable again. "I was with the Arcane Agency. Advertising, public relations, and so on."

"Oh, well," I said. "Hollywood is at least as phony, so I shouldn't sneer."

I couldn't help it, however. Those Madison Avenue characters gave me a pain in the rear end. Using the good Art to puff some self-important nobody, or to sell a product whose main virtue is its total similarity to other brands of the same. The SPCA has cracked down on training nixies to make fountains spell out words, or cramming young salamanders into glass tubes to light up Broadway, but I can still think of better uses for slick paper than trumpeting Ma Chère perfume. Which is actually a love potion anyway, though you know what postal regulations are.

"You don't understand," she said. "It's part of our economy—part of our whole society. Do you think the average backyard warlock is capable of repairing, oh, say a lawn sprinkler? Hell, no! He'd probably let loose the water elementals and flood half a township if it weren't for the inhibitory spells. And we, Arcane, undertook the campaign to convince the Hydros they had to respect our symbols. I told you it's psychosomatic when you're dealing with these really potent beings. For that job, I had to go down in an aqualung!"

I stared at her with more respect. Ever since mankind found how to degauss the ruinous effects of cold iron, and the goetic age began, the world has needed some pretty bold people. Apparently she was one of them.

Abrams brought in two plates of rations. He looked wistful, and I would have invited him to join us except that our mission was secret and we had to thresh out the details.

Captain Graylock 'chanted the coffee into martinis—not quite dry enough—and the dog food into steaks—a turn too well done; but you can't expect the finer sensibilities in a woman, and it was the best chow I'd had in a month. She relaxed a bit over the brandy, and I learned that her repellent crispness was simply armor against the slick types she dealt with, and we found out that our first names were Steven and Virginia. But then dusk had become dark outside, and we must be going.

III

YOU MAY THINK it was sheer lunacy, sending two people, one of them a woman, into an enemy division on a task like this. It would seem to call for a Ranger brigade, at least. But present-day science had transformed war as well as industry, medicine, and ordinary life. Our mission was desperate in any event, and we wouldn't have gained enough by numbers to make reinforcements worthwhile.

You see, while practically anyone can learn a few simple cantrips, to operate a presensitized broomstick or vacuum cleaner or turret lathe or whatever, only a small minority of the human race can qualify as adepts. Besides years of study and practice, that takes inborn talent. It's kind of like therianthropy: if you're one of the rare persons with chromosomes for that, you can change into your characteristic animal almost by instinct; otherwise you need a transformation performed on you by powerful outside forces.

My scientific friends tell me that the Art involves regarding the universe as a set of Cantorian infinities. Within any given class, the part is equal to the whole and so on. One good witch could do all the runing we were likely to need; a larger party would simply be more liable to detection, and would risk valuable personnel. So Vanbrugh had very rightly sent us two alone.

The trouble with sound military principles is that sometimes you personally get caught in them.

Virginia and I turned our backs on each other while we changed clothes. She got into an outfit of slacks and combat jacket, I into the elastic knit garment which would fit me as well in wolf-shape. We put on our helmets, hung our equipment around us, and turned about. Even in the baggy green battle garb she looked good.

"Well," I said tonelessly, "shall we go?"

I wasn't afraid, of course. Every recruit is immunized against fear when they put the geas on him. But I didn't like the prospect.

12

"The sooner the better, I suppose," she answered. Stepping to the entrance, she whistled.

Her stick swooped down and landed just outside. It had been stripped of the fancy chrome, but was still a neat job. The foam-rubber seats had good shock absorbers and well-designed back rests, unlike Army transport. Her familiar was a gigantic tomcat, black as a furry midnight, with two malevolent yellow eyes. He arched his back and spat indignantly. The weatherproofing spell kept rain off him, but he didn't like this damp air.

Virginia chucked him under the chin. "Oh, so, Svartalf," she murmured. "Good cat, rare sprite, prince of darkness, if we outlive this night you shall sleep on cloudy cushions and lap cream from a golden bowl." He cocked his ears and raced his motor.

I climbed into the rear seat, snugged my feet in the stirrups, and leaned back. The girl mounted in front of me and crooned to the stick. It swished upward, the ground fell away and the camp was hidden in gloom. Both of us had been given witch-sight—infrared vision, actually—so we didn't need lights.

When we got above the clouds, we saw a giant vault of stars overhead and a swirling dim whiteness below. I also glimpsed a couple of P-56's circling on patrol, fast jobs with six brooms each to lift their weight of armor and machine guns. We left them behind and streaked northward. I rested the BAR on my lap and sat listening to the air whine past. Underneath us, in the rough-edged murk of the hills, I spied occasional flashes, an artillery duel. So far no one had been able to cast a spell fast enough to turn or implode a shell. I'd heard rumors that General Electric was developing a gadget which could recite the formula in microseconds, but meanwhile the big guns went on talking.

Trollburg was a mere few miles from our position. I saw it as a vague sprawling mass, blacked out against our cannon and bombers. It would have been nice to have an atomic weapon just then, but as long as the Tibetans keep those antinuclear warfare prayer wheels turning, such thoughts must remain merely science-fictional. I felt my belly muscles tighten. The cat bottled out his tail and swore. Virginia sent the broomstick slanting down.

We landed in a clump of trees and she turned to me. "Their outposts must be somewhere near," she whispered. "I didn't dare try landing on a rooftop; we could have been seen too easily. We'll have to go in from here."

I nodded. "Okay. Gimme a minute."

I turned the flash on myself. How hard to believe that transforming had depended on a bright full moon till only ten years ago! Then Wiener showed that the process was simply one of polarized light of the right wavelengths, triggering the pineal gland, and the Polaroid Corporation made another million dollars or so from its WereWish Lens. It's not easy to keep up with this fearful and wonderful age we live in, but I wouldn't trade.

The usual rippling, twisting sensations, the brief drunken dizziness and half-ecstatic pain, went through me. Atoms reshuffled into whole new molecules, nerves grew some endings and lost others, bone was briefly fluid and muscles like stretched rubber. Then I stabilized, shook myself, stuck my tail out the flap of the skin-tight pants, and nuzzled Virginia's hand.

She stroked my neck, behind the helmet. "Good boy," she whispered. "Go get 'em."

I turned and faded into the brush.

A lot of writers have tried to describe how it feels to be were, and every one of them has failed, because human language doesn't have the words. My vision was no longer acute, the stars were blurred above me and the world took on a colorless flatness. But I heard with a clarity that made the night almost a roar, way into the supersonic; and a universe of smells roiled in my nostrils, wet grass and teeming dirt, the hot sweet little odor of a scampering field mouse, the clean tang of oil and guns, a faint harshness of smoke— Poor stupefied humanity, half-dead to such earthy glories!

The psychological part is the hardest to convey. I was a wolf, with a wolf's nerves and glands and instincts, a wolf's sharp but limited intelligence. I had a man's memories and a man's purposes, but they were unreal, dreamlike. I must make an effort of trained will to hold to them and not go hallooing off after the nearest jackrabbit. No wonder weres had a bad name in the old days, before they themselves understood the mental changes involved and got the right habits drilled into them from babyhood.

I weigh a hundred and eighty pounds, and the conservation of mass holds good like any other law of nature, so I was a pretty big wolf. But it was easy to flow through the bushes and meadows and gullies, another drifting shadow. I was almost inside the town when I caught a near smell of man.

I flattened, the gray fur bristling along my spine, and waited. The sentry came by. He was a tall bearded fellow with gold earrings that glimmered wanly under the stars. The turban wrapped around his helmet bulked monstrous against the Milky Way.

I let him go and followed his path until I saw the next one. They were placed around Trollburg, each pacing a hundred-yard arc and meeting his opposite number at either end of it. No simple task to—

Something murmured in my ears. I crouched. One of their aircraft ghosted overhead. I saw two men and a couple of machine guns squatting on top of the carpet. It circled low and lazily, above the ring of sentries. Trollburg was well guarded.

Somehow, Virginia and I had to get through that picket. I wished the transformation had left me with full human reasoning powers. My wolf-impulse was simply to jump on the nearest man, but that would bring the whole garrison down on my hairy ears.

Wait—maybe that was what was needed!

I loped back to the thicket. The Svartalf cat scratched at me and zoomed up a tree. Virginia Graylock started, her pistol sprang into her hand, then she relaxed and laughed a bit nervously. I could work the flash hung about my neck, even as I was, but it went more quickly with her fingers.

"Well?" she asked when I was human again. "What'd you find out?"

I described the situation, and saw her frown and bite her lip. It was really too shapely a lip for such purposes. "Not so good," she reflected. "I was afraid of something like this."

"Look," I said, "can you locate that afreet in a hurry?"

"Oh, yes. I've studied at Congo U. and did quite well at witch-smelling. What of it?"

"If I attack one of those guards and make a racket doing it, their main attention will be turned that way. You should have an even chance to fly across the line unobserved, and once you're in the town your Tarnkappe—"

She shook her red head. "I didn't bring one. Their detection systems are as good as ours. Invisibility is actually obsolete."

"Mmm—yeah, I suppose you're right. Well, anyhow, you can take advantage of the darkness to get to the afreet house. From there on, you'll have to play by ear."

"I suspected we'd have to do something like this," she replied. With a softness that astonished me: "But Steve, that's a long chance for you to take."

"Not unless they hit me with silver, and most of their cartridges are plain lead. They use a tracer principle like us; every tenth round is argent. I've got a ninety percent probability of getting home free.''

"You're a liar," she said. "But a brave liar."

I wasn't brave at all. It's inspiring to think of Valley Forge, or the Alamo, or San Juan Hill, or Casablanca where our outnumbered Army stopped three Panther divisions of von Ogerhaus' Afrika Korps—but only when you're safe and comfortable yourself. Down underneath the antipanic geas, a cold knot was in my guts. Still, I couldn't see any other way to do the job, and failure to attempt it would mean courtmartial.

"I'll run their legs off once they start chasing me," I told her. "When I've shaken 'em, I'll try to circle back and join you."

"Okay." Suddenly she rose on tiptoe and kissed me. The impact was explosive.

I stood for a moment, looking at her. "What are you doing Saturday night?" I asked, a mite shakily.

She laughed. "Don't get ideas, Steve. I'm in the Cavalry."

"Yeah, but the war won't last forever." I grinned at her, a reckless fighting grin that made her eyes linger. Acting experience is often useful.

We settled the details as well as we could. She herself had no soft touch: the afreet would be well guarded, and was plenty dangerous in itself. The chances of us both seeing daylight were nothing to feel complacent about.

I turned back to wolf-shape and licked her hand. She rumpled my fur. I slipped off into the darkness.

I had chosen a sentry well off the highway, across which there would surely be barriers. A man could be seen to either side of my victim, tramping slowly back and forth. I glided behind a stump near the middle of his beat and waited for him.

When he came, I sprang. I caught a dark brief vision of eyes and teeth in the bearded face, I heard him yelp and smelled the upward spurt of his fear, then we shocked together. He went down on his back, threshing, and I snapped for the throat. My jaws closed on his arm, and blood was hot and salty on my tongue.

He screamed again. I sensed the call going down the line. The two nearest Saracens ran to help. I tore out the gullet of the first man and bunched myself for a leap at the next.

He fired. The bullet went through me in a jag of pain and the impact sent me staggering. But he didn't know how to deal with a were. He should have dropped on one knee and fired steadily till he got to the silver bullet; if necessary, he should have fended me off, even pinned me with his bayonet, while he shot. This one kept running toward me, calling on the Allah of his heretical sect.

My tissues knitted as I plunged to meet him. I got past the bayonet and gun muzzle, hitting him hard enough to knock the weapon loose but not to bowl him over. He braced his legs, grabbed my neck, and hung on.

I swung my left hind leg back of his ankle and shoved. He fell with me on top, the position an infighting werewolf always tries for. My head swiveled; I gashed open his arm and broke his grip.

Before I could settle the business, three others had piled on me. Their trench scimitars went up and down, in between my ribs and out again. Lousy training they'd had. I snapped my way free of the heap—half a dozen by then—and broke loose.

Through sweat and blood I caught the faintest whiff of Chanel No. 5, and something in me laughed. Virginia had sped past the confusion, riding her stick a foot above ground, and was inside Trollburg. My next task was to lead a chase and not stop a silver slug while doing so.

I howled, to taunt the men spilling from outlying houses, and let them have a good look at me before making off across the fields. My pace was easy, not to lose them at once; I relied on zigzags to keep me unpunctured. They followed, stumbling and shouting.

As far as they knew, this had been a mere commando raid. Their pickets would have re-formed and the whole garrison been alerted. But surely none except a few chosen officers knew about the afreet, and none of those knew we'd acquired the information. So they had no way of telling what we really planned. Maybe we *would* pull this operation off—

Something swooped overhead, one of their damned carpets. It rushed down on me like a hawk, guns spitting. I made for the nearest patch of woods.

Into the trees! Given half a break, I could—

They didn't give it. I heard a bounding behind me, caught the acrid smell, and whimpered. A weretiger could go as fast as I.

For a moment I remembered an old guide I'd had in Alaska, and wished to blazes he were here. He was a were-Kodiak bear. Then I whirled and met the tiger before he could pounce.

He was a big one, five hundred pounds at least. His eyes smoldered above the great fangs, and he lifted a paw that could crack my spine like a dry twig. I rushed in, snapping, and danced back before he could strike.

Part of me heard the enemy, blundering around in the underbrush trying to find us. The tiger leaped. I evaded him and bolted for the nearest thicket. Maybe I could go where he couldn't. He ramped through the woods behind me, roaring.

I saw a narrow space between a pair of giant oaks, too small for him, and hurried that way. But it was too small for me also. In the half second that I was stuck, he caught up. The lights exploded and went out.

IV

I WAS NOWHERE and nowhen. My very body had departed from me, or I from it. How could I think of infinite eternal dark and cold and emptiness when I had no senses? How could I despair when I was nothing but a point in spacetime? . . . No, not even that, for there was nothing else, nothing to find or love or hate or fear or be related to in any way whatsover. The dead were less alone than I, for I was all which existed.

This was my despair.

But on the instant, or after a quadrillion years, or both or neither, I came to know otherwise. I was under the regard of the Solipsist. Helpless in unconsciousness, I could but share that egotism so ultimate that it would yield no room even to hope. I swirled in the tides and storms of thoughts too remote, too alien, too vast for me to take in save as I might brokenly hear the polar ocean while it drowned me.

—danger, this one—he and those two—somehow they can be a terrible danger—not now (scornfully) *when they merely help complete the ruin of a plan already bungled into wreck—no, later, when the next plan is ripening, the great one of which this war was naught but an early leaf—something about them warns thinly of danger—could I only scan more clearly into time!— they must be diverted, destroyed, somehow dealt with before their potential has grown—but I cannot originate anything yet— maybe they will be slain by the normal chances of war—if not, I must remember them and try later—now I have too much else to do, saving those seeds I planted in the world—the birds of the enemy fly thick across my fields, hungry crows and eagles to guard them—* (with ever wilder hate) *my snares shall take you yet, birds—and the One Who loosed you!*

So huge was the force of that final malevolence that I was cast free.

V

I OPENED MY EYES. For a while I was aware entirely of the horror. Physical misery rescued me, driving those memories back to where half-forgotten nightmares dwell. The thought flitted by me that shock must have made me briefly delirious.

A natural therianthrope in his beast shape isn't quite as invulnerable as most people believe. Aside from things like silver—biochemical poisons to a metabolism in that semifluid state—damage which stops a vital organ will stop life; amputations are permanent unless a surgeon is near to sew the part back on before its cells die; and so on and so on, no pun intended. We are a hardy sort, however. I'd taken a blow that probably broke my neck. The spinal cord not being totally severed, the damage had healed at standard therio speed.

The trouble was, they'd arrived and used my flash to make me human before the incidental hurts had quite gone away. My head drummed and I retched.

"Get up." Someone stuck a boot in my ribs.

I lurched erect. They'd removed my gear, including the flash. A score of them trained their guns on me. Tiger Boy stood close. In man-shape he was almost seven feet tall and monstrously fat. Squinting through the headache, I saw he wore the insignia of an emir—which was a military rank these days rather than a title, but pretty important nevertheless.

"Come," he said. He led the way, and I was hustled along behind.

I saw their carpets in the sky and heard the howling of their own weres looking for spoor of other Americans. I was still too groggy to care very much.

We entered the town, its pavement sounding hollow under the boots, and went toward the center. Trollburg wasn't big, maybe five thousand population once. Most of the streets were empty. I saw a few Saracen troops, anti-aircraft guns poking into the sky, a dragon lumbering past with flames flickering around its jaws

20

and cannon projecting from the armored howdah. No trace of the civilians, but I knew what had happened to them. The attractive young women were in the officers' harems, the rest dead or locked away pending shipment to the slave markets.

By the time we got to the hotel where the enemy headquartered, my aches had subsided and my brain was clear. That was a mixed blessing under the circumstances. I was taken upstairs to a suite and told to stand before a table. The emir sat down behind it, half a dozen guards lined the walls, and a young pasha of Intelligence seated himself nearby.

The emir's big face turned to that one, and he spoke a few words—I suppose to the effect of "I'll handle this, you take notes." He looked back at me. His eyes were the pale tiger-green.

"Now then," he said in good English, "we shall have some questions. Identify yourself, please."

I told him mechanically that I was called Sherrinford Mycroft, Captain, AUS, and gave him my serial number.

"That is not your real name, is it?" he asked.

"Of course not!" I replied. "I know the Geneva Convention, and you're not going to cast name-spells on me. Sherrinford Mycroft is my official johnsmith."

"The Caliphate has not subscribed to the Geneva Convention," said the emir quietly, "and stringent measures are sometimes necessary in a jehad. What was the purpose of this raid?"

"I am not required to answer that," I said. Silence would have served the same end, delay to gain time for Virginia, but not as well.

"You may be persuaded to do so," he said.

If this had been a movie, I'd have told him I was picking daisies, and kept on wisecracking while they brought out the thumbscrews. In practice it would have fallen a little flat.

"All right," I said. "I was scouting."

"A single one of you?"

"A few others. I hope they got away." That might keep his boys busy hunting for a while.

"You lie," he said dispassionately.

"I can't help it if you don't believe me," I shrugged.

His eyes narrowed. "I shall soon know if you speak truth," he said. "If not, may Eblis have mercy on you."

I couldn't help it, I jerked where I stood and sweat pearled out, on my skin. The emir laughed. He had an unpleasant laugh, a sort of whining growl deep in his fat throat, like a tiger playing with its kill.

"Think over your decision," he advised, and turned to some papers on the table.

It grew most quiet in that room. The guards stood as if cast in bronze. The young shavetail dozed beneath his turban. Behind the emir's back, a window looked out on a blankness of night. The sole sounds were the loud tickings of a clock and the rustle of papers. They seemed to deepen the silence.

I was tired, my head ached, my mouth tasted foul and thirsty. The sheer physical weariness of having to stand was meant to help wear me down. It occurred to me that the emir must be getting scared of us, to take this much trouble with a lone prisoner. That was kudos for the American cause, but small consolation to me.

My eyes flickered, studying the tableau. There wasn't much to see, standard hotel furnishings. The emir had cluttered his desk with a number of objects: a crystal ball useless because of our own jamming, a fine cut-glass bowl looted from somebody's house, a set of nice crystal wineglasses, a cigar humidor of quartz glass, a decanter full of what looked like good Scotch. I guess he just liked crystal.

He helped himself to a cigar, waving his hand to make the humidor open and a Havana fly into his mouth and light itself. As the minutes crawled by, an ashtray soared up from time to time to receive from him. I guessed that everything he had was 'chanted so it would rise and move easily. A man that fat, paying the price of being a really big werebeast, needed such conveniences.

It was very quiet. The light glared down on us. It was somehow hideously wrong to see a good ordinary GE saintelmo shining on those turbaned heads.

I began to get the forlorn glimmerings of an idea. How to put it into effect I didn't yet know, but just to pass the time I began composing some spells.

Maybe half an hour had passed, though it seemed more like half a century, when the door opened and a fennec, the small fox of the African desert, trotted in. The emir looked up as it went into a closet, to find darkness to use its flash. The fellow who came out was, naturally, a dwarf barely one foot high. He prostrated himself and spoke rapidly in a high thready voice.

"So." The emir's chins turned slowly around to me. "The

report is that no trace was found of other tracks than yours. You have lied."

"Didn't I tell you?" I asked. My throat felt stiff and strange. "We used owls and bats. I was the lone wolf."

"Be still," he said tonelessly. "I know as well as you that the only werebats are vampires, and that vampires are—what you say—4-F in all armies."

That was true. Every so often, some armchair general asks why we don't raise a force of Draculas. The answer is routine: they're too light and flimsy; they can't endure sunshine; if they don't get a steady blood ration they're apt to turn on their comrades; and you can't possibly use them around Italian troops. I swore at myself, but my mind had been too numb to think straight.

"I believe you are concealing something," went on the emir. He gestured at his glasses and decanter, which supplied him with a shot of Scotch, and sipped judiciously. The Caliphate sect was also heretical with respect to strong drink; they maintained that while the Prophet forbade wine, he said nothing about beer, gin, whisky, brandy, rum, or akvavit.

"We shall have to use stronger measures," the emir said at last. "I was hoping to avoid them." He nodded at his guards.

Two held my arms. The pasha worked me over. He was good at that. The werefennec watched avidly, the emir puffed his cigar and went on with his paperwork. After a long few minutes, he gave an order. They let me go, and even set forth a chair for me, which I needed badly.

I sat breathing hard. The emir regarded me with a certain gentleness. "I regret this," he said. "It is not enjoyable." Oddly, I believed him. "Let us hope you will be reasonable before we have to inflict permanent injuries. Meanwhile, would you like a cigar?"

The old third degree procedure. Knock a man around for a while, then show him kindness. You'd be surprised how often that makes him blubber and break.

"We desire information about your troops and their plans," said the emir. "If you will cooperate and accept the true faith, you can have an honored position with us. We like good men in the Caliphate." He smiled. "After the war, you could select your harem out of Hollywood if you desired."

"And if I don't squeal—" I murmured.

He spread his hands. "You will have no further wish for a harem. The choice is yours."

"Let me think," I begged. "This isn't easy."

"Please do," he answered urbanely, and returned to his papers.

I sat as relaxed as possible, drawing the smoke into my throat and letting strength flow back. The Army geas could be broken by their technicians only if I gave my free consent, and I didn't want to. I considered the window behind the emir. It was a two-story drop to the street.

Most likely, I'd just get myself killed. But that was preferable to any other offer I'd had.

I went over the spells I'd haywired. A real technician has to know at least one arcane language—Latin, Greek, classical Arabic, Sanskrit, Old Norse, or the like—for the standard reasons of sympathetic science. Paranatural phenomena are not strongly influenced by ordinary speech. But except for the usual tag-ends of incantations, the minimum to operate the gadgets of daily life, I was no scholar.

However, I knew one slightly esoteric dialect quite well. I didn't know if it would work, but I could try.

My muscles tautened as I moved. It was a shuddersome effort to be casual. I knocked the end of ash off my cigar. As I lifted the thing again, it collected some ash from the emir's.

I got the rhyme straight in my mind, put the cigar to my lips, and subvocalized the spell.

"Ashes-way of the urningbay,
upward-way ownay eturningray,
as-way the arksspay do yflay,
ikestray imhay in the eye-way!"

I closed my right eye and brought the glowing cigar end almost against the lid.

The emir's El Fumo leaped up and ground itself into *his* right eye.

He screamed and fell backward. I soared to my feet. I'd marked the werefennec, and one stride brought me over to him. I broke his vile little neck with a backhanded cuff and yanked off the flash that hung from it.

The guards howled and plunged for me. I went over the table and down on top of the emir, snatching his decanter en route. He clawed at me, wild with pain, I saw the ghastliness in his eye socket, and meanwhile I was hanging on to the vessel and shouting:

"Ingthay of ystalcray,
ebay a istralmay!
As-way I-way owthray,
yflay ouyay osay!"

As I finished, I broke free and hurled the decanter at the guards. It was lousy poetics, and might not have worked if the fat man hadn't already sensitized his stuff. As if was, the ball, the ashtray, the bowl, the glasses, the humidor, and the window-panes all took off after the decanter. The air was full of flying glass.

I didn't stay to watch the results, but went out that window like an exorcised devil. I landed in a ball on the sidewalk, bounced up, and began running.

VI

SOLDIERS WERE AROUND. Bullets sleeted after me. I set a record reaching the nearest alley. My witch-sight showed me a broken window, and I wriggled through that. Crouching beneath the sill, I heard the pursuit go by.

This was the back room of a looted grocery store, plenty dark for my purposes. I hung the flash around my neck, turned it on myself, and made the changeover. They'd return in a minute, and I didn't want to be vulnerable to lead.

Wolf, I snuffled around after another exit. A rear door stood half open. I slipped through into a courtyard full of ancient packing cases. They made a good hideout. I lay there, striving to control my lupine nature which wanted to pant, while they swarmed through the area.

When they were gone again, I tried to consider my situation. The temptation was to hightail out of this poor, damned place. I could probably make it, and had technically fulfilled my share of the mission. But the job wasn't really complete, and Virginia was alone with the afreet—if she still lived—and—

When I tried to recall her, the image came as a she-wolf and a furry aroma. I shook my head angrily. Weariness and desperation were submerging my reason and letting the animal instincts take over. I'd better do whatever had to be done fast.

I cast about. The town smells were confusing, but I caught the faintest sulfurous whiff and trotted cautiously in that direction. I kept to the shadows, and was seen twice but not challenged. They must have supposed I was one of theirs. The brimstone reek grew stronger.

They kept the afreet in the courthouse, a good solid building. I went through the small park in front of it, snuffed the wind carefully, and dashed over street and steps. Four enemy soldiers sprawled on top, throats cut open, and the broomstick was parked by the door. It had a twelve-inch switchblade in the handle, and Virginia had used it like a flying lance.

The man side of me, which had been entertaining stray romantic thoughts, backed up in a cold sweat; but the wolf grinnned. I poked at the door. She'd 'chanted the lock open and left it that way. I stuck my nose in, and almost had it clawed off before Svartalf recognized me. He jerked his tail curtly, and I passed by and across the lobby. The stinging smell was coming from upstairs. I followed it through a thick darkness.

Light glowed in a second-floor office. I thrust the door ajar and peered in. Virginia was there. She had drawn the curtains and lit the elmos to see by. She was still busy with her precautions, started a little on spying me but went on with the chant. I parked my shaggy behind near the door and watched.

She'd chalked the usual figure, same as the Pentagon in Washington, and a Star of David inside that. The Solly bottle was at the center. It didn't look impressive, an old flask of hard-baked clay with its hollow handle bent over and returning inside—merely a Klein bottle, with Solomon's seal in red wax at the mouth. She'd loosened her hair, and it floated in a ruddy cloud about the pale beautiful face.

The wolf of me wondered why we didn't just make off with this crock of It. The man reminded him that undoubtedly the emir had taken precautions and would have sympathetic means to uncork it from afar. We had to put the demon out of action . . . somehow . . . but nobody on our side knew a great deal about his race.

Virginia finished her spell, drew the bung, and sprang outside the pentacle as smoke boiled from the flask. She almost didn't make it, the afreet came out in such a hurry. I stuck my tail between my legs and snarled. She was scared, too, trying hard not to show that but I caught the adrenalin odor.

The afreet must bend almost double under the ceiling. He was a monstrous gray thing, nude, more or less anthropoid but with wings and horns and long ears, a mouthful of fangs and eyes like hot embers. His assets were strength, speed, and physical near-invulnerability. Turned loose, he could break any attack of Vanbrugh's, and inflict frightful casualties on the most well-dug-in defense. Controlling him afterward, before he laid the countryside waste, would be a problem. But why should the Saracens care? They'd have exacted a geas from him, that he remain their ally, as the price of his freedom.

He roared something in Arabic. Smoke swirled from his mouth. Virginia looked tiny under those half-unfurled bat membranes. Her voice was less cool than she would have preferred: "Speak English, Marid. Or are you too ignorant?"

The demon huffed indignantly. "O spawn of a thousand baboons!" My eardrums flinched from the volume. "O thou white and gutless infidel thing, which I could break with my least finger, come in to me if thou darest!"

I was frightened, less by the chance of his breaking loose than by the racket he was making. It could be heard for a quarter mile.

"Be still, accursed of God!" Virginia answered. That shook him a smidgen. Like most of the hell-breed, he was allergic to holy names, though only seriously so under conditions that we couldn't reproduce here. She stood hands on hips, head tilted, to meet the gaze that smoldered down upon her. "Suleiman bin-Daoud, on whom be peace, didn't jug you for nothing, I see. Back to your prison and never come forth again, lest the anger of Heaven smite you!"

The afreet fleered. "Know that Suleiman the Wise is dead these three thousand years," he retorted. "Long and long have I brooded in my narrow cell, I who once raged free through earth and sky and will now at last be released to work my vengeance on the puny sons of Adam." He shoved at the invisible barrier, but one of that type has a rated strength of several million p.s.i. It would hold firm—till some adept dissolved it. "O thou shameless unveiled harlot with hair of hell, know that I am Rashid the Mighty, the glorious in power, the smiter of rocs! Come in here and fight like a man!"

I moved close to the girl, my hackles raised. The hand that touched my head was cold. "Paranoid type," she whispered. "A lot of these harmful Low Worlders are psycho. Stupid, though. Trickery's our single chance. I don't have any spells to compel him directly. But—" Aloud, to him, she said: "Shut up, Rashid, and listen to me. I also am of your race, and to be respected as such."

"Thou?" He hooted with fake laughter. "Thou of the Marid race? Why, thou fish-faced antling, if thou'dst come in here I'd show thee thou'rt not even fit to—" The rest was graphic but not for any gentlewere to repeat.

"No, hear me," said the girl. "Look and hearken well." She made signs and uttered a formula. I recognized the self-geas against telling a falsehood in the particular conversation. Our courts still haven't adopted it—Fifth Amendment—but I'd seen it used in trials abroad.

The demon recognized it, too. I imagine the Saracen adept

who pumped a knowledge of English into him, to make him effective in this war, had added other bits of information about the modern world. He grew more quiet and attentive.

Virginia intoned impressively: "I can speak nothing to you except the truth. Do you agree that the name is the thing?"

"Y-y-yes," the afreet rumbled. "That is common knowledge."

I scented her relief. First hurdle passed! He had *not* been educated in scientific goetics. Though the name is, of course, in sympathy with the object, which is the principle of nymic spells and the like—nevertheless, only in this century has Korzybski demonstrated that the word and its referent are not identical.

"Very well," she said. "My name is Ginny."

He started in astonishment. "Art thou indeed?"

"Yes. Now will you listen to me? I came to offer you advice, as one jinni to another. I have powers of my own, you know, albeit I employ them in the service of Allah, the Omnipotent, the Omniscient, the Compassionate."

He glowered, but supposing her to be one of his species, he was ready to put on a crude show of courtesy. She couldn't be lying about her advice. It did not occur to him that she hadn't said the counsel would be good.

"Go on, then, if thou wilst," he growled. "Knowest thou that tomorrow I fare forth to destroy the infidel host?" He got caught up in his dreams of glory. "Aye, well will I rip them, and trample them, and break and gut and flay them. Well will they learn the power of Rashid the bright-winged, the fiery, the merciless, the wise, the . . ."

Virginia waited out his adjectives, then said gently: "But Rashid, why must you wreak harm? You earn nothing thereby except hate."

A whine crept into his bass. "Aye, thou speakest sooth. The whole world hates me. Everybody conspires against me. Had he not had the aid of traitors, Suleiman had never locked me away. All which I have sought to do has been thwarted by envious ill-wishers— Aye, but tomorrow comes the day of reckoning!"

Virginia lit a cigaret with a steady hand and blew smoke at him. "How can you trust the emir and his cohorts?" she asked. "He too is your enemy. He only wants to make a cat's-paw of you. Afterward, back in the bottle!"

"Why . . . why . . ." The afreet swelled till the spacewarp barrier creaked. Lightning crackled from his nostrils. It hadn't occurred to him before; his race isn't bright; but of course a

trained psychologist would understand how to follow out
paranoid logic.

"Have you not known enmity throughout your long days?"
continued Virginia quickly. "Think back, Rashid. Was not the
very first thing you remember the cruel act of a spitefully envious
world?"

"Aye—it was." The maned head nodded, and the voice
dropped very low. "On the day I was hatched . . . aye, my
mother's wingtip smote me so I reeled."

"Perhaps that was accidental," said Virginia.

"Nay. Ever she favored my older brother—the lout!"

Virginia sat down cross-legged. "Tell me about it," she
urged. Her tone dripped sympathy.

I felt a lessening of the great forces that surged within the
barrier. The afreet squatted on his hams, eyes half-shut, going
back down a memory trail of millennia. Virginia guided him, a
hint here and there. I didn't know what she was driving at, surely
you couldn't psychoanalyze the monster in half a night, but—

"—Aye, and I was scarce turned three centuries when I fell
into a pit my foes must have dug for me."

"Surely you could fly out of it," she murmured.

The afreet's eyes rolled. His face twisted into still more
gruesome furrows. "It was a pit, I say!"

"Not by any chance a lake?" she inquired.

"Nay!" His wings thundered. "No such damnable thing . . .
'twas dark, and wet, but—nay, not wet either, a cold which
burned . . ."

I saw dimly that the girl had a lead. She dropped long lashes to
hide the sudden gleam in her gaze. Even as a wolf, I could realize
what a shock it must have been to an aerial demon, nearly
drowning, his fires hissing into steam, and how he must ever
after deny to himself that it had happened. But what use could
she make of—

Svartalf the cat streaked in and skidded to a halt. Every hair on
him stood straight, and his eyes blistered me. He spat something
and went out again with me in his van.

Down in the lobby I heard voices. Looking through the door, I
saw a few soldiers milling about. They'd come by, perhaps to
investigate the noise, seen the dead guards, and now they must
have sent for reinforcements.

Whatever Ginny was trying to do, she needed time for it. I
went out that door in one gray leap and tangled with the Saracens. We boiled into a clamorous pile. I was almost pinned flat

by their numbers, but kept my jaws free and used them. Then Svartalf rode that broomstick above the fight, stabbing.

We carried a few of their weapons back into the lobby in our jaws, and sat down to wait. I figured I'd do better to remain wolf and be immune to most things than have the convenience of hands. Svartalf regarded a tommy gun thoughtfully, propped it along a wall, and crouched over it.

I was in no hurry. Every minute we were left alone, or held off the coming attack, was a minute gained for Ginny. I laid my head on my forepaws and dozed off. Much too soon I heard hobnails rattle on pavement.

The detachment must have been a good hundred. I saw their dark mass, and the gleam of starlight off their weapons. They hovered for a while around the squad we'd liquidated. Abruptly they whooped and charged up the steps.

Svartalf braced himself and worked the tommy gun. The recoil sent him skating back across the lobby, swearing, but he got a couple. I met the rest in the doorway.

Slash, snap, leap in, leap out, rip them and gash them and howl in their faces! After a brief whirl of teeth they retreated. They left half a dozen dead and wounded.

I peered through the glass in the door and saw my friend the emir. He had a bandage over his eye, but lumbered around exhorting his men with more energy than I'd expected. Groups of them broke from the main bunch and ran to either side. They'd be coming in the windows and the other doors.

I whined as I realized we'd left the broomstick outside. There could be no escape now, not even for Ginny. The protest became a snarl when I heard glass breaking and rifles blowing off locks.

That Svartalf was a smart cat. He found the tommy gun again and somehow, clumsy though paws are, managed to shoot out the lights. He and I retreated to the stairway.

They came at us in the dark, blind as most men are. I let them fumble around, and the first one who groped to the stairs was killed quietly. The second had time to yell. The whole gang of them crowded after him.

They couldn't shoot in the gloom and press without potting their own people. Excited to mindlessness, they attacked me with scimitars, which I didn't object to. Svartalf raked their legs and I tore them apart—whick, snap, clash, Allah Akbar and teeth in the night!

The stair was narrow enough for me to hold, and their own casualties hampered them, but the sheer weight of a hundred

brave men forced me back a tread at a time. Otherwise one could
have tackled me and a dozen more have piled on top. As things
were, we gave the houris a few fresh customers for every foot we
lost.

I have no clear memory of the fight. You seldom do. But it
must have been about twenty minutes before they fell back at an
angry growl. The emir himself stood at the foot of the stairs,
lashing his tail and rippling his gorgeously striped hide.

I shook myself wearily and braced my feet for the last round.
The one-eyed tiger climbed slowly toward us. Svartalf spat.
Suddenly he zipped down the banister past the larger cat and
disappeared in the gloom. Well, he had his own neck to think
about—

We were almost nose to nose when the emir lifted a paw full of
swords and brought it down. I dodged somehow and flew for his
throat. All I got was a mouthful of baggy skin, but I hung on and
tried to work my way inward.

He roared and shook his head till I swung like a bell clapper. I
shut my eyes and clamped on tight. He raked my ribs with those
long claws. I skipped away but kept my teeth where they were.
Lunging, he fell on me. His jaws clashed shut. Pain jagged
through my tail. I let go to howl.

He pinned me down with one paw, raising the other to break
my spine. Somehow, crazed with the hurt, I writhed free and
struck upward. His remaining eye was glaring at me, and I bit it
out of his head.

He screamed! A sweep of one paw sent me kiting up to slam
against the banister. I lay with the wind knocked from me while
the blind tiger rolled over in his agony. The beast drowned the
man, and he went down the stairs and wrought havoc among his
own soldiers.

A broomstick whizzed above the melee. Good old Svartalf!
He'd only gone to fetch our transportation. I saw him ride toward
the door of the afreet, and rose groggily to meet the next wave of
Saracens.

They were still trying to control their boss. I gulped for breath
and stood watching and smelling and listening. My tail seemed
ablaze. Half of it was gone.

A tommy gun began stuttering. I heard blood rattle in the
emir's lungs. He was hard to kill. *That's the end of you, Steve
Matuchek,* thought the man of me. *They'll do what they should
have done in the first place, stand beneath you and sweep you
with their fire, every tenth round argent.*

The emir fell and lay gasping out his life. I waited for his men to collect their wits and remember me.

Ginny appeared on the landing, astride the broomstick. Her voice seemed to come from very far away. "Steve! Quick! Here!"

I shook my head dazedly, trying to understand. I was too tired, too canine. She stuck her fingers in her mouth and whistled. That fetched me.

She slung me across her lap and hung on tight as Svartalf piloted the stick. A gun fired blindly from below. We went out a second-story window and into the sky.

A carpet swooped near. Svartalf arched his back and poured on the Power. That Cadillac had legs! We left the enemy sitting there, and I passed out.

VII

WHEN I CAME TO, I was prone on a cot in a hospital tent. Daylight was bright outside; the earth lay wet and steaming. A medic looked around as I groaned. "Hello, hero," he said. "Better stay in that position for a while. How're you feeling?"

I waited till full consciousness returned before I accepted a cup of bouillon. "How am I?" I whispered; they'd humanized me, of course.

"Not too bad, considering. You had some infection of your wounds—a staphylococcus that can switch species for a human or canine host—but we cleaned the bugs out with a new antibiotic technique. Otherwise, loss of blood, shock, and plain old exhaustion. You should be fine in a week or two."

I lay thinking, my mind draggy, most of my attention on how delicious the bouillon tasted. A field hospital can't lug around the equipment to stick pins in model bacteria. Often it doesn't even have the enlarged anatomical dummies on which the surgeon can do a sympathetic operation. "What technique do you mean?" I asked.

"One of our boys has the Evil Eye. He looks at the germs through a microscope."

I didn't inquire further, knowing that *Reader's Digest* would be waxing lyrical about it in a few months. Something else nagged at me. "The attack . . . have they begun?"

"The— Oh. That! That was two days ago, Rin-Tin-Tin. You've been kept under asphodel. We mopped 'em up along the entire line. Last I heard, they were across the Washington border and still running."

I sighed and went back to sleep. Even the noise as the medic dictated a report to his typewriter couldn't hold me awake.

Ginny came in the next day, with Svartalf riding her shoulder. Sunlight striking through the tent flap turned her hair to hot copper. "Hello, Captain Matuchek," she said. "I came to see how you were, soon as I could get leave."

34

I raised myself on my elbows, and whistled at the cigaret she offered. When it was between my lips, I said slowly: "Come off it, Ginny. We didn't exactly go on a date that night, but I think we're properly introduced."

"Yes." She sat down on the cot and stroked my hair. That felt good. Svartalf purred at me, and I wished I could respond.

"How about the afreet?" I asked after a while.

"Still in his bottle." She grinned. "I doubt if anybody'll ever be able to get him out again, assuming anybody would want to."

"But what did you *do?*"

"A simple application of Papa Freud's principles. If it's ever written up, I'll have every Jungian in the country on my neck, but it worked. I got him to spinning out his memories and illusions, and soon found he had a hydrophobic complex— which is fear of water, Rover, not rabies—"

"You can call me Rover," I growled, "but if you call me Fido, gives a paddling."

She didn't ask why I assumed I'd be sufficiently close in future for such laying on of hands. That encouraged me. Indeed, she blushed, but went on: "Having gotten the key to his personality, I found it simple to play on his phobia. I pointed out how common a substance water is and how difficult total dehydration is. He got more and more scared. When I showed him that all animal tissue, including his own, is about eighty percent water, that was that. He crept back into his bottle and went catatonic."

After a moment, she added thoughtfully: "I'd like to have him for my mantelpiece, but I suppose he'll wind up in the Smithsonian. So I'll simply write a little treatise on the military uses of psychiatry."

"Aren't bombs and dragons and elfshot gruesome enough?" I demanded with a shudder.

Poor simple elementals! They think they're fiendish, but ought to take lessons from the human race.

As for me, I could imagine certain drawbacks to getting hitched with a witch, but— "C'mere, youse."

She did.

I don't have many souvenirs of the war. It was an ugly time and best forgotten. But one keepsake will always be with me, in spite of the plastic surgeons' best efforts. As a wolf, I've got a stumpy tail, and as a man I don't like to sit down in wet weather.

That's a hell of a thing to receive a Purple Heart for.

VIII

HERE WE REACH one of the interludes. I'll skip over them fast. They were often more interesting and important to us—to Ginny and me—than the episodes which directly involved our Adversary. The real business of people is not strife or danger or melodrama; it's work, especially if they're so fortunate as to enjoy what they do; it's recreation and falling in love and raising families and telling jokes and stumbling into small pleasant adventures.

But you wouldn't care especially about what happened to us in those departments. You have your personal lives. Furthermore, a lot of it is nobody's business but ours. Furthermore yet, I have only this one night to 'cast. Any longer, and the stress might have effects on me. I don't take needless chances with the unknown; I've been there.

Finally, the big events do matter to you. He's also your Adversary.

Let me therefore just use the interludes to put the episodes in context. Okay?

This first period covers roughly two years. For several months of them Ginny and I remained in service, though we didn't see combat again. Nor did we see each other, which was worse on two counts. Reassignment kept shuffling us around.

Not that the war lasted that long. The kaftans had been beaten off the Caliphate. It disintegrated like a dropped windowpane, in revolutions, riots, secessions, vendettas, banditry, and piece-meal surrenders. America and her allies didn't need armed forces to invade enemy-held territory. They did need them, and urgently, for its occupation, to restore order before famine and plague broke loose. Our special talents had Ginny and me hopping over half the world—but not in company.

We spent a barrel of pay on postage. Nevertheless I took a while to decide I really had better propose; and while her answer was tender, it wasn't yes. Orphaned at a rather early age, she'd grown to womanhood with a need for warmth—and a capacity for it—which required that tough career-girl shell to guard her from hurt. She would not contract a marriage that she wasn't certain could be for life.

I was discharged somewhat before her and went home to reweave threads torn loose by the war. Surprisingly few showed in the United States. Though the invaders had overrun nearly half, throughout most of that conquest they were present only a short while before we rolled them back, and in that while we kept them too busy to wreak the degree of harm that luckless longer-held corners like Trollburg suffered. Civil government followed on the heels of the Army, more rapid and efficient in its work than I'd have expected. Or maybe civilization itself was responsible. Technology can produce widespread devastation, but likewise quick recoveries.

Thus I returned to a country which, apart from various shortages that soon disappeared, looked familiar. On the surface, I mean. The psyche was something else again. Shocked to their souls by what had happened, I suppose, shocked more deeply than they knew, a significant part of the population had come unbalanced. What saved us from immediate social disaster was doubtless the variety of their eccentricities. So many demagogues, self-appointed prophets, would-be necromancers, nut cultists in religion and politics and science and dieting and life style and Lord knows what else, tended to cancel each other out. A few of them did grow ominously, like the Johannine Church, of which much more anon.

However, that didn't happen in a revolutionary leap. Those of us who weren't afflicted with some fanaticism—and we were the majority, remember—seldom worried more than peripherally. We figured the body politic would stop twitching in the natural course of events. Meanwhile we had our careers and dreams to rebuild; we had the everydays to get through.

Myself, I went back to Hollywood and resumed werewolfing for Metro-Goldwyn-Merlin. That proved a disappointment. It was a nuisance wearing a fake brush over my bobbed tail, for me and the studio alike. They weren't satisfied with my performances, either; nor was I. For instance, in spite of honestly trying, I couldn't get real conviction into my role in *Dracula, Frankenstein, the Wolf Man, the Mummy, and the Thing Meet Paracelsus*. Not that I look down on pure entertainment, but I was discovering a newborn wish to do something more significant.

So there began to be mutual hints about my resignation. Probably only my medals delayed a crisis. But war heroes were a dime a coven. Besides, everybody knows that military courage is a large part training and discipline, another large part the antipanic geas; and the latter is routinely lifted upon discharge, because civilians *need* a touch of timidity. I don't claim any more than the normal share of natural guts.

About that time Ginny was demobbed. She came straight to visit me. That was quite a reunion. She wouldn't accept my repeated proposals—"Not yet, Steve, dear; not till we see what we're both like under ordinary conditions; don't you understand?"—but I seemed to be running well out in front.

In the course of several days, besides the expected things, we did considerable serious talking. She drew to the forefront of my mind what my true ambition was: taming Fire and Air to create an antigravity spell powerful enough that men could reach the planets. In fact, I'd set out to be an engineer. But funds ran low in my freshman year, and a talent scout happened to see me in some amateur theatricals, and one thing led to another. Like most people, I'd drifted through life.

Ginny was not like most people. However, she'd been doing some rethinking too. She was welcome back at Arcane, but wondered if she really wanted to work for a large organization. Wouldn't her own independent consulting agency give her freedom to explore her own ideas? For that she needed further goetic knowledge, and the obvious way to acquire it was to go for a Ph.D.

And . . . between our savings and our GI, we could both now afford a return to college.

The clincher came when, after some correspondence, Trismegistus University offered her an instructorship—since she already had an M.A. from Congo—while she did her advanced studies. I fired off an application to its school of engineering and was accepted. A few weeks later, Steven Matuchek and MGM parted ways with many polite noises, and he and Virginia Graylock boarded a supercarpet for the Upper Midwest.

At first everything went like lampwork. We found us decent inexpensive rooms, not far apart. Classes were interesting. We

spent most of our free waking hours together. Her resistance to
an early marriage was eroding at such a rate that I extrapolated
she'd accept me by Christmas and we'd hold the wedding right
after the spring finals.

But then we felt the kicker. Right in the belly.

We'd known that the generally good faculty was saddled with
a pompous mediocrity of a president, Bengt Malzius, whose
chief accomplishment had been to make the trustees his yes-
men. What he said, went. As a rule that didn't affect anybody on
a lower level, at least not much. But in the past year he had
decreed that academic personnel, without exception, must take a
geas to obey every University regulation while their contracts
were in force.

Few persons objected strongly. By and large, the rules were
the standard ones; and salaries were good; and the new compul-
sion was intended as a partial check on the rebelliousness,
nuttiness, and outright nihilism that had been growing to a
disturbing extent of late, not only among students but among
faculties. Ginny went along.

We'd been around for a couple of weeks when someone
notcied we were going steady, and blabbed. Ginny was called
into the president's presence. He showed her the fine print in his
regulations, that she had not thought to read.

Students and faculty, right down to the instructor level, were
not permitted to date each other.

We had a grim session that evening.

Naturally, next day I stormed past every clerk and secretary to
confront Malzius in his office. No use. He wasn't going to revise
the book for us. "Bad precedent, Mr. Matuchek, bad precedent." I agreed furiously that it was, indeed, a bad president.
The rule would have had to be stricken altogether, as the geas
didn't allow special dispensations. Nor did it allow for the case
of a student from another school, so it was pointless for me to
transfer.

The sole solution, till Ginny's contract expired in June, would
have been for me to drop out entirely, and her cold-iron determination wouldn't hear of that. Lose a whole year? What was I, a
wolf or a mouse? We had a big fat quarrel about it, right out in
public. And when you can only meet by chance, or at official
functions, it isn't just easy to kiss and make up.

Oh, sure, we were still "good friends" and still saw each
other at smokers, teas, certain lectures . . . real *dolce vita*.

Meanwhile, as she stated with the icy logic I knew was defensive but never could break past, we were human. From time to time she would be going out with some bachelor colleague, wishing he were me, and I'd squire an occasional girl around—

That's how matters stood in November.

IX

THE SKY WAS full of broomsticks and the police were going nuts trying to handle the traffic. The Homecoming game always attracts an overflow crowd, also an overflow of high spirits. These I did not share. I edged my battered prewar Chevvy past a huge two-hundred-dragonpower Lincoln with sky-blue handle, polyethylene straw, and blatting radio. It sneered at me, but I got to the vacant rack first. Dismounting, I pocketed the runekey and mooched glumly through the mob.

The Weather Bureau kachinas are obliging about game nights. There was a cool crisp tang to the air, and dry leaves scrittled across the sidewalks. A harvest moon was rising like a big yellow pumpkin over darkened campus buildings. I thought of Midwestern fields and woods, damp earthy smells and streaming mists, out beyond the city, and the wolf part of me wanted to be off and away after jackrabbits. But with proper training a were can control his reflexes and polarized light doesn't have to cause more than a primitive tingle along his nerves.

For me, the impulse was soon lost in bleaker thoughts. Ginny, my darling! She should have been walking beside me, face lifted to the wind and long hair crackling in the thin frost; but my only companion was an illegal hip flask. Why the hell was I attending the game anyhow?

Passing Teth Caph Sameth frat house, I found myself on the campus proper. Trismegistus was founded after the advent of modern science, and its layout reflects that fact. The largest edifice houses the Language Department, because exotic tongues are necessary for the more powerful spells—which is why so many African and Asian students come here to learn American slang; but there are two English halls, one for the arts college and one for Engineering Poetics. Nearby is the Therioanthropology Building, which always has interesting displays of foreign technique: this month it was Eskimo, in honor of the

visiting angekok Dr. Ayingalak. A ways off is Zoology, carefully isolated inside its pentagonal fence, for some of those long-
legged beasties are not pleasant neighbors. The medical school
has a shiny new research center, courtesy of the Rockefeller
Foundation, from which has already come such stunning ad-
vances as the Polaroid filter-lenses that make it possible for those
afflicted with the Evil Eye to lead normal lives.

The law school is unaffected. Their work has always been of
the other world.

Crossing the Mall, I went by the grimy little Physical Sciences
Building just in time for Dr. Griswold to hail me. He came
puttering down the steps, a small wizened fellow with goatee and
merry blue eyes. Somewhere behind their twinkle lay a look of
hurt bafflement; he was a child who could never quite understand why no one else was really interested in his toys.

"Ah, Mr. Matuchek," he said. "Are you attending the
game?"

I nodded, not especially sociable, but he tagged along and I
had to be polite. That wasn't to polish any apples. I was in his
chemistry and physics classes, but they were snaps. I simply
hadn't the heart to rebuff a nice, lonely old geezer.

"Me too," he went on. "I understand the cheerleaders have
planned something spectacular between halves."

"Yeah?"

He cocked his head and gave me a birdlike glance. "If you're
having any difficulty, Mr. Matuchek . . . if I can help
you . . . that's what I'm here for, you know."

"Everything's fine," I lied. "Thanks anyway, sir."

"It can't be easy for a mature man to start in with a lot of
giggling freshmen," he said. "I remember how you helped me
in that . . . ah . . . unfortunate incident last month. Believe me,
Mr. Matuchek, I am grateful."

"Oh, hell, that was nothing. I came here to get an education."
And to be with Virginia Graylock. But that's impossible now. I
saw no reason to load my troubles on him. He had an ample
supply already.

Griswold sighed, perhaps feeling my withdrawal. "I often
feel so useless," he said.

"Not in the least, sir," I answered with careful heartiness.
"How on Midgard would—oh, say alchemy, be practical without a thorough grounding in nuclear physics? You'd either get a
radioactive isotope that could kill you, or blow up half a
county."

"Of course, of course. You understand. You know something of the world—more than I, in all truth. But the students . . . well, I suppose it's only natural. They want to speak a few words, make a few passes, and get what they desire, just like that, without bothering to learn the Sanskrit grammar or the periodic table. They haven't realized that you never get something for nothing."

"They will. They'll grow up."

"Even the administration . . . this University simply doesn't appreciate the need for physical science. Now at California, they're getting a billion-volt Philosopher's Stone, but here—" Griswold shrugged. "Excuse me. I despise self-pity."

We came to the stadium, and I handed over my ticket but declined the night-seeing spectacles, having kept the witchsight given me in basic training. My seat was on the thirty-yard line, between a fresh-faced coed and an Old Grad already hollering himself raw. An animated tray went by, and I bought a hot dog and rented a crystal ball. But that wasn't to follow the details of play. I muttered over the globe and peered into it and saw Ginny.

She was seated on the fifty, opposite side, the black cat Svartalf on her lap, her hair a shout of red against the human drabness around. That witchcraft peculiarly hers was something more old and strong than the Art in which she was so adept. Even across the field and through the cheap glass gazer, she made my heart stumble.

Tonight she was with Dr. Alan Abercrombie, assistant professor of comparative mantics, sleek, blond, handsome, the lion of the tiffins. He's been paying her a lot of attention while I smoldered alone.

Quite alone. I think Svartalf considers my morals no better than his. I had every intention of fidelity, but when you've parked your broomstick in a moonlit lane and a cute bit of fluff is snuggled against you . . . those round yellow eyes glowing from a nearby tree are remarkably style-cramping. I soon gave up and spent my evenings studying or drinking beer.

Heigh-ho. I drew my coat tighter about me and shivered in the wind. That air smelled wrong somehow . . . probably only my bad mood, I thought, but I'd sniffed trouble in the future before now.

The Old Grad blasted my ears off as the teams trotted out into the moonlight, Trismegistus' Gryphons and the Albertus Magnus Wyverns. The very old grads say they can't get used to so many four-eyed runts wearing letters. Apparently a football team was composed of dinosaurs back before the goetic age. But of course the Art is essentially intellectual and has given its own tone to sports—

This game had its interesting points. The Wyverns levitated off and their tiny quarterback turned out to be a werepelican. Dushanovitch, in condor shape, nailed him on our twenty. Andrevski is the best line werebuck in the Big Ten, and held them for two downs. In the third, Pilsudski got the ball and became a kangaroo. His footwork was beautiful as he dodged a tackle—the guy had a Tarnkappe, but you could see the footprints advance—and passed to Mstislav. The Wyverns swooped low, expecting Mstislav to turn it into a raven for a field goal, but with lightning a-crackle as he fended off their counterspells, he made it into a pig . . . greased. (These were minor transformations, naturally, a quick gesture at an object already sensitized, not the great and terrible Words I was to hear before dawn.)

A bit later, unnecessary roughness cost us fifteen yards: Domingo accidentally stepped on a scorecard which had blown to the field and drove his cleats through several of the Wyverns' names. But no real harm was done, and they got the same penalty when Thorsson was carried away by the excitement and tossed a thunderbolt. At the end of the first half, the score was Trismegistus 13, Albertus Magnus 6, and the crowd was nearly ripping the benches loose.

I pulled my hat back off my ears, gave the Old Grad a dirty look, and stared into the crystal. Ginny was more of a fan than I, she was jumping and hollering, hardly seeming to notice that Abercrombie had an arm around her. Or perhaps she didn't mind—? I took a long, resentful drag at my flask.

The cheering squad paraded out onto the field. Their instruments wove through an elaborate aerial maneuver, drumming and tootling, while they made the traditional march to the Campus Queen. I'm told it's also traditional that she ride forth on a unicorn to meet them, but for some reason that was omitted this year.

The hair rose stiff on my neck and I felt the blind instinctive tug of Skinturning. Barely in time I hauled myself back toward human and sat in a cold sweat. The air was suddenly rotten with danger. Couldn't *anyone* else smell it?

I focused my crystal on the cheering squad, looking for the source, only dimly aware of the yell—

"Aleph, beth, gimel, daleth, he, vau,
Nomine Domini, bow, wow, wow!

Melt 'em in the fire and stick 'em with pins,
Trimegistus always wins—''
MacIlwraith!

"Hey, what's wrong, mister?'' The coed shrank from me, and I realized I was snarling.

"Oh . . . nothing . . . I hope.'' With an effort I composed my face and kept it from sprouting a snout.

The fattish blond kid down among the rooters didn't look harmful, but a sense of lightning-shot blackness swirled about his future. I'd dealt with him before, and—

Though I didn't snitch on him at the time, he was the one who had almost destroyed Griswold's chemistry class. Premed freshman, rich boy, not a bad guy at heart but with an unfortunate combination of natural aptitude for the Art and total irresponsibility. Medical students are notorious for merry pranks such as waltzing an animated skeleton through the girls' dorm, and he wanted to start early.

Griswold had been demonstrating the action of a catalyst, and MacIlwraith had muttered a pun-spell to make a cat boil out of the test tube. However, he slipped quantitatively and got a saber-toothed tiger. Because of the pun, it listed to starboard, but it was nonetheless a vicious, panic-raising thing. I ducked into a closet, used my pocket moonflash, and transformed. As a wolf I chased Pussy out the window and into a tree till somebody could call the Exorcism Department.

Having seen MacIlwraith do it, I took him aside and warned him that if he disrupted the class again I'd chew him out in the most literal sense. Fun is fun, but not at the expense of students who really want to learn and a pleasant elderly anachronism who's trying to teach them.

—"TEAM!''

The cheerleader waved his hands and a spurt of many-colored fire jumped out of nothingness. Taller than a man it lifted, a leaping glory of red, blue, yellow, haloed with a wheel of sparks. Slitting my eyes, I could just discern the lizardlike form, white-hot and supple, within the aura.

The coed squealed. "Thrice-blessed Hermes,'' choked the Old Grad. "What is that? A demon?''

"No, a fire elemental,'' I muttered. "Salamander. Hell of a dangerous thing to fool around with.''

My gaze ran about the field as the burning shape began to do its tricks, bouncing, tumbling, spelling out words in long flame-bands. Yes, they had a fireman close by in full canonicals, making the passes that kept the creature harmless. The situation ought to be okay. I lit a cigaret, shakily. It is not well to raise Loki's pets, and the stink of menace to come was acrid in my nostrils.

A good show, but— The crystal revealed Abercrombie clapping. Ginny, though, sat with a worried frown between the long green eyes. She didn't like this any better than I. Switch the ball back to MacIlwraith, fun-loving MacIlwraith.

I was perhaps the single member of the audience who saw what happened. The boy gestured at his baton. It sprouted wings. The fat fireman, swaying back and forth with his gestures, was a natural target for a good healthy goose.

"Yeowp!"

He rocketed heavenward. The salamander wavered. All at once it sprang on high, thinning out till it towered over the walls. We glimpsed a spinning, dazzling blur, and the thing was gone.

My cigaret burst luridly into flame. I tossed it from me. Hardly thinking, I jettisoned my hip flask. It exploded from a touch of incandescence and the alcohol burned blue. The crowd howled, hurling away their smokes, slapping at pockets where matches had kindled, getting rid of bottles. The Campus Queen shrieked as her thin dress caught fire. She got it off in time to prevent serious injury and went wailing across the field. Under different circumstances, I would have been interested.

The salamander stopped its lunatic shuttling and materialized between goalposts that began to smoke: an intolerable blaze, which scorched the grass and roared. The fireman dashed toward it, shouting the spell of extinguishment. From the salamander's mouth licked a tongue of fire, I heard a distinct Bronx cheer, then it was gone again.

The announcer, who should have been calming the spectators, screeched as it flickered before his booth. That touched off the panic! In one heartbeat, five thousand people were clawing and trampling, choking each other in the gates, blind with the maniac need to escape.

I vaulted across benches and an occasional head, down to the field. There was death on those jammed tiers. "Ginny! Ginny, come here where it's safe!"

She couldn't have heard me above the din, but came of herself, dragging a terrified Abercrombie by one wrist. We faced each other in a ring of ruin. She drew the telescoping wand from her purse.

The Gryphons came boiling out of their locker room. Boiling

is the right word: the salamander had materialized down there and playfully wrapped itself around the shower pipes.

Sirens hooted under the moon and police broomsticks shot above us, trying to curb the stampede. The elemental flashed for a moment across one besom. The rider dove it till he could jump off, and the burning stick crashed on the grass.

"God!" exclaimed Abercrombie. "The salamander's loose!"

"Tell me more," I snorted. "Ginny, you're a witch. Can you do anything about this?"

"I can extinguish the brute if it'll hold still long enough for me to recite the spell," she said. Disordered ruddy hair had tumbled past her pale, high-boned face to the fur-clad shoulders. "That's our one chance—the binding charm is broken, and it knows that!"

I whirled, remembering friend MacIlwraith, and collared him. "Were you possessed?" I shouted.

"I didn't do anything," he gasped. His teeth rattled as I shook him.

"Don't hand me that guff. I saw!"

He collapsed on the ground. "It was only for fun," he whimpered. "I didn't know—"

Well, I thought grimly, that was doubtless true. There's the trouble with the Art: with every blind powerful force man uses, fire or dynamite or atomic energy or goetics. Any meathead can learn how to begin something; these days, they start them in the third grade with spelling bees. But it's not always so easy to halt the something.

Student pranks were a standing problem at Trismegistus, as at all colleges. They were usually harmless, like sneaking into the dorms after curfew with Tarnkappen, or 'chanting female lingerie out through the windows. Sometimes they could be rather amusing, like the time the statue of a revered and dignified former president was animated and marched downtown singing bawdy songs. Often they fell quite flat, as when the boys turned Dean Hornsby into stone and it wasn't noticed for three days.

This one had gotten out of hand. The salamander could ignite this entire city.

I turned to the fireman, who was jittering about trying to flag down a police broom. In the dim shifty light, none of the riders saw him. "What'd you figure to do?" I asked.

"I gotta report back for duty," he said harshly. "And we'll need a water elemental, I guess."

"I have experience with the Hydros," offered Ginny. "I'll come along."

"Me too," I said at once.

Abercrombie glowered. "What can *you* do?"

"I'm were," I snapped. "In wolf shape I can't easily be harmed by fire. That might turn out useful."

"Wonderful, Steve!" Ginny smiled at me, the old smile which had so often gone between us. Impulsively, I grabbed her to me and kissed her.

She didn't waste energy on a slap. I collected an uppercut that tumbled me on my stern. "Not allowed," she clipped. That double-damned geas! I could see misery caged within her eyes, but her mind was compelled to obey Malzius' rules.

"That's . . . ah . . . no place for a woman . . . a lady as charming as you," murmured Abercrombie. "Let me take you home, my dear."

"I've work to do," she said impatiently. "What the devil is wrong with those cops? We've got to get a lift out of here."

"Then I shall come too," said Abercrombie. "I am not unacquainted with blessings and curses, though—ha!—I fear that ever-filled purses are a trifle beyond my scope. In any event, the Treasury Department frowns on them."

Even in that moment, with riot thundering and hell let loose on earth, I was pleased to note that Ginny paid no attention to his famous wit. She scowled abstractedly and looked around. The Campus Queen was huddled near the benches, wearing somebody's overcoat. Ginny grinned and waved her wand. The Campus Queen shucked the coat and ran toward us. Thirty seconds later, three police broomsticks had landed. The fireman commandeered them and our party was whirled over the stadium and into the street.

During that short hop, I saw three houses ablaze. The salamander was getting around!

X

WE GATHERED AT the district police station, a haggard and sooty crew with desperate eyes. The fire chief and police chief were there, and a junior officer going crazy at the switchboard. Ginny, who had collected her own broom at her lodgings, arrived with Svartalf on one shoulder and the *Handbook of Alchemy and Metaphysics* under her arm. Abercrombie was browbeating the terrified MacIlwraith till I told him to lay off.

"My duty—" he began. "I'm a proctor, you know."

I suppose it's necessary to have witch-smellers on campus, to make sure the fellows don't 'chant up liquor in the frat houses or smuggle in nymphs. And every year somebody tries to get by an exam with a familiar under his coat whispering the answers from a cribsheet. Nevertheless, I don't like professional nosy parkers.

"You can deal with him later," I said, and gave the boy a push out the door. "The salamander can fight back."

President Malzius huffed into the room. "What is the meaning of this?" he demanded. His pince-nez bobbed above full jowls. "I'll have you know, sir, I was preparing a most important address. The Lions Totem is holding a luncheon tomorrow, and—"

"Might not be any lunch," grunted the cop who had fetched him. "We got a salamander loose."

"Sala— No! It's against the rules! It is positively forbidden to—"

The man at the switchboard looked toward us. "It's just kindled the Methodist church at Fourteenth and Elm," he said. "And my God, all our equipment is already in service."

"Impossible!" cried Malzius. "A demon can't go near a church."

"How stupid does a man have to be to get your job?" Ginny fairly spat. "This *isn't* a demon. It's an elemental." When her temper was again sheathed in ice, she continued slowly: "We haven't much hope of using a Hydro to put out the salamander,

49

but we can raise one to help fight the fires. It'll always be three jumps behind, but at least the whole city won't be ruined."

"Unless the salamander gets too strong," cut in Abercrombie. His face was colorless and he spoke through stiff lips. "Then it can evaporate the Hydro."

"Summon two water beings," stammered Malzius. "Summon a hundred. I'll waive the requirement of formal application for permission to—"

"That possibility is limited, sir," Abercrombie told him. "The restraining force required is an exponential function of the total embodied mass. There probably aren't sufficient adepts in this town to control more than three at a time. If we raised four . . . we'd flood the city, and the salamander need merely skip elsewhere."

"Alan—" Ginny laid her handbook on the desk and riffled its pages. Abercrombie leaned over her shoulder, remembering to rest one hand carelessly on her hip. I choked back my prize cusswords. "Alan, for a starter, can you summon one Hydro and put it to work at plain fire fighting?"

"Of course, gorgeous one," he smiled. "That is a, ha, elemental problem."

She gave him a worried glance. "They can be as tricky as Fire or Air," she warned. "It's not enough just to know the theory."

"I have some small experience," he preened. "During the war— After this is over, come around to my place for a drink and I'll tell you about it." His lips brushed her cheek.

"Mr. Matuchek!" yelled Malzius. "Will you please stop growing fangs?"

I shook myself and suppressed the rage which had been almost as potent as moonlight.

"Look here," said the police chief. "I gotta know what's going on. You longhairs started this trouble and I don't want you making it worse."

Seeing that Ginny and Pretty Boy were, after all, legitimately busy, I sighed and whistled for a cigaret. "Let me explain," I offered. "I leaned a few things about the subject, during the war. An elemental is not the same as a demon. Any kind of demon is a separate being, as individual as you and I. An elemental is part of the basic force involved: in this case, fire, or more accurately energy. It's raised out of the basic energy matrix, given temporary individuality, and restored to the matrix when the adept is through with it."

"Huh?"

"Like a flame. A flame only exists potentially till someone lights a fire, and goes back to potential existence when you put the fire out. And the second fire you light, even on the same log, is not identical with the first. So you can understand why an elemental isn't exactly anxious to be dismissed. When one breaks loose, as this one did, it does its damnedest to stay in this world and to increase its power."

"But how come can it burn a church?"

"Because it's soulless, a mere physical force. Any true individual, human or otherwise, is under certain constraints of a . . . a moral nature. A demon is allergic to holy symbols. A man who does wrong has to live with his conscience in this world and face judgment in the next. But what does a fire care? And that's what the salamander is—a glorified fire. It's only bound by the physical laws of nature and paranature."

"So how do you, uh, put one out?"

"A Hydro of corresponding mass could do it, by mutual annihilation. Earth could bury it or Air withdraw from its neighborhood. Trouble is, Fire is the swiftest of the lot; it can flick out of an area before any other sort of elemental can injure it. So we're left with the dismissal spell. But that has to be said in the salamander's presence, and takes about two minutes."

"Yeah . . . and when the thing hears you start the words, it'll burn you down or scram. *Very* nice. What're we gonna do?"

"I don't know, chief," I said, "except it's like kissing a sheep dog." I blew hard and immediately smacked my lips. "You got to be quick. Every fire the critter starts feeds it more energy and makes it that much stronger. There's a limit somewhere—the square-cube law—but by then, it could be too powerful for humans to affect it."

"And what'd happen next?"

"Ragnarök. . . . No, I suppose not quite. Men would naturally raise correspondingly strong counter-elementals, like Hydros. But think of the control difficulties, and the incidental damage. Compared to that, the Caliphists were pikers."

Ginny turned from the desk. Abercrombie was chalking a pentagram on the floor while a sputtering Malzius had been deputized to sterilize a pocket knife with a match. (The idea was to draw a little blood from somebody. It can substitute for the usual powders, since it contains the same proteins.) The girl laid a hand on mine. "Steve, we'd take too long getting hold of every local adept and organizing them," she said. "I'm afraid the same's true of the state police or the National Guard. God knows what the salamander will do while this office is calling for help. We, though, you and I, we could at least keep track of it, with less danger to ourselves than most. Are you game?''

"Sure," I agreed. "It can't hurt me in my wolf shape . . . not permanently . . . not if I'm careful. But you're staying put."

"Ever hear about the oath of my order? Come on.''

As we went out the door, I gave Abercrombie a smug look. He had nicked his wrist and sprinkled the Signs; now he was well into the invocation. I felt cold dampness swirl through the room.

Outside, the night remained autumnally sharp, the moon high. Roofs made a saw-toothed silhouette against the leaping red glare at a dozen points around us, and sirens howled in the streets. Overhead, across the small indifferent stars, I saw what looked like a whirl of dry leaves, refugees fleeing on their sticks.

Svartalf jumped to the front end of Ginny's Cadillac, and I took the saddle behind hers. We whispered skyward.

Below us, blue fire spat and the station lights went out. Water poured into the street, a solid roar of it with President Malzius bobbing like a cork in the torrent.

"Unholy Sathanas!" I choked. "What's happened now?''

Svartalf ducked the stick low. "That idiot," groaned Ginny. "He let the Hydro slop clear over the floor . . . short circuits—'' She made a few rapid passes with her wand. The stream quieted, drew into itself, became a ten-foot-high blob glimmering in the moonlight. Abercrombie scuttled out and started it squelching toward the nearest fire.

I laughed. "Go visit his place and listen to him tell about his vast experience," I said.

"Don't kick a man when he's down," Ginny snapped. "You've pulled your share of boners, Steve Matuchek.''

Svartalf whisked the broom aloft again and we went above the chimney pots. *Oof!* I thought. Could she really be falling for that troll? A regular profile, a smooth tongue, and proximity. . . . I bit back an inward sickness and squinted ahead, trying to find the salamander.

"There!" Ginny yelled over the whistle of cloven air. Svartlaf bottled his tail and hissed.

The University district is shabby-genteel: old pseudo-Gothic caves of wood which have slipped from mansions to rooming houses, fly-specked with minor business establishments. It had begun burning merrily, a score of red stars flickering in the darkness between street lamps. Rushing near, we saw one of the stars explode in a white puff of steam. The Hydro must have clapped a sucker onto a fireplug and blanketed the place. I had a brief heretical thought that the salamander was doing a public service by eliminating those architectural teratologies. But lives and property were involved—

Tall and terrible, the elemental wavered beside the house on which it was feeding. It had doubled in size, and its core was too bright to look at. Flames whirled about the narrow head.

Svartalf braked and we hovered a few yards off, twenty feet in the air and level with the hungry mouth. Ginny was etched wild against night by that intolerable radiance. She braced herself in the stirrups and began the spell, her voice almost lost in the roar as the roof caved in. *"O Indra, Abaddon, Lucifer, Moloch, Hephaestos, Loki—"*

It heard. The seething eyes swung toward us and it leaped.

Svartalf squalled when his whiskers shriveled—perhaps only hurt vanity—and put the stick through an Immelmann turn and whipped away. The salamander bawled with the voice of a hundred blazing forests. Suddenly the heat scorching my back was gone, and the thing had materialized in front of us.

"That way!" I hollered, pointing. "In there!"

I covered Ginny's face and buried my own against her back as we went through the plate-glass front of Stub's Beer Garden. The flame-tongue licked after us, recoiled, and the salamander ramped beyond the door.

We tumbled off the broom and looked around. The tavern was empty, full of a fire-spattered darkness; everyone had fled. I saw a nearly full glass of beer on the counter and tossed it off.

"You might have offered me a drink," said Ginny. "Alan would have." Before I could recover enough to decide whether she was taunting or testing me, she went on in a rapid whisper: "It isn't trying to escape. It's gained power—confidence—it means to kills us!"

Even then, I wanted to tell her that red elflocks and a soot-smudge across an aristocratic nose were particularly enchanting. But the occasion didn't seem appropriate. "Can't get in here," I panted. "Can't do much more than ignite the building by thermal radiation, and that'll take a while. We're safe for the moment."

"Why . . . oh, yes, of course. Stub's is cold-ironed. All these college beer parlors are, I'm told."

"Yeah." I peered out the broken window. The salamander peered back, and spots danced before my eyes. "So the clientele won't go jazzing up the brew above 3.2— Quick, say your spell.''

Ginny shook her head. ''It'll just flicker away out of earshot. Maybe we can talk to it, find out—''

She trod forth to the window. The thing crouched in the street extended its neck and hissed at her. I stood behind my girl, feeling boxed and useless. Svartalf, lapping spilled beer off the counter, looked toward us and sneered.

''Ohé, Child of Light!'' she cried.

A ripple went down the salamander's back. Its tail switched restlessly, and a tree across the way kindled. I can't describe the voice that answered: crackling, bellowing, sibilant, Fire given a brain and a throat. ''Daughter of Eve, what have you to say to the likes of Me?''

''I command you by the Most High, return to your proper bonds and cease from troubling the world.''

''Ho—oh, ho, ho, ho!'' The thing sat back on its haunches— asphalt bubbled—and shuddered its laughter into the sky. *''You* command me, combustible one?''

''I have at my beck powers so mighty they could wither your puny spark into the nothingness whence it came. Cease and obey, lest worse befall you than dismissal.''

I think the salamander was, for a moment, honestly surprised. ''Greater than *Me?''* Then it howled so the tavern shook. ''You dare say there are mightier forces than Fire? Than Me, who am going to consume the earth?''

''Mightier and more beautiful, O Ashmaker. Think. You cannot even enter this house. Water will extinguish you. Earth will smother you, Air alone can keep you alive. Best you surrender now—''

I remembered the night of the afreet. Ginny must be pulling the same trick—feeling out the psychology of the thing that raged and flared beyond the door—but what could she hope to gain?

''More beautiful!'' The salamander's tail beat furrows in the street. It threw out bursting fireballs and a rain of sparks, red, blue, yellow, a one-being Fourth of July. I thought crazily of a child kicking the floor in a tantrum.

''More beautiful! Stronger! You dare say— Haaaaa—'' Teeth of incandescence gleamed in a mouth that was jumping fire. ''We shall see how beautiful you are when you lie a choked corpse!'' Its head darted to the broken glass front. It could not pass the barrier of cold iron, but it began to suck air, in and out. A furnace wave of heat sent me gasping back.

"My God . . . it's going to use up our oxygen. . . . Stay here!" I sprang for the door. Ginny shrieked, but I scarcely heard her "No!" as I went through.

Moonlight flooded me, cool and tingling between the unrestful guttering fires. I crouched to the hot sidewalk and felt a shudder when my body changed.

Wolf I was, but a wolf that my enemy could not kill . . . I hoped. My abbreviated tail thrust against the seat of my pants, and I remembered that some injuries are beyond the healing powers of even the therio shape.

Pants! Hell and damnation! In the excitement, I'd forgotten. Have you ever tried being a wolf while wrapped in shirt, trousers, underwear, and topcoat designed for a man?

I went flat on my moist black nose. My suspenders slid down and wrapped themselves about my hind legs. My tie tripped me in front and my coat gleefully wrapped everything into a bundle.

Frantic, I rolled over and tore at the cloth with my fangs. The salamander grew aware of me. Its tail slammed across my back. For a moment of searing pain, hair and skin scorched with the fabric. But that burning shredded it and I was free. The labile molecules of my body rebuilt themselves in seconds. The salamander had turned its attention away, deeming me out of action. Hardly realizing what I did, I snatched with my jaws a shoe which had dropped from my now smaller foot, laid it on the salamander's nearest white-hot toe, and bore down with both forepaws.

It bellowed and swung around to attack me afresh. That mouth gaped wide enough to bite me in half. I skittered aside. The monster paused, gauged the distance, flicked into nothingness, and materialized right on top of me.

This time I had no escape. Weighted down, I inhaled the fire that cooked my flesh. Agony sent my being whirling out of me like another flame.

XI

ALONENESS WAS NOT broken by the face which looked upon me, a face for which I have no words save that it was huge and its eyes were those of a corpse. But then, I did not see it, nor feel the cold which was deeper and stabbed me more cruelly than any I had known since last the thought-voice came through not-space and not-time to shake the senses I did not have. And the end of every hope and every faith was upon me.

"Be proud, Steven. I myself have worked to bring the death of you and your companions. To that end, I myself planted a prank in the head of a fool; for know, only thus may we safely work in the world, and I would not trust the subtleties of this one task to any minion. Pleasing though the general destruction is, material harm to men is not the true aim, and indeed my maneuverings to encompass the doom of you twain could prove costly if they provoke retaliation from the Other Side. But the danger to ours that you represent has become ever more clear as time runs toward a certain moment. I cannot know when that moment waits or what lineaments it will bear; but I know you must not be part of it."

That which was I would have cringed, were it not less than a point in nothingness.

"And yet," tolled through me, "and yet, Steven, you need not be dead. I forebode that the woman Virginia can be a worse enemy than you. Yes, I forebode that, lacking her, you are no threat to the Plan; but she, without you, might well prove so, if not as great a menace as you two conjoined. How this may be, there is no augury. But note her skills and her Gift; note that she has not twice been trapped like you; note what a spirit she bears within her. Vengefulness for you may drive her to search below the appearance of things. Or she may take some other course. I cannot tell what. But I see that although you burn, she is not absolutely inescapably caught.

"Would you live, and live well, Steven?"

Fainter than light from the farthest star flickered out of me: —
What must I do?

"Take my service. Accept my geas. The salamander will
release you before irreparable injury has occurred. When your
hurts have knit, the geas will make you do a single thing—
nothing else for a long, rich lifetime. You will call her outside,
stand well clear, and distract her wariness for the moment the
salamander will need to materialize upon her as it did upon you.

"If you refuse this, return to the instant of your own cremation
alive."

Virginia was more than infinitely remote, and I had no body to
feel with nor tongue to speak yea or nay. But the focus that was I
considered her within the anguish it had known; and it became
absolute rage, to match the absolute hate that had stormed it free
of another timelessness; and the not-scene exploded back into
the void whence it had come.

XII

I *think* THAT MY fury overcame my torment to the degree that I started fighting. I am told I got a fang-grip on the obvious place to bite a beast that is sitting on you, and did not let go. But the pain was too great for me to recall anything other than itself.

Then the salamander had vanished. The street lay bare, dark except for the moon and a distant unbroken lamp and the uneasy red glow from kindled houses, quiet except for the crackle and crash of their burning. When I'd recovered to the point of having a functional nose, what I first noticed was the acrid smoke.

That took several minutes. Barely enough unseared tissue remained to provide a DNA pattern for reconstructing the rest. When sanity returned, my shaggy head was in Ginny's lap. She was stroking it and crying. I licked her hand, feebly, with a tongue like dried-out leather. If a man, I'd have stayed a while where she had me. But being a wolf with lupine instincts, I struggled to sit up and uttered a faint, hoarse yip.

"Steve . . . almighty Father, Steve, you saved our lives," Ginny whispered. "Another couple of minutes and we'd have been suffocating. My throat still feels like mummy dust."

Svartalf trotted from the bar, looking as smug as a cat with singed whiskers is able. He meowed. Ginny gave a shaken laugh and explained:

"But you owe this fellow a pint of cream or something. He may have tipped the scales for you, same as you did for us. At least, he showed me a way to help you."

I cocked my ears.

"He manned the beer taps," she said. "I filled pitcher after pitcher and threw them out the door at the salamander. They discommoded it. It shifted around. That may've taken the heat off you, and the pressure, till you could manage to use your bite." She gripped my ruff. "And what an epic that was, those seconds while you clung!"

Beer! I wavered to my feet and back inside Stub's. They

followed me, puzzled until I whined and pointed with my muzzle at the nearest glass. "Oh, I see." Ginny snapped her fingers. "You're thirsty. No, you're dehydrated!"

She drew me a quart. I lapped it down in a cataract and signaled for more. She shook her head. "You may have forced the salamander to skip, but we have to deal with it yet. The rest will be plain water."

My therio metabolism redistributed the fluid and brought me back to complete health. My first truly clear thought was that I hoped no more beer would have to be spent on fighting the elemental. My second was that whatever the means, we'd better apply them soon.

Penalties attach to everything. The trouble with being were is that in the other shape you have, essentially, an animal brain, with a superficial layer of human personality. Or in plain language, as a wolf I'm a rather stupid man. I was only able to realize I'd better reassume the human form . . . so I trotted to the open doorway where the moonlight could touch me, and did.

Ever see a cat grin? "Omigawd!" I yelped, and started to change back.

"Hold on," said Ginny crisply. "If you must fret about my maidenly modesty, here." She peeled off her scorched but serviceable fur coat. I doubt if one has ever been donned faster than by me. It was a pretty tight fit around the shoulders but went low enough—if I was careful. Though the night wind nipped my bare shanks, my face was of salamander temperature.

That was one reason I dismissed from among my worries the vision I had had. Another was the immediacy of the peril that confronted us, now and in the flesh. Besides, even more than on the previous occasion, the physical pain which followed the restoration of consciousness had blurred memory of so insubstantial an experience. Finally, I don't suppose I wanted to think further about it.

The idea flitted through my head: Twice I've had a similar illusion while passed out. Maybe I should see a psychiatrist? No, that'd be silly. This can't be more than an idiosyncratic reaction to a kind of trauma that isn't likely to hit me again in my life.

I forgot about the matter.

Instead, I asked quickly, "Now where? The damned critter could be anyplace."

"I think it'll hang around the campus," Ginny said. "Ample grazing, and it's not particularly smart. Let's get moving."

She fetched her stick from the smoldering barroom and we

lifted. "So far," I said, "we've done nothing but waste time."

"N-no, not entirely. I did get a line on its mind." We cleared the rooftops and Ginny looked back around at me. "I wasn't sure of the precise form into which it had been conjured. You can mold the elemental forces into almost anything. But apparently the cheerleader was satisfied to give it a knowledge of English and a rudimentary intelligence. Add to that the volatile nature of Fire, and what have you got? A child."

"Some child," I muttered, hugging her coat to me.

"No, no, Steve, this is important. It has all the child's limiting traits. Improvidence, carelessness, thoughtlessness . . . A wise salamander would lie low, gathering strength slowly. It'd either realize it couldn't burn the entire planet, or if it didn't know, would never think of such a thing. Because what would it use for oxygen afterward?

"Remember, too, its fantastic vanity. It went into an insane rage when I said that powers existed more strong and beautiful than it, and the crack about beauty hurt as much as the one about strength.

"Short span of attention. It could have destroyed either you first, or Svartalf and me first, before taking care of the minor nuisance the other provided. Instead, it let its efforts be split. And it could have gritted its teeth when you took that mouthful, standing the pain for the short time needed to weight you down firmly again till you—you were dead." Her voice wavered at that, and she hastened on:

"At the same time, within that short span, if nothing distracts it, it focuses on one issue only, to the exclusion of any parts of a larger whole." She nodded thoughtfully. The long blowing hair tickled my face. "I don't know how, but some way its psychology must provide us with a lever."

My own vanity is not small. "I wasn't such a minor nuisance," I grumbled.

Ginny smiled and reached to pat my cheek. "All right, Steve, all right. I like you just the same, and now I *know* you'd make a good husband."

That left me in a comfortable glow until I wondered precisely what she was thinking of.

We spotted the salamander below us, igniting a theater, but it flicked away as I watched, and a mile off it appeared next to the medical research center. Glass brick doesn't burn so well. As we neared, I saw it petulantly kick the wall and vanish again. Ignorant and impulsive . . . a child . . . a brat from hell!

Sweeping over the campus, we saw lights in the Administration Building. "Probably that's become headquarters for our side," said Ginny. "We'd better report." Svartalf landed us on the Mall in front of the place and strutted ahead up the stairs.

A squad of cops armed with fire extinguishers guarded the door. "Hey, there!" One of them barred our path. "Where you going?"

"To the meeting," said Ginny, smoothing her tresses.

"Yeah?" The policeman's eye fell on me. "Really dressed for it, too, aren't you? Haw, haw, haw!"

I'd had about my limit for this night. I wered and peeled off his own trousers. As he lifted his billy, Ginny turned it into a small boa constrictor. I switched back to human; we left the squad to its problems and went down the hall.

The faculty meeting room was packed. Malzius had summoned every one of his professors. As we entered, I heard his orotund tones: "—disgraceful. The authorities won't so much as listen to me. Gentlemen, it is for us to vindicate the honor of Gown against Town." He blinked when Ginny and Svartalf came in, and turned a beautiful Tyrian purple as I followed in the full glory of mink coat and stubbly chin. *"Mister* Matuchek!"

"He's with me," said Ginny curtly. "We were out fighting the salamander while you sat here."

"Possibly something other than brawn, even lupine brawn, is required," smiled Dr. Alan Abercrombie. "I see that Mr. Matuchek lost his pants in a more than vernacular sense."

Like Malzius, he had changed his wet clothes for the inevitable tweeds. Ginny gave him a cold look. "I thought you were directing the Hydro," she said.

"Oh, we got enough adepts together to use three water elementals," he said. "Mechanic's work. I felt my job was here. We can readily control the fires—"

"If the salamander weren't always lighting fresh ones," clipped Ginny. "And each blaze it starts, it gets bigger and stronger, while you sit here looking beautiful."

"Why, thank you, my dear," he laughed.

I jammed my teeth together so they hurt. She had actually smiled back at him.

"Order, order!" boomed President Malzius. "Please be seated, Miss Graylock. Have you anything to contribute to the discussion?"

"Yes. I understand the salamander now." She took a place at

the end of the table. That was the last vacant chair, so I hovered miserably in the background wishing her coat had more buttons.

"Understand it sufficiently well to extinguish it?" asked Professor van Linden of Alchemy.

"No. But I know how it thinks."

"We're more interested in how it operates," said van Linden. "How can we make it hold still for a dismissal?" He cleared his throat. "Obviously, we must first know by what process it shuttles around so fast—"

"Oh, that's simple," piped Griswold. He was drowned by van Linden's fruity bass:

"—which is, of course, by the well-known affinity of Fire for Quicksilver. Since virtually every home these days has at least one thermometer—"

"With due respect, my good sir," interrupted Vittorio of Astrology, "you are talking utter hogwash. It is a simple matter of the conjunction of Mercury and Neptune in Scorpio—"

"You're wrong, sir!" declared van Linden. "Dead wrong! Let me show you the *Ars Thaumaturgica.*" He glared around after his copy, but it had been mislaid and he had to use an adaptation of the Dobu yam-calling chant to find it. Meanwhile Vittorio was screaming:

"No, no, no! The conunction, with Uranus opposing in the ascendant . . . as I can easily prove—" He went to the blackboard and started to draw a diagram.

"Oh, come now!" snorted Jasper of Metaphysics. "I don't understand how you can both be so wrong. As I showed in the paper I read at the last Triple-A-S meeting, the intrinsic nature of the matrix—"

"That was disproved ten years ago!" roared van Linden. "The affinity—"

"Ding an sich—"

"—up Uranus—"

I sidled over and tugged at Griswold's sleeve. He pattered into a corner with me. "Okay, how does the bloody thing work?" I asked.

"Oh . . . merely a question of wave mechanics," he whispered. "According to the Heisenberg uncertainty principle, a photon has a finite probability of being at any point of space. The salamander uses a simple diffraction process to change the spatial coordinates of psi squared, in effect going from point to point without crossing the intervening distance, much like an electron making a quantum jump, although, to be sure, the analogy is not precise due to the modifying influence of—''

"Never mind," I sighed. "This confab is becoming a riot. Wouldn't we do better to—"

"—stick by the original purpose," agreed Abercrombie, joining us. Ginny followed. Van Linden blacked Vittorio's eye while Jasper threw chalk at both of them. Our rump group went over near the door.

"I've already found the answer to our problem," said Abercrombie, "but I'll need help. A transformation spell. We'll turn the salamander into something we can handle more easily."

"That's dangerous," said Ginny. "You'll need a really strong T-spell, and that sort can backfire. What happens then is unpredictable."

Abercrombie straightened himself with a look of pained nobility. "For you, my dear, no hazard is too great."

She regarded him with admiration. It does take guts to use the ultimate runes. "Let's go," she said. "I'll help."

Griswold plucked at my arm. "I don't like this, Mr. Matuchek," he confided. "The Art is too unreliable. There ought to be some method grounded in nature and nature's quantitative laws."

"Yeah," I said disconsolately. "But what?" I paddled after Ginny and Abercrombie, who had their heads together over the handbook. Griswold marched beside me and Svartalf made a gesture with his tail at the Trismegistus faculty. They were too embroiled to notice.

We went out past an enraged but well-cowed squad of cops. The Physical Sciences hall stood nearby, and its chemistry division held stuff that would be needed. We entered an echoing gloom.

The freshman lab, a long room full of workbenches, shelves, and silence, was our goal. Griswold switched on the lights and Abercrombie looked around. "But we'll have to bring the salamander here," he said. "We can't do anything except in its actual presence."

"Go ahead and make ready," the girl told him. "I know how to fetch the beast. A minor transformation—" She laid out some test tubes, filled them with various powders, and sketched her symbols on the floor. Those ball-point wands are handy.

"What's the idea?" I asked.

"Oh, get out of the way," she snapped. I told myself she was only striking at her own weariness and despair, but it hurt. "We'll use its vanity, of course. I'll prepare some Roman candles and rockets and stuff . . . shoot them off, and naturally it'll come to show it can do more spectacular things.''

Griswold and I withdrew into a corner. This was big-league play. I was frankly scared, and the little scientist's bony knees were beating a tattoo in march time. Even Ginny—yes, sweat beaded that smooth forehead. If this didn't work, we here were probably done for: either the salamander or the backlash of the spell could finish us. And we had no way of knowing whether the beast had grown too strong for a transformation.

The witch got her fireworks prepared, and went to an open window and leaned out. Hissing balls of blue and red, streamers of golden sparks, flew skyward and exploded.

Abercrombie had completed his diagrams. He turned to smile at us. "It's all right," he said. "Everything under control. I'm going to turn the salamander's energy into matter. E equals m c squared, you know. Just light me a Bunsen burner, Matuchek, and set a beaker of water over it. Griswold, you turn these lights off and the Polaroid bulbs on. We need polarized radiation.''

We obeyed, though I hated to see an old and distinguished man acting as lab assistant to this patronizing slick-paper adman's dream. "You *sure* it'll work?" I asked.

"Of course," he smiled. "I've had experience. I was in the Quartermaster Corps during the war.''

"Yeah," I said, "but turning dirt into K rations isn't the same thing as transforming that monster. You and your experience!''

Suddenly and sickly, remembering how he had bungled with the Hydro, I realized the truth. Abercrombie was confident, unafraid—because he didn't *know* enough!

For a minute I couldn't unfreeze my muscles. Griswold fiddled unhappily with some metallic samples. He'd been using them the other day for freshman experiments, trying to teach us the chemical properties; Lord, it seemed a million years ago. . . .

"Ginny!" I stumbled toward her where she stood at the window throwing rainbows into the air. "My God, darling, stop—''

Crack! The salamander was in the room with us.

I lurched back from it, half-blinded. Grown hideously bigger, it filled the other end of the lab, and the bench tops smoked.

"Oh, so!" The voice of Fire blasted our eardrums. Svartalf shot to a shelf top and upset bottles of acid onto the varmint. It didn't notice. "So, small moist pests, you would try to outdo Me!''

Abercrombie and Ginny lifted their wands and shouted the few brief words of transformation.

Crouched back into my corner, peering through a sulfurous reek of fumes, I saw Ginny lurch and then jump for safety. She must have sensed the backlash. There came a shattering explosion and the air was full of flying glass.

My body shielded Griswold, and the spell didn't do more to me than turn me lupine. Ginny was on her hands and knees behind a bench, half-unconscious . . . but unhurt, unhurt, praise the good Powers forever. Svartalf—a Pekingese dog yapped on the shelf. Abercrombie was gone, but a chimpanzee in baggy tweeds scuttered wailing toward the door.

A fire-blast rushed before the ape. He whirled, screamed, and shinnied up a steam pipe. The salamander arched its back and howled with laughter.

"You would use your tricks on Me? Almighty Me, terrible Me, beautiful Me? Ha, they bounce off like water from a hot skillet! And I, I, I am the skillet which is going to fry you!"

Somehow, the low-grade melodrama of its speech was not in the least ridiculous. For this was the childish, vainglorious, senselessly consuming thing which was loose on earth to make ashes of men and the homes of men.

Under the Polaroids, I switched back to human and rose to my feet behind a bench. Griswold turned on a water faucet and squirted a jet with his finger. The salamander hissed in annoyance—yes, water still hurt, but we had too little liquid here to quench it, you'd need a whole lake by this time— It swung its head, gape-mouthed, aimed at Griswold, and drew a long breath.

All is vanity. . . .

I reeled over to the Bunsen burner that was heating a futile beaker of water. Ginny looked at me through scorched bangs. The room roiled with heat, sweat rivered off me. I didn't have any flash of genius, I acted on raw instinct and tumbled memories.

"Kill us," I croaked. "Kill us if you dare. Our servant is more powerful than you. He'll hound you to the ends of creation."

"Your servant?" Flame wreathed the words.

"Yeah . . . I mean yes . . . our servant, that Fire which fears not water!"

The salamander stepped back a pace, snarling. It was not yet so strong that the very name of water didn't make it flinch. "Show me!" it chattered. "Show me! I dare you!"

"Our servant . . . small, but powerful," I rasped. "Brighter and more beautiful than you, and above taking harm from the Wet Element." I staggered to the jars of metal samples and grabbed a pair of tongs. "Have you the courage to look on him?"

The salamander bristled. "Have I the *courage?* Ask rather, does it dare confront Me?"

I flicked a glance from the corner of my eye. Ginny had risen and was gripping her wand. She scarcely breathed, but her eyes were narrowed.

There was a silence. It hung like a world's weight in that room, smothering what noises remained: the crackle of fire, Abercrombie's simian gibber, Svartalf's indignant yapping. I took a strip of magnesium in the tongs and held it to the burner flame.

It burst into a blue-white actinic radiance from which I turned dazzled eyes. The salamander was less viciously brilliant. I saw the brute accomplish the feat of simultaneously puffing itself up and shrinking back.

"Behold!" I lifted the burning strip. Behind me, Ginny's rapid mutter came: *"O Indra, Abaddon, Lucifer—"*

The child mind, incapable of considering more than one thing at a time . . . but for how long a time? I had to hold its full attention for the hundred and twenty seconds required.

"Fire," said the salamander feverishly. "Only another fire, one tiny piece of that Force from which I came."

"Can you do this, buster?"

I plunged the strip into the beaker. Steam puffed from the water, it boiled and bubbled—and the metal went on burning!

"—abire ex orbis terrestris—"

"Mg plus H_2O yields MgO plus H_2," whispered Griswold reverently.

"Keek-eek-eek!" said Abercrombie.

"Yip-yip-yip!" said Svartalf.

"It's a trick!" screamed the salamander. "It's impossible! If even I cannot— No!"

"Stay where you are!" I barked in my best Army manner. "Do you doubt that my servant can follow you wherever you may flee?"

"I'll kill that little monster!"

"Go right ahead, chum," I agreed. "Want to fight the duel under the ocean?"

Whistles skirled above our racket. The police had seen through these windows.

"I'll show you, I will!" The roar was almost a sob. I ducked behind the bench, pulling Griswold with me. A geyser of flame rushed where I had been.

"Nyaah, nyaah, nyaah," I called. "You can't catch me! Scaredy-cat!"

Svartalf gave me a hard look.

The floor trembled as the elemental came toward me, not going around the benches but burning its way through them. Heat clawed at my throat. I spun down toward darkness.

And it was gone. Ginny cried her triumphant *"Amen!"* and displaced air cracked like thunder.

I lurched to my feet. Ginny fell into my arms. The police entered the lab and Griswold hollered something about calling the fire department before his whole building whiffed off in smoke. Abercrombie scampered out a window and Svartalf jumped down from the shelf. He forgot that a Pekingese isn't as agile as a cat, and his popeyes bubbled with righteous wrath.

XIII

OUTSIDE, THE MALL was cool and still. We sat on dewed grass and looked at the moon and thought what a great and simple wonder it is to be alive.

The geas held us apart, but tenderness lay on Ginny's lips. We scarcely noticed when somebody ran past us shouting that the salamander was gone, nor when church bells began pealing the news to men and Heaven.

Svartalf finally roused us with his barking. Ginny chuckled. "Poor fellow. I'll change you back as soon as I can, but now I've more urgent business. Come on, Steve."

Griswold, assured that his priceless hall was safe, followed us at a tactful distance. Svartalf merely sat where he was . . . too shocked to move, I guess, at the idea that there could be more important affairs than turning him back into a cat.

Dr. Malzius met us halfway, under one of the campus elms. Moonlight spattered his face and gleamed in the pince-nez. "My dear Miss Graylock," he began, "is it indeed true that you have overcome that menace to society? Most noteworthy. Accept my congratulations. The glorious annals of this great institution of which I have the honor to be president—"

Ginny faced him, arms akimbo, and nailed him with surely the chilliest gaze he had ever seen. "The credit belongs to Mr. Matuchek and Dr. Griswold," she said. "I shall so inform the press. Doubtless you'll see fit to recommend a larger appropriation for Dr. Griswold's outstanding work."

"Oh, now, really," stammered the scientist. "I didn't—"

"Be quiet, you ninnyhammer," whispered Ginny. Aloud: "Only through his courageous and farsighted adherence to the basic teachings of natural law— Well, you can fill in the rest for yourself, Malzius. I don't think you'd be awfully popular if you went on starving his department."

"Oh . . . indeed . . . after all—" The president expanded himself. "I have already given careful consideration to the idea. Was going to recommend it at the next meeting of the board, in fact."

"I'll hold you to that," Ginny said. "Next: this stupid rule against student-faculty relationships. Mr. Matuchek will shortly be my husband—"

Whoosh! I tried to regain my breath.

"My dear Miss Graylock," sputtered Malzius, "decorum . . . propriety . . . why, he isn't even decent!"

I realized with horror that somehow, in the hullabaloo, I'd lost Ginny's coat.

A pair of cops approached, dragging a hairy form that struggled in their arms. A third man carried the garments the chimp had shed. "Begging your pardon, Miss Graylock." The tone was pure worship. "We found this monkey loose and—"

"Oh, yes." She laughed. "We'll have to restore him. But not right away. Steve needs those pants worse."

I got into them like a snake headed down a hole. Ginny turned back to smile with angelic sweetness at Malzius.

"Poor Dr. Abercrombie," she sighed. "These things will happen when you deal with paranatural forces. Now I believe, sir, that you have no rule against faculty members conducting research."

"Oh, no," said the president shakily. "Of course not. On the contrary! We expect our people to publish—"

"To be sure. Well, I have in mind a most interesting research project involving transformations. I'll admit it's a teeny bit dangerous. It could backfire as Dr. Abercrombie's spell did." Ginny leaned on her wand and regarded the turf thoughtfully. "It could even . . . yes, there's even a small possibility that it could turn *you* into an ape, dear Dr. Malzius. Or, perhaps, a worm. A long slimy one. But we mustn't let that stand in the way of science, must we?"

"What? But—"

"Naturally," purred the witch, "if I were allowed to conduct myself as I wish with my fiancé, I wouldn't have time for research."

Malzius took a bare fifty words to admit defeat. He stumped off in tottery grandeur while the last fire-glow died above the campus roofs.

Ginny gave me a slow glance. "The rule can't officially be stricken till tomorrow," she murmured. "Think you can cut a few classes then?"

"Keek-eek-eek," said Dr. Alan Abercrombie. Then Svartalf arrived full of resentment and chased him up the tree.

XIV

A SHORT INTERLUDE this time. We finished our first academic year okay. Ginny was proud of my straight A's in shamanistics and calculus, and assisted me over some humps in arcane languages. (Griswold did me a similar service for electronics.) She had to modify her own plan of further study somewhat, if we were to get married in June.

You might think a former high-salaried New York witch would be anything but innocent. Certainly Ginny had a temper and her special kind of sophistication. However, quite apart from a stubbornly loyal and clean personality, she'd concentrated on those branches of the Art which require maidenhood. That kind of specialist commands fees in proportion to rarity.

Now my fire-and-ice girl was to become only another bride. And what's so only about that? Next year she could acquire the techniques necessary to compensate for being wedded.

We couldn't entirely hide our roles in snuffing the salamander from the news media; but with the eager cooperation of Malzius, who kept blaring about how the University Team had saved this fair city, we managed to obfuscate it so that we soon dropped out of the public eye. Griswold was conscience-stricken at receiving more credit than he thought he deserved, and indignant at our receiving less than we deserved, till we pointed out that the first was essential to getting his department modernized and the second to protecting our privacy. Besides, if we wanted to be sure the rule on dating was rescinded, and that conditions at Trismegistus would remain tolerable for us in other respects, we had to give Malzius tacit cooperation in rescuing his pride and not getting stuck with a craven image.

So, in brief, that winter and spring were wonderful and full of wonder. I could skip well ahead, but can't help dwelling on— oh, at least the moment when:

"No," I said to my bride's business associate. "You are not coming along on the honeymoon."

He laid back his ears. "Mneowrr!" he said resentfully.

"You'll do fine by yourself in this apartment for a month," I
told him. "The superintendent has promised to feed you every
evening, the same time as he sets out the milk for the Brownie.
And don't forget, when the Brownie comes in here, you are not
to chase after him. After the last time you did that, three times in
a row when Ginny and I went out to dinner, the Good People
sweetened our martinis."

Svartalf glowered, yellow-eyed, and switched his tail. I
imagine that was cat for, Well, dammit, anything the size of a
mouse, which scuttles like a mouse, has got to expect to be
treated like a mouse.

"He'll be here to dust and change *your* litterbox," I reminded
Svartalf in my sternest voice. "You'll have the run of the place,
and you can fly up the chimney on the whisk broom anytime you
want fresh air. But the Brownie is off limits, bucko, and if I come
back and hear you've been after him, I'll take wolf-shape and
tree you. Understand?"

Svartalf jerked his tail at me, straight upward.

Virginia Graylock, who had for an incredible few hours been
Mrs. Steven Matuchek, entered the living room. I was so
stunned by the view of tall slenderness in a white dress, straight
aristocratic features and red hair shouting down to her shoulders,
that the voice didn't register except as a symphonic accompani-
ment. She had to repeat: "Darling, are you absolutely sure we
can't take him? His feelings are hurt."

I recovered enough to say, "His feelings are made of tool
steel. It's okay if he wants to share our bed when we get back, I
guess—within reason—but fifteen pounds of black witchcat on
my stomach when I'm honeymooning is out of reason. Besides,
what's worse, he'd prefer your stomach."

Ginny blushed. "It will be odd without my familiar, after
these many years. If he promised to behave—"

Svartalf, who had been standing on a table, rubbed against her
hip and purred. Which was not a bad idea, I thought. However, I
had my foot down and wasn't about to lift it. "He's incapable of
behaving," I said. "And you won't need him. We're going to
forget the world and its work, aren't we? I'm not going to study
any texts, nor visit any of my fellow theriomorphs, even that
were-coyote family down at Acapulco who invited us to drop in.
It's going to be just us two, and I don't want any pussy—" I
braked as fast as possible. She didn't notice, only sighed a little,
nodded, and stroked a soothing hand across the cat's back.

"Very well, dear," she said. With a flick of her earlier self: "Enjoy wearing the family pants while you can."

"I intend to do so all the time," I bragged.

She cocked her head. "*All* the time?" Hastily: "We'd best be on our way. Everything's packed."

"Check, mate," I agreed. She stuck out her tongue at me. I patted Svartalf. "So long, chum. No grudges, I trust?" He bit a piece out of my hand and said he supposed not. Ginny hugged him, seized my arm, and hurried me out.

The home to which we'd be coming back was a third-floor apartment near Trismegistus University. Our wedding this morning had been quiet, a few friends at the church, a luncheon afterward at somebody's house, and then we made our farewells. But Ginny's connections in New York and mine in Hollywood have money. Several people had clubbed together to give us a Persian carpet: a somewhat overwhelming present, but show me the bridal couple who don't like a touch of luxury.

It lay on the landing, its colors aglow in the sun. Our baggage was piled in the rear. We snuggled down side by side on cushions of polymerized sea foam. Ginny murmured the command words. We started moving so smoothly I didn't notice when we were airborne. The carpet wasn't as fast or flashy as a sports-model broomstick, but the three hundred dragonpower spell on it got us out of the city in minutes.

Midwestern plains rolled green and enormous beneath us, here and there a river like argent ribbon; but we were alone with birds and clouds. No wind of our passage got by the force screen. Ginny slipped off her dress. She had a sunsuit beneath it, and now I understand transistor theory; the absence of material has as real an existence as the presence. We sunbathed on our way south, stopped at twilight for supper at a charming little restaurant in the Ozarks, but decided not to stay in a broomotel. Instead, we flew on. The carpet was soft and thick and roomy. I started to raise the convertible top, but Ginny said we'd keep warm if we flew low, and she was right. Stars crowded the sky, until a big yellow Southern moon rose to drown half of them, and the air was murmurous, and we could hear crickets chorus from the dark earth below, and nothing else is any of your business.

XV

I KNEW EXACTLY where I was bound. A wartime friend of mine, Juan Fernandez, had put his Army experience to good use. He'd been in the propaganda section, and done many excellent scripts. These days, instead of preparing nightmares to send the enemy, he was broadcasting a popular dream series, and his sponsors were paying him accordingly. In fact, everyone loved Fernandez except the psychoanalysts, and they're obsolete now that scientific research has produced some really efficient antipossession techniques. Last year he had built a lodge in the country of his ancestors. It stood entirely by itself on the Sonora coast, at one of the loneliest spots on Midgard and one of the most beautiful. Fernandez had offered me the use of it this month, and Ginny and I had set our wedding date accordingly.

We glided down about noon the next day. Westward the Gulf of California burned blue and molten white. Surf broke on a wide strip of sand beach, cliffs rose tier upon tier, finally the land itself rolled off to the east, dry, stark, and awesome. The lodge made a spot of green, perched on a bluff just above the strand.

Ginny clapped her hands. "Oh! I wouldn't have believed it!"

"You Easterners don't know what big country is," I said smugly.

She shaded her eyes against the sun-dazzle and pointed. "What's that, though?"

My own gaze traveled no further than her arm, but I remembered. Atop a cliff, about a mile north of the lodge and several hundred feet higher, crumbling walls surrounded a rubble heap; the snag of a tower stood at the northwest angle, to scowl among winds. "La Fortaleza," I said. "Spanish work, seventeenth century. Some don had an idea he could exploit this area for profit. He erected the castle as a strong point and residence, brought a wife here from Castile. But everything went wrong and the place was soon abandoned."

"Can we explore it?"

"If you like."

Ginny laid a hand on my shoulder. "What's wrong, Steve?"

"Oh . . . nothing. I don't care for the Fortaleza myself. Even as a human by daylight, I sense wrongness. I went over there once after dark, wolf-shape, and it stank. Not so much in a physical way, but— Oh, forget it."

She said soberly: "The Spaniards enslaved the Indians in those times, didn't they? I imagine a lot of human agony went into that castle."

"And left a residuum. Yeah, probably. But hell, it was long ago. We'll have a look around. The ruins are picturesque, and the view from there is tremendous."

"If you really are worried about ghosts—"

"Forget it, darling! I'm not superstitious!"

And we landed at the lodge and did indeed forget it.

The place was built in cloister style, white walls and red tile roof enclosing a courtyard where a fountain played. But there was also a garden surrounding the outside, green with leaves and grass, red and white and purple and gold with flower beds. We were quite alone. The grounds were elementalized for Earth and Water, hence needed no attendants; the other two elemental forces kept the house air-conditioned, and an expensive cleanliness spell had also been put on it. Since Ginny was now temporarily out of the goetic game, she prepared a Mexican lunch from the supplies we'd brought along. She was so beautiful in shorts, halter, and frilly apron that I hadn't the heart to offer to teach her to cook. She exclaimed aloud when the dirty dishes floated back to the kitchen and followed them to watch them dive into soapy water and frisk around. "It's the most up-to-date automatic dishwasher I've heard of!" she cried.

So we had plenty of time for an afternoon of surf bathing. At sunset we climbed back a stairway hewn from the yellow rock, ravenous, and I prepared steaks by introducing them to a charcoal fire but allowing no further conversation. Afterward we moved onto a patio overlooking the sea. We sat in deck chairs, holding hands, and the stars came out to greet us.

"Let's Skinturn at moonrise and frolic a bit," I suggested. "You'd make a delightful lady wolf. Or, hm, I wou— Never mind!"

She shook her head. "I can't, Steve, dear."

"Sure, you can. You'd need a T-spell, of course, but—"

"That's just it. You have lycanthropic genes; all you need to change species is polarized light. But for me it's a major transformation, and . . . I don't know . . . I don't feel able to do it. I can't even remember the formulas. I guess I'm not able, any more. My knowledge has gotten even fuzzier than I expected. I'll need refresher courses in the most elementary things. Right now, only a professional could change me.''

I sighed. I'd been looking forward to wolfing it. You don't really know the world till you've explored it with animal as well as human senses, and Ginny was certainly a part of the world— Whoa, there! "Okay," I said. "Later, when you're an adept again.''

"Of course. I'm sorry, darling. If you want to run off by yourself, werewise, go ahead.''

"Not without you.''

She chuckled. "You might get fleas, anyhow.'' She was leaning over to nibble my ear when we both heard the footsteps.

I rose to my feet, muttering inhospitable things. A form, shadowy under the velvet sky, approached us over a path which snaked inland. Who the devil, I thought. Someone from the village, ten miles hence? But— My nose in human shape is dull by my wolf standards, but suddenly caught a smell I didn't like. It wasn't an unpleasant odor; indeed, its pungency seemed at once to heighten Ginny's half-visible beauty to an unbearable degree. And yet something in me bristled.

I stepped forward as the stranger reached our patio. He was medium-tall for a Mexican, which made him shorter than me. He moved so gracefully, no more loud than smoke, that I wondered if he could be a werecougar. A dark cape over an immaculate white suit garbed the supple body. His wide-brimmed hat made the face obscure, till he took it off and bowed. Then light from a window touched him. I had never met a handsomer man, high cheekbones, Grecian nose, pointed chin, wide-set eyes of a gold-flecked greenish gray. His skin was whiter than my wife's, and the sleek hair was ashblond. I wondered if he was a Mexican national, let alone of native stock.

"Buenas noches, señor," I said curtly. "Pardón, pero no hablamos español." Which was not quite true, but I didn't want to make polite chitchat.

The voice that answered was tenor or contralto, I couldn't decide which, but music in any case. "I' faith, good sir, I speak as many tongues as needful. I pray forgiveness, yet having observed from afar that this house was lighted, methought its master had returned, and I did come with neighborly greeting.''

His pronunciation was as archaic as the phrasing: the vowels, for instance, sounded Swedish, though the sentences didn't have a Swedish rhythm. At the moment, however, I was surprised by the words themselves. "Neighbor?"

"My sister and I have made abode within yon ancient castle."

"What? But— Oh." I stopped. Fernandez hadn't mentioned anything like this, but then, he himself hadn't been here for months. The Fortaleza and grounds belonged to the Mexican government, from which he had purchased several acres for his hideaway. "Did you buy it?"

"A few rooms were made a right comfortable habitation for us, sir," he evaded. "I hight Amaris Maledicto." The mouth, so cleanly shaped that you scarcely noticed how full it was, curved into an altogether charming smile. Had it not been for the odor low in my nostrils, I might have been captivated. "You and your fair lady are guests of Señor Fernandez? Be welcome."

"We've borrowed the lodge." Ginny's voice was a tad breathless. I stole a glance, and saw by the yellow windowlight that her eyes were full upon his, and brilliant. "Our . . . our name . . . Virginia. Steven and Virginia . . . Matuchek." I thought, with a cold sort of puzzlement, that brides were supposed to make a great show of being Mrs. So-and-So, not play it down in that fashion. "It's very kind of you to walk this far. Did your . . . your sister . . . come too?"

"Nay," said Maledicto. "And truth to tell, however glad of your society, 'tis belike well she was spared the sight of such loveliness as is yours. 'Twould but excite envy and wistfulness."

From him, somehow, unbelievably, in that flowering night above the great dim sea, under stars and sheer cliffs, that speech to another man's wife wasn't impudent, or affected, or anything except precisely right. By the half-illumination on the patio, I saw Ginny blush. Her eyes broke free of Maledicto's, the lashes fluttered birdlike, she answered confusedly: "It's kind of you . . . yes . . . won't you sit down?"

He bowed again and flowed into a chair. I plucked at Ginny's dress, drew her back toward the house and hissed furiously: "What the devil are you thinking of? Now we won't get rid of this character for an hour!"

She shook free with an angry gesture I remembered from past quarrels. "We have some cognac, Señor Maledicto," she said. It would have been her best smile she gave him, slow and sideways, except that the faintest tremble remained upon her lips. "I'll get it. And would you like a cigar? Steve brought some Perfectos."

I sat down while she bustled inside. For a moment I was too outraged to speak. Maledicto took the word. "A charming lass, sir. A creature of purest delight."

"My *wife*," I growled. "We came here for privacy."

"Oh, misdoubt me not!" His chuckle seemed to blend with the sea-murmur. Where he sat, in shadow, I could only make him out as a white and black blur, those oblique eyes glowing at me. "I understand, and shall not presume upon your patience. Mayhap later 'twould please you to meet my sister—"

"I don't play bridge."

"Bridge? Oh, aye, indeed, I remember. 'Tis a modern game with playing cards." His hand sketched an airy dismissal. "Nay, sir, our way is not to force ourselves unwanted. Indeed, we cannot visit save where some desire for us exists, albeit unspoken. 'Twas but . . . how should a man know aught from our dwelling, save that neighbors had arrived? And now I cannot churlishly refuse your lady's courtesy. But 'tis for a short time only, sir."

Well, that was as soft an answer as ever turned away wrath. I still couldn't like Maledicto, but my hostility eased till I could analyze my motives. Which turned out to be largely reaction to a third wheel. Something about him, maybe the perfume he used, made me desire Ginny more than ever before.

But my rage came back as she hovered over him with the cognac, chattered too loudly and laughed too much and insisted on having the Maledictos to dinner tomorrow! I hardly listened to their conversation. He talked smoothly, wittily, never quite answering my questions about himself. I sat and rehearsed what I'd say after he left.

Finally he rose. "I must not keep you," he said. "Moreover, 'tis a stony path to the Fortaleza, one with which I am not well familiar. Thus I must go slowly, lest I lose my way."

"Oh! But that could be dangerous." Ginny turned to me. "You've been over the trail, Steve. Show him home."

"I'd not afford you that trouble," demurred Maledicto.

"It's the least we can do. I insist, Amaris. It won't take you long, Steve. You said you felt like a run in the moonlight, and look, the moon is almost due up."

"Okay, okay, okay!" I snapped, as ungraciously as possible. I could, indeed, turn wolf on the way back, and work some of my temper off. If I tried to argue with her now, the way I felt, our second night would see one Armageddon of a quarrel. "Let's go."

He kissed her hand. She said farewell, in a soft, blurry voice, like a schoolgirl in love for the first time. He had a flashlight; it made a small, bobbing puddle of radiance before us, picking out stones and clumps of sagebrush. The moonglow on the eastern ridges grew stronger. I felt it tingle along my nerves. For a while, as we wound across the mountainside, only the scrunch of our shoes made any noise.

"You brought no torch of your own, sir," he said at last. I grunted. Why should I tell him of my witch-sight—to say nothing of the fact that I was a werewolf who in my alternate species had no need of flashlights? "Well, you shall take mine back," he continued. "The way were perilous otherwise."

That I knew. An ordinary human would blunder off the trail, even in bright moonlight. It was a dim, nearly obliterated path, and the land was gnarled and full of shadows. If he then got excited, the man would stumble around lost till dawn—or, quite probably, go off a precipice and smash his skull.

"I will call for it tomorrow evening." Maledicto sighed happily. "Ah, sir, 'tis rare good you've come. New-wedded folk are aye overflowingly full of love, and Cybelita has long been as parched as Amaris."

"Your sister?" I asked.

"Yes. Would you care to meet her this eventide?"

"No."

Silence fell again. We dipped into a gut-black ravine, rounded a crag, and could no more see the lodge. Nothing but the dim sheen of waters, the moonglow opposite, the suddenly very far and cold stars, lit that country. I saw the broken walls of the Fortaleza almost over my head, crowning their cliff like teeth in a jaw. Maledicto and I might have been the last living creatures on Midgard.

He stopped. His flashlight snapped out. "Good night, Señor Matuchek!" he cried. His laughter rang evil and beautiful.

"What?" I blinked bewildered into the murk that had clamped on me. "What the hell do you mean? We're not at the castle yet!"

"Nay. Proceed thither if thou wilt. And if thou canst."

I heard his feet start back down the path. They didn't crunch the gravel any more. They were soft and rapid, like the feet of a bounding animal.

Back toward the lodge.

A moment I stood as if cast in lead. I could hear the faintest movement of air, rustling dry sagebrush, the ocean. Then my heartbeat shook all other noises out of me.

"Ginny!" I screamed.

I whirled and raced after him. My toes caught a rock, I pitched over, bloodied my hands with the fall. I staggered up, the bluffs and gullies flung my curses back at me, I went stumbling down a slope and through brush and cactus.

Again my foot snagged on something and I fell. This time I cracked my head against a boulder. The impact wasn't serious, but pain speared through me, lights burst, and for a minute or two I lay half-stunned.

And I felt a new presence in the night.

And through the hopeless aloneness that streamed from it and into my heart and marrow, I felt wire-taut expectation.

—success in my grasp, this third time—both of them, he dead and she corrupted, afterward broken by remorse—safety from the threat that can be seen over them like a stormcloud as that certain moment draws nigh—safety at last—

And the thought jagged more dreadfully sharp than any pain: Maledicto couldn't affect her by himself, not that strongly anyhow, not overcoming the love and pride and decency of her . . . no, the Tempter has worked in person on my girl—

I did not know what evil was intended. But in one flash, the vision of her alone with Maledicto burned me free of everything else, of hurt, weakness, the sense and even for a while the memory of a sneering Observer. I howled forth my rage and desperation, sprang erect, and ran.

That was sheer berserkergang. I didn't consciously notice what I was doing. Doubtless this had been planned, so I'd fall over a cliff to my death. But half-animal instincts and reflexes— I suppose—guarded me.

Presently I'd exhausted my wind and had to stop and gasp a while. That forced pause gave my sanity a chance to take over.

Glaring around, I saw neither castle nor lodge. I'd lost my way.

XVI

MY GAZE swept down the slope to the drop-off. The sea was a wan glimmer beyond. More of my wits came back. Maledicto had adroitly removed me from the scene, perhaps murdered me: if I were the untrained unspecial Homo sapiens he assumed. But I had a little more in reserve than he knew, such as witch-sight. I mumbled the formula and felt the retinal changes. At once I could see for miles. The view was blurred, of course; the human eyeball can't focus infrared wavelengths very well; but I could recognize landmarks. I set a general course and made for home.

With nightmare slowness. Maledicto had gone faster than human.

Nearly full, the moon broke over the hills.

The change was on me before I had overtly willed it. I didn't stop to undress, bundle my clothes and carry them in my mouth. My wolf-jaws ripped everything to rags except the elastic-banded shorts, and I went shadow-swift over the mountainside. If you think a giant bobtailed wolf in shorts is ridiculous, you're probably right; but it didn't occur to me just then.

I couldn't see as far with lupine eyes. However, I could smell my own trail, in bruised vegetation, vivid as a cry. I found the path and drank another scent. Now I knew what the undertone of Maledicto's odor had been.

Demon.

I'd never caught that exact whiff before, and my wolf brain wasn't up to wondering about his species. Nor did it wonder what he desired of Ginny. There was only room in my narrow skull for hate, and for hurrying.

The lodge came into view. I sprang onto the patio. No one was about. But the master bedroom faced the sea, its window open to the moonbeams. I went through in a leap.

He had her in his arms. She was still pressing him away, resisting, but her eyes were closed and her strength faded. "No," she whispered. "No, help, don't, Amaris, Amaris,

Amaris.'' Her hands moved to his throat, slid to his neck, drew his face to hers. They swayed downward together in the gloom.

I howled, once, and sank my teeth in him.

His blood did not taste human. It was like liquor, it burned and sang within me. I dared not bite him again. Another such draught and I might lie doglike at his feet, begging him to stroke me. I willed myself human.

The flow of transformation took no longer than he needed to release Ginny and turn around. Despite his surprise, he didn't snarl back at me. A shaft of moonlight caught his faerie visage, blazed gold in his eyes, and he was laughing.

My fist smashed forward with my weight behind it. Poor, slow man-flesh, how shall it fight the quicksilver life of Air and Darkness? Maledicto flickered aside. He simply wasn't there. I caromed into a wall and fell down, my knuckles one crumple of anguish.

His laughter belled above me. ''And this puling thing should deserve as lively a wench as thee? Say but the word, Virginia, and I whip him to his kennel.''

''Steve. . . .'' She huddled back in a corner, not coming to me. I reeled onto my feet. Maledicto grinned, put an arm about Ginny's waist, drew her to him. She shuddered, again trying to pull away. He kissed her, and she made a broken sound and the motions of resistance started again to become motions of love. I charged. Maledicto shoved with his free hand. I went down, hard. He set a foot on my head and held me.

''I'd liefer not break thy bones,'' he said, ''but if thou'rt not so gentle as to respect the lady's wishes—''

''*Wishes?*'' Ginny broke from him. ''God in Heaven!'' she wailed. ''Get out!''

Maledicto chuckled. ''I must needs flee the holy names, if a victim of mine invoke them in full sincerity,'' he murmured. ''And yet thou seest that I remain here. Thine inmost desire is to me, Virginia.''

She snatched a vase and hurled it at him. He fielded it expertly, dropped it to shatter on me, and went to the window. ''Oh, aye, this time the spell has been broken,'' he said. ''Have no fear, though. At a more propitious hour, I shall return.''

There was a moment's rippling, and he had gone over the sill. I crawled after him. The patio lay white and bare in the moonlight.

I sat down and held my head. Ginny flung herself sobbing beside me. A long time passed. Finally I got up, switched on the light, found a cigaret, and slumped on the edge of the bed. She crouched at my knees, but I didn't touch her.

"What was it?" I asked.

"An incubus." Her head was bent, I saw just the red hair flowing down her back. She had put on her frilliest nightgown while we were gone—for whom? Her voice came small and thin. "He . . . it . . . it must haunt the ruins. Came over with the Spaniards. . . . Maybe it was responsible for their failure to—"

I dragged smoke into my lungs. "Why hasn't it been reported?" I wondered aloud, dully. And: "Oh, yeah, sure. It must have a very limited range of operation. A family curse on a family now extinct, so it's confined to the home and lands of that old don. Since his time, no one has been here after dark."

"Until we—" Her whisper trailed off.

"Well, Juan and his wife, with occasional guests." I smoked more fiercely. "You're the witch. You have the information. I barely know that an incubus is an erotic demon. Tell me, why did it never bother the Fernandezes?"

She began to weep afresh, deep hopeless gasps. I thought that despair had combined with the earlier loss of witchpower to drive her thaumaturgic training clean out of reach. My own mind was glass-clear as I continued. "Because it did speak the truth, I suppose, about holy symbols being a shield for people who really want to be shielded. Juan and his wife are good Catholics. They wouldn't come here without hanging crucifixes in every room. And neither of them wishes to be unfaithful to the other."

The face she raised was wild. "Do you think that I—"

"Oh, not consciously. If we'd thought to put up some crosses when we arrived, or offered an honest prayer, we'd have been safe too. We might never have known there was an incubus around. But we had too much else to think about, and it's too late now. Subconsciously, I suppose, you must have toyed with the idea that a little vacation from strict monogamy could do no one any harm—"

"Steve!" She scrambled stiffly to her feet. "On our honeymoon! You could say such a thing!"

"Could and did." I ground out the cigaret, wishing it were Maledicto's face. "How else could it lay a spell on you?"

"And you— Steve— Steve, I love you. Nobody else but you."

"Well, you better rev up the carpet," I sighed. "Fly to, oh, I imagine Guaymas is the nearest town big enough to have an exorcist on the police force. Report this and ask for protection.

Because if I remember my demonology, it can follow you anywhere, once you've come under its influence.''

''But nothing happened!'' She cried that as if I were striking her: which, in a sense, I was.

''No, there wasn't time. Then. And, of course, you'd have been able to bounce any demon off with a purely secular spell, if you'd possessed your witch-powers. But those are gone. Until you relearn them, you'll need an exorcist guard, every hour of the day you aren't in a church. Unless—'' I rose too.

''What?'' She caught me with cold frantic hands. I shook her off, blinded by the double hurt to my manhood, that Maledicto had whipped me in fight and almost seduced my bride. ''Steve, what are you thinking?''

''Why, that I might get rid of him myself.''

''You *can't!* You're no warlock, and he's a demon!''

''I'm a werewolf. It may be a fair match.'' I shuffled into the bathroom, where I began to dress my wounds. They were superficial, except for swollen knuckles. She tried to help, but I gestured her away from me.

I knew I wasn't rational. Too much pain and fury filled me. I had some vague idea of going to the Fortaleza, whither Maledicto had presumably returned. In wolf-shape, I'd be as fast and strong as he. Of course, I dare not bite . . . but if I could switch to human as occasion warranted, use the unarmed combat techniques I'd learned in the Army. . . . The plan was as hopeless as any men ever coughed forth, but my own demon was driving me.

Ginny sensed it: that much witchcraft remained to her, if it was not simply inborn. She was quite pale in the unmerciful glare of the saintelmo, she shivered and gulped, but after a while she nodded. ''If you must. We'll go together.''

''No!'' the roar burst from my gullet. ''Be off to Guaymas, I said! Haven't I troubles enough? Let me alone till I can decide if I want you back!''

Another instant she stared at me. May I never again see such eyes. Then she fled.

I went out on the patio and became a wolf. The demon stench was thick on the air. I followed it over the mountainside.

XVII

THE EARTH WAS a dazzle of moonlight. My nose caught smells of dust, sage, cactus, kelp, and salt more remotely; my ears heard a bat's sonar squeak, the terrified scuttering of a jackrabbit; my pelt tingled with sensations for which men have no words. I felt my human torture no longer. The lupine brain could only hold clean, murderous carnivore thoughts. It was like being reborn. I understand that some psychiatrists have gotten good results by turning their patients temporarily into animals.

Presently the old watchtower lifted its corroded outline across the moon. Every nerve abristle for attack, I entered what had been a gateway. The courtyard lay empty around me. Sand had blown in during the centuries, weeds thrust between the flagstones, a shard of paving jutted here and there. Near the center was a heap which had been a building. Cellars lay underneath. I'd explored them a trifle, once, not deeply enough to come on the lair of the incubus.

I bayed my challenge.

It rustled in the tower door. A white form stepped out. My heart made one leap, and I crouched back. I thought wildly, Could I slash his jugular on the first bite, it wouldn't matter if I swallowed that drug-blood, he would be dead. . . .

Laughter ran around me on soft little feet. She made another stride outward, so that she could stand under a cataract of moonlight, impossibly white against the black moldering walls. "Good even, fair youth," she said. "I had not hoped for this fortune."

Her scent entered my lungs and my veins. I growled, and it turned into a whine. I wagged the stump of my tail. She came to me and scratched me behind the ears. I licked her arm; the taste was dizzying. Somewhere in a thunderful wilderness, I thought it was no use remaining lupine. The currents of change ran through me. I stood up a man.

She was as tall and ripplesome as Amaris, and she had the

same strange pointed face and eyes that fluoresced under the moon. But the pale hair fell past her waist in a cloud, and she wore a gown obviously woven by stingy spiders, on a figure that— Oh, well, I won't try to describe it. I suppose half the fun was simply in the way it moved.

"Cybelita . . . I presume?" I managed to husk.

"And thou art Steven." A slender hand fell upon mine and lingered. "Ah, welcome!"

I wet my lips. "Er . . . is your brother at home?"

She swayed closer. "What matters that?"

"I . . . uh . . ." I thought crazily that one can't politely explain one's business to a lady's brother as being to kill him. And after all, well, anyhow— "Look here," I blurted. "You, he, you've got to leave us alone!"

Cybelita smiled yieldingly. "Ah, thy grief is mine, Steven. And yet, canst thou not find it in thy heart to pity us? Knowest thou what damnation in truth consists of? To be a creature in whom the elements exist unblent—Fire of lust, Air of impulse, Water of wantonness, and the dark might of Earth—to be of such a nature, yet doomed to slink like a rat in these ruins, and howl to empty skies, and hunger and hunger for three hundred years! If thou wert starving, and two folk passing by spread a feast, wouldst thou not take such few crumbs as they could well spare?"

I croaked something about the analogic fallacy.

" 'Tis not malignancy," she pleaded. She drew close, her arms reached to my shoulders and her bosom nudged mine. " 'Tis need which forces us. And after all, Steven, ye mortals are not perfect either. Were ye saints with never an impure thought, no demon could venture near. We are drawn by that in ye which is akin to ourselves."

"Uh, well, yes," I choked. "You have two points there . . . a point, I mean. Yes."

Cybelita laughed anew. "But la, sweet youth! Here I stand in moonlight, embracing the most beautiful unclothed lad in this world—"

"Oh, my God!" I remembered that my outfit was a pair of skivvies. Since she didn't shrink away, my exclamation must not have counted as a prayer.

"—and discourse on metaphysic! Nay, now thou'rt a-flush." Cybelita pirouetted from me. "I'd not have the advantage of thee. That's not true friendship. Let us be alike in garb."

She snapped her fingers and the gown vanished. Not that it made any big difference, except morally, and by then morals seemed irrelevant.

"And now, come, come, my darling. My wolf, thou'rt my first *loup-garou*—had I suspected so new a wonder, no time would have been wasted on the woman— Come!" She threw herself against me. I don't know exactly what made me respond to her kiss. It was like being caught in a rose-colored cyclone.

Somehow I found a last resting place in the fragments of my will power. "No! I have a wife!"

Cybelita laughed less pleasantly. "Ha! Where thinkest thou Amaris has been since the moment thou left the wench alone?"

I made one garroted sound.

" 'Tis happened now," she purred. "What's done can ne'er be undone. Blame not thy wife. She is but mortal. Shouldst thou be more?"

I previewed Purgatory for about a minute. Then, hardly aware what was happening, I snatched Cybelita to me. My kisses broke her lips a little and I tasted the demon blood. "Come," she crooned, "my lover, my lover, bear me to the tower. . . ."

I picked her up and started across the courtyard.

"Steve!"

Ginny's scream was a knife driven through me.

I dropped my burden. Cybelita landed on her lovely tokus and said a most unlovely word. I gaped at Ginny. She crouched on our Persian carpet, it hovered over the broken gateway, her red hair tumbled past her bare shoulders and I knew, in that moment when I had already lost her to Amaris (for it could nevermore be the same between us two), that she was all I would ever want.

Cybelita rose. She looked bleached in the moonlight. I had no further desire for her. To hell with her.

To hell itself with her.

She sneered toward Ginny, turned back and opened her arms to me. I said: "Defend yourself!" and became a wolf.

Cybelita skipped back from my lunge. I heard Ginny cry out again, as if from another existence. My whole attention was on the succubus. Cybelita's body pulsed, grayed, suddenly she was a wolf too. She grinned shamelessly at me and her femaleness hit me like a club.

I didn't take the offer. I went for her throat. We rolled over and fought. She was tough, but hadn't been trained in combat lycanthropy. I know the judo breaks for my animal-shape, too. I got under her jaws and clamped my teeth where I wanted them.

The demon blood was sweet and horrible to taste. But this time it couldn't rouse my wishes. The powers in me of Love, for my wife, and Hate, for the thing I fought, were too strong. Or, if you insist on outmoded terms, my glands were supplying enough testosterone and adrenalin to swamp whatever hormone was in that ichor.

I killed her.

In the last fragmented second, I heard—not with my ears—the shriek of the foul spirit within. I felt—not with my nerves—the space-time turbulence as it struggled to change the mathematical form of its Schrödinger function, thus fleeing to the Low Continuum where it belonged and leaving me with the exchange mass. But my fangs had been too quick and savage. The body perished and the soulless demon was no more.

I lay by the wolf corpse, gasping. It writhed horribly through shapes of woman, man, horned and tailed satanoid. When its last cohesive forces were spent, it puffed away in gas.

Piece by tattered piece, my wits returned. I lay across Ginny's dear lap. Moonlight poured cool over us, under friendly stars, down to a castle which was nothing but piled stones. Ginny laughed and wept and held me close.

I became a man again and drew her to me. "It's okay, darling," I breathed. "Everything's okay. I finished her. I'll get Amaris next."

"What?" Her wet face lifted from my breast toward my lips. "Don't you n-n-n-know? You have!"

"Huh?"

"Yes. Some of my education c-c-came back to me . . . after you'd gone." She drew a shaking breath. "Incubi and succubi are identical. They change their sex as . . . as . . . in-dicated. . . . Amaris and that hussy were the same!"

"You mean she didn't—he didn't—you didn't—" I let out a yell which registered on seismographs in Baja California. And yet that noise was the most fervent prayer of thanks which Our Father had ever gotten from me.

Not that I hadn't been prepared to forgive my dearest, having had experience of the demon's power. But learning that there wasn't anything which needed to be forgiven was like a mountain off my back.

"Steve!" cried Ginny. "I love you too, but my ribs aren't made of iron!"

I climbed to my feet. "It's done with," I whispered, incredulous. In a moment: "More than done with. We actually came out ahead of the game."

"How's that?" she asked, still timid but with a sunrise in her eyes.

"Well," I said, "I guess we've had a useful lesson in humility. Neither of us turns out to own a more decorous subconscious mind than the average person."

An instant's chill possessed me. I thought: No average persons would have come as near falling as we did . . . on the second night after their wedding! Nor would we ourselves. More than the resources of a petty demon was marshaled against us. More than chance brought us to its haunts. Something else wanted us destroyed.

I believe, now, that that Force was still at hand, watching. It could not strike at us directly. No new agents of temptation were near, and we were fire-tempered against them anyway. It could not again use our latent suspicions and jealousies to turn us on each other; we were as purged of those as common mortals can be.

But did it, in its time-abiding craftiness, *withdraw* the last evil influences from around and within us—did it free us of aches and weariness—and itself depart?

I don't know. I do know that suddenly the night was splendor, and my love for Ginny rose in a wave that left no room in me for anything else, and when many days later I remembered that encounter on the sea cliff, it was as vague to me as the former ones and I dismissed it with the same casual half-joke: "Funny how a bonk on the conk always gives me that particular hallucination."

There in the courtyard, I looked upon her, drew her to me, and said—my throat so full of unshed tears that the words came hoarse— "In what counts, darling, I learned how you do care for me. You followed me here, not knowing what might be waiting, when I'd told you to run for safety. . . ."

Her tousled head rubbed my shoulder. "I learned likewise about you, Steve. It's a good feeling."

We walked onto the carpet. "Home, James," I said. After a pause, when James was airborne: "Uh, I suppose you're dead tired."

"Well, actually not. I'm too keyed up yet . . . no, by gosh, I'm too happy." She squeezed my hand. "But you, poor dear—"

"I feel fine," I grinned. "We can sleep late tomorrow."

''Mister Matuchek! What are you thinking?''

''The same as you, Mrs. Matuchek.''

I imagine she blushed in the moonlight. ''So I see. Very good, sir.''

Which turned out to be a prophecy.

XVIII

AFTER WE RETURNED to our apartment we took summer jobs, quitting when classes reopened in fall. Like most newlyweds, we ran into budgetary difficulties: nothing too serious, but we had to sell the carpet, for instance, when Ginny got pregnant. Otherwise, that first couple of married years, we lived unspectacular lives, except when we were alone together.

And then a nurse led me to the bed where my darling lay. Always fair-hued, she was white after her battle, and the beautiful bones stood sharply in her face. But her hair was fire across the pillow, and though the lids drooped on her eyes, that green had never shone brighter.

I bent and kissed her, as gently as I could. "Hi, there," she whispered.

"How are you?" was the foolish single thing that came to me to say.

"Fine." She regarded me for a moment before, abruptly, she grinned. "But you look as if couvade might be a good idea."

As a matter of fact, some obstetricians do put the father to bed when a child is being born. Our doctor followed majority opinion in claiming that I'd give my wife the maximum possible sympathetic help by just sweating it out in the waiting room. I'd studied the subject frantically enough, these past months, to become somewhat of an authority. A first birth for a tall slim girl like Ginny was bound to be difficult. She took the prospect with her usual coolness, unbending only to the extent of casting runes to foretell the sex of the child, and that only so we wouldn't be caught flat-footed for a name.

"How do you like your daughter?" she asked me.

"Gorgeous," I said.

"Liar," she chuckled. "The man never lived who wasn't horrofied when they told him he'd sired that wrinkled blob of red protoplasm." Her hand reached for mine. "But she will be lovely, Steve. She can't help being. It's so lovely between us.''

I told myself that I would *not* bawl right in front of the mothers in this room. The nurse saved me with a crisp: ''I think we had better let your wife rest, Mr. Matuchek. And Dr. Ashman would like to finish things so he can go home.''

He was waiting for me in the naming office. When I had passed through the soundproof door, the nurse sealed it behind me with wax and a davidstar. This was an up-to-date hospital where they took every care. Thomas Ashman was a grizzled, craggy six-footer with a relaxed manner, at present a bit droopy from weariness. I saw that beneath the impressive zodiacal traceries on his surgical gown, he'd been wearing white duck pants and a tee shirt—besides his amulet, of course.

We shook hands. ''Everything's good,'' he assured me. ''I've gotten the lab report. You understand that, with no therianthropes on the maternal side, none of your children will ever be a natural werewolf. But since this one has inherited the complete recessive gene complex from you, she'll take transformation spells quite easily. A definite advantage, expecially if she goes in for a thaumaturgic career like her mother. It does mean, however, that certain things should be guarded against. She'll be more subject to paranatural influences than most people are.''

I nodded. Ginny and I had certainly had an undue share of adventures we didn't want.

''Marry her off right,'' Ashman joked, ''and you'll have werewolf grandchildren.''

''If she takes after her old lady,'' I said, ''Lord help any poor boy we tried to force on her!'' I felt as idiotic as I sounded. ''Look, Doctor, we're both tired. Let's make out the birth certificates and turn in.''

''Sure.'' He sat down at the desk. The parchments were already inscribed with parental names, place and date, and the file number they bore in common. ''What're you calling her?''

''Valeria.''

''Yes, I suppose your wife would pick something like that. Her idea, wasn't it? Any middle name?''

''Uh . . . Mary. My decision—for my own mother—'' I realized I was babbling again.

''Good thought. She can take refuge in it if she doesn't like the fancy monicker. Though I suspect she will.'' He typed out the information, signed, gave me the document, and dropped the carbon in an out box. Rather more ceremoniously, he laid down the primary certificate that bore her fingerprints. "And the true name?"

"Victrix."

"Hm?"

"Ginny always liked it. Valeria Victrix. The last Roman legion in Britain." The last that stood against Chaos, she had said in one of her rare wholly serious moments.

Ashman shrugged. "Well, it isn't as if the kid's going to use it."

"I hope she never has to!"

"That'd imply a bad emergency," he agreed. "But don't fret. I see too many young husbands, shaken up by what they've undergone, be knocked for a loop at the grim possibilities they have to face now. Really, though, this is nothing more than another sensible precaution, like a vaccination."

"I know," I said. "Wish they'd had the idea when I was born." It isn't likely that anyone will try nymic tricks against an ordinary peaceful citizen, but you've seen how my career has gotten turbulent every once in a while, and maintaining the counterspells is a bloody nuisance—not always reliable, either. Medical science is one of the few areas where I'll admit that genuine progress gets made.

Ashman dipped an eagle quill in a well of oak-gall ink. "By the bird of thy homeland and the tree of the lightning," he intoned, "under their protection and God's, child of this day, be thy true name, known on this earth but to thy parents, thy physician, and thee when thou shalt come of age: Victrix; and may thou bear it in honor and happiness while thy years endure. Amen." He wrote, dusted sand from Galilee across the words, and stood up again. "This one I'll file personally," he said. Yawning: "Okay, that's all."

We repeated our handshake. "I'm sorry you had to deliver her at such an unsanctified hour," I said.

"Nothing we GP's aren't used to," he answered. The sleepiness left him. He regarded me very steadily. "Besides, in this case I expected it."

"Huh?"

"I'd heard something about you and your wife already," Ashman said. "I looked up more. Cast a few runes of my own. Maybe you don't know it yourself, but that kid was begotten on the winter solstice. And, quite apart from her unusual heredity, there's something else about her. I can't identify it. But I felt pretty sure she'd be born this night—because a full moon was due on Matthewsmas. I'm going to watch her with a great deal of interest, Mr. Matuchek, and I suggest you take extra special care of her. . . . Good night, now.''

XIX

NOTHING SPECTACULAR HAPPENED to us in the following three years. Or so you would have thought; but you are somebody else. For our little circle, it was when the world opened up for our taking and, at the same time, buckled beneath our feet.

To start with, Valeria was unexpected. We found out later that Svartalf had been chasing the Brownie again and, in revenge, the Good Folk had turned Ginny's pills to aspirin. Afterward I've wondered if more didn't lie behind the incident than that. The Powers have Their ways of steering us toward situations that will serve Their ends.

At first Ginny intended to go ahead according to our original plan, as soon as the youngster was far enough along that a babysitter could handle things by day. And she did take her Ph.D. in Arcana, and had some excellent job offers. But once our daughter was part of our home, well, mama's emancipation kept getting postponed. We weren't about to let any hireling do slobwork on Valeria! Not yet, when she was learning to smile, when she was crawling everywhere around, when her noises of brook and bird were changing into language—later, later.

I quite agreed. But this meant giving up, for a while if not forever, the condition we'd looked forward to: of a smart young couple with a plump double income, doing glamorous things in glamorous places among glamorous people. I did propose trying to take up my Hollywood career again, but would have been astounded if Ginny had been willing to hear word one of that idea. "Do you imagine for half a second," she said, "that I'd want a mediocre player of Silver Chief and Lassie, when I could have a damn good engineer?" Personally, I don't think the pictures I made were that all bad; but on the whole, her answer relieved me.

A newly created B.Sc. doesn't step right into the kind of challenging project he hopes for, especially when he's older than the average graduate. I had to start out with what I could get. By luck—we believed then—that was unexpectedly good.

The Nornwell Scryotronics Corporation was among the new outfits in the booming postwar communications and instrument business. Though small, it was upward bound on an exponential curve. Besides manufacture, it did R & D, and I was invited to work on the latter. This was not simply fascinating in itself, it was a long step toward my ultimate professional goal. Furthermore, an enlightened management encouraged us to study part time for advanced degrees, on salary. That pay wasn't bad, either. And before long, Barney Sturlason was my friend as much as he was my boss.

The chief drawback was that we had to stay in this otherwise dull city and endure its ghastly Upper Midwestern winters. But we rented a comfortable suburban house, which helped. And we had each other, and little Valeria. Those were good years. It's just that nobody else would find an account of them especially thrilling.

That's twice true when you consider what went on meanwhile at large. I suppose mankind has always been going to perdition in a roller coaster and always will be. Still, certain eras remind you of the old Chinese curse: "May you live in interesting times!"

Neither Ginny nor I had swallowed the propaganda guff about how peace and happiness would prevail forevermore once the wicked Caliphate had been defeated. We knew what a legacy of wretchedness all wars must leave. Besides, we knew this conflict was more a symptom than a cause of the world's illness. The enemy wouldn't have been able to overrun most of the Eastern Hemisphere and a chunk of the United States if Christendom hadn't been divided against itself. For that matter, the Caliphate was nothing but the secular arm of a Moslem heresy; we had plenty of good Allah allies.

It did seem reasonable, though, to expect that afterward people would have learned their lesson, put their religious quarrels aside, and settled down to reconstruction. In particular, we looked for the Johannine Church to be generally discredited and fade away. True, its adherents had fought the Caliph too, had in fact taken a leading role in the resistance movements in the occupied countries. But wasn't its challenge to the older creeds—to the whole basis of Western society—what had split and weakened our civilization in the first place? Wasn't its example what had stimulated the rise of the lunatic Caliphist ideology in the Middle East?

I now know better than to expect reasonableness in human affairs.

Contrary to popular impression, the threat didn't appear suddenly. A few men warned against it from the beginning. They pointed out how the Johnnies had become dominant in the politics of more than one nation, which thereupon stopped being especially friendly to us, and how in spite of this they were making converts throughout America. But most of us hardly listened. We were too busy repairing war damage, public and personal. We considered those who sounded the alarm to be reactionaries and would-be tyrants (which some, perhaps, were). The Johannine theology might be nuts, we said, but didn't the First Amendment guarantee its right to be preached? The Petrine churches might be in trouble, but wasn't that their problem? And really, in our scientific day and age, to talk about subtle, pervasive dangers in a religious-philosophical system . . . a system which emphasized peacefulness almost as strongly as the Quakers, which exalted the commandment to love thy neighbor above every other—well, it just might be that our materialistic secular society and our ritualistic faiths would benefit from a touch of what the Johnnies advocated.

So the movement and its influence grew. And then the activist phase began: and somehow orderly demonstrations were oftener and oftener turning into riots, and wildcat strikes were becoming more and more common over issues that made less and less sense, and student agitation was paralyzing campus after campus, and person after otherwise intelligent person was talking about the need to tear down a hopelessly corrupt order of things so that the Paradise of Love could be built on the ruins . . . and the majority of us, that eternal majority which wants nothing except to be left alone to cultivate its individual gardens, wondered how the country could have started to disintegrate overnight.

Brother, it did not happen overnight. Not even over Walpurgis Night.

XX

I CAME HOME early that June day. Our street was quiet, walled in between big old elms, lawns, and houses basking in sunlight. The few broomsticks in view were ridden by local women, carrying groceries in the saddlebags and an infant or two strapped in the kiddie seat. This was a district populated chiefly by young men on the way up. Such tend to have pretty wives, and in warm weather these tend to wear shorts and halters. The scenery lightened my mood no end.

I'd been full of anger when I left the turbulence around the plant. But here was peace. My roof was in sight. Ginny and Val were beneath it. Barney and I had a plan for dealing with our troubles, come this eventide. The prospect of action cheered me. Meanwhile, I was home!

I passed into the open garage, dismounted, and racked my Chevvy alongside Ginny's Volksbesen. As I came out again, aimed at the front door, a cannonball whizzed through the air and hit me. "Daddy! Daddy!"

I hugged my offspring close, curly yellow hair, enormous blue eyes, the whole works. She was wearing her cherub suit, and I had to be careful not to break the wings. Before, when she flew, it had been at the end of a tether secured to a post, and under Ginny's eye. What the deuce was she doing free—?

Oh. Svartalf zoomed around the corner of the house on a whisk broom. His back was arched, his tail was raised, and he used bad language. Evidently Ginny had gotten him to supervise. He could control the chit fairly well, no doubt, keep her in the yard and out of trouble . . . until she saw Daddy arrive.

"Okay!" I laughed. "Enough. Let's go in and say boo to Mother."

"Wide piggyback?"

For Val's birthday last fall I'd gotten the stuff for an expensive spell and had Ginny change me. The kid was used to playing with me in my wolf form, I'd thought; but how about a piggyback ride, the pig being fat and white and spotted with flowers? The local small fry were still talking about it. "Sorry, no," I had to tell her. "After that performance of yours, you get the Air Force treatment." And I carried her by her ankles, squealing and wiggling, while I sang,

"Up in the air, junior birdman,
Up in the air, upside down—"

Ginny came into the living room, from the workroom, as we did. Looking behind her, I saw why she'd deputized the supervision of Val's flytime. Washday. A three-year-old goes through a lot of clothes, and we couldn't afford self-cleaning fabrics. She had to animate each garment singly, and make sure they didn't tie themselves in knots or something while they soaped and rinsed and marched around to dry off and so forth. And, since a parade like that is irresistible to a child, she had to get Val elsewhere.

Nonetheless, I wondered if she wasn't being a tad reckless, putting her familiar in charge. Hitherto, she'd done the laundry when Val was asleep. Svartalf had often shown himself to be reliable in the clutch. But for all the paranatural force in him, he remained a big black tomcat, which meant he was not especially dependable in dull everyday matters. . . . Then I thought, What the blazes, since Ginny stopped being a practicing witch, the poor beast hasn't had much excitement; he hasn't even got left a dog or another cat in the whole neighborhood that dares fight him; this assignment was probably welcome; Ginny always knows what she's doing; and—

"—and I'm an idiot for just standing here gawping," I said, and gathered her in. She was dressed like the other wives I'd seen, but if she'd been out there too I wouldn't have seen them.

She responded. She knew how.

"What's a Nidiot?" Val asked from the floor. She pondered the matter. "Well, Daddy's a *good* Nidiot."

Svartalf switched his tail and looked skeptical.

I relaxed my hold on Ginny a trifle. She ran her fingers through my hair. "Wow," she murmured. "What brought that on, tiger?"

"Daddy's a woof," Val corrected her.

"You can call me tiger today," I said, feeling happier by the minute.

Ginny leered. "Okay, pussycat."

"Wait a bit—"

She shrugged. The red tresses moved along her shoulders.

"Well, if you insist, okay, Lame Thief of the Waingunga."

Val regarded us sternly. "When you fwoo wif you' heads," she directed, "put 'em outside to melt."

The logic of this, and the business of getting the cherub rig off her, took time to unravel. Not until our offspring was bottoms up on the living-room floor, watching cartoons on the crystal ball, and I was in the kitchen watching Ginny start supper, did we get a chance to talk.

"How come you're home so early?" she asked.

"How'd you like to reactivate the old outfit tonight?" I replied.

"Which?"

"Matuchek and Graylock—no, Matuchek and Matuchek—Troubleshooters Extraordinary, Licensed Confounders of the Ungodly."

She put down her work and gave me a long look. "What are you getting at, Steve?"

"You'll see it on the ball, come news time," I answered. "We aren't simply being picketed any more. They've moved onto the grounds. They're blocking every doorway. Our personnel had to leave by skylight, and rocks got thrown at some of them."

She was surprised and indignant, but kept the coolness she showed to the world outside this house. "You didn't call the police?"

"Sure, we did. I listened in, along with Barney, since Roberts thought a combat veteran might have some useful ideas. We can get police help if we want it. The demonstrators have turned into trespassers; and windows are broken, walls defaced with obscene slogans, that sort of thing. Our legal case is plenty clear. Only the opposition is out for trouble. Trouble for us, as much as possible, but mainly they're after martyrs. They'll resist any attempt to disperse them. Just like the fracas in New York last month. A lot of these characters are students too. Imagine the headlines: Police Brutality Against Idealistic Youths. Peaceful Protesters Set On With Clubs and Geas Casters.

"Remember, this is a gut issue. Nornwell manufactures a lot of police and defense equipment, like witchmark fluorescers and basilisk goggles. We're under contract to develop more kinds. The police and the armed forces serve the Establishment. The establishment is evil. Therefore Nornwell must be shut down."

"Quod erat demonstrandum about," she sighed.

"The chief told us that an official move to break up the

invasion would mean bloodshed, which might touch off riots at the University, along Merlin Avenue—Lord knows where it could lead. He asked us to stop work for the rest of the week, to see if this affair won't blow over. We'd probably have to, anyway. Quite a few of our men told their supervisors they're frankly scared to come back, the way things are.''

The contained fury sparked in her eyes. "If you knuckle under," she said, "they'll proceed to the next on their list."

"You know it," I said. "We all do. But there is that martyrdom effect. There are those Johnny priests ready to deliver yet another sanctimonious sermon about innocent blood equals the blood of the Lamb. There's a country full of well-intentioned bewildered people who'll wonder if maybe the Petrine churches aren't really on the way out, when the society that grew from them has to use violence against members of the Church of Love. Besides, let's face the fact, darling, violence has never worked against civil disobedience."

"Come back and tell me that after the machine guns have talked," she said.

"Yeah, sure. But who'd want to preserve a government that resorts to massacre? I'd sooner turn Johnny myself. The upshot is, Nornwell can't ask the police to clear its property for it."

Ginny cocked her head at me. "You don't look too miserable about this."

I laughed. "No. Barney and I brooded over the problem for a while and hatched us quite an egg. I'm actually enjoying myself by now, sort of. Life's been too tame of late. Which is why I asked if you'd like to get in on the fun."

"Tonight?"

"Yes. The sooner the better. I'll give you the details after our young hopeful's gone to bed."

Ginny's own growing smile faded. "I'm not sure I can get a sitter on notice that short. This is final exam week at the high school."

"Well, if you can't, what about Svartalf?" I suggested. "You won't be needing a familiar, and he can do the elementary things, keep guard, dash next door and yowl a neighbor awake if she gets collywobbles—"

"She might wake up and want us," Ginny objected, not too strongly.

I disposed of that by reminding her we'd bought a sleep watcher for Val, after a brief period when she seemed to have occasional nightmares. The little tin soldier didn't merely stand by her bed, the dream of him stood with his musket at the edge of her dreams, ready to chase away anything scary. I don't believe gadgets can substitute for parental love and presence; but they help a lot.

Ginny agreed. I could see the eagerness build up in her. Though she'd accepted a housewife's role for the time being, no race horse really belongs on a plowing team.

In this fashion did we prepare the way for hell to break loose, literally.

XXI

THE NIGHT FELL MOONLESS, a slight haze dulling the stars. We left soon after, clad alike in black sweaters and slacks, headlights off. Witch-sight enabled us to make a flight that was safe if illegal, high over the city's constellated windows and lamps until our stick swung downward again toward the industrial section. It lay still darker and emptier than was normal at this hour. I saw practically no tiny bluish glimmers flit around the bulks of shops and warehouses. The Good Folk were passing up their nocturnal opportunity for revels and curious window-peeking when man wasn't around. That which was going on had frightened them.

It centered on Nornwell's grounds. They shone forth, an uneasy auroral glow in the air. As we neared, the wind that slid past, stroking and whispering to me, bore odors—flesh and sweat, incense, an electric acridity of paranatural energies. The hair stood erect along my spine. I was content not be be in wolf-shape and get the full impact of that last.

The paved area around the main building was packed close to solid with bodies. So was the garden that had made our workers' warm-weather lunches pleasant; nothing remained of it except mud and cigaret stubs. I estimated five hundred persons altogether, blocking any except aerial access. Their mass was not restless, but the movement of individuals created an endless rippling through it, and the talk and footshuffle gave those waves a voice.

Near the sheds, our lot was less crowded. Scattered people there were taking a break from the vigil to fix a snack or flake out in a sleeping bag. They kept a respectful distance from a portable altar at the far end: though from time to time, someone would kneel in its direction.

I whistled, long and low. "That's arrived since I left." Ginny's arms caught tighter around my waist.

A Johannine priest was holding service. Altitude or no, we couldn't mistake his white robe, high-pitched minor-key chanting, spread-eagle stance which he could maintain for hours, the tau crucifix that gleamed tall and gaunt behind the altar, the four talismans—Cup, Wand, Sword, and Disc—upon it. Two acolytes swung censers whence came the smoke that sweetened and, somehow, chilled the air.

"What's he up to?" I muttered. I'd never troubled to learn much about the new church. Or the old ones, for that matter. Not that Ginny and I were ignorant of modern scientific discoveries proving the reality of the Divine and things like absolute evil, atonement, and an afterlife. But it seemed to us that so little is known beyond these bare hints, and that God can have so infinitely many partial manifestations to limited human understanding, that we might as well call ourselves Unitarians.

"I don't know," she answered. Her tone was bleak. "I studied what's public about their rites and doctrines, but that's just the top part of the iceberg, and it was years ago for me. Anyhow, you'd have to be a communicant—no, a lot more, an initiate, ultimately an adept, before you were told what a given procedure really means."

I stiffened. "Could he be hexing our side?"

Whetted by alarm, my vision swept past the uneasy sourceless illumination and across the wider scene. About a score of burly blue policemen were posted around the block. No doubt they were mighty sick of being jeered at. Also, probably most of them belonged to traditional churches. They wouldn't exactly mind arresting the agent of a creed which said that their own creeds were finished.

"No," I replied to myself, "he can't be, or the cops'd have him in the cooler this minute. Maybe he's anathematizing us. He could do that under freedom of religion, I suppose, seeing as how man can't control God but can only ask favors of Him. But actually casting a spell, bringing goetic forces in to work harm—"

Ginny interrupted my thinking aloud. "The trouble is," she said, "when you deal with these Gnostics, you don't know where their prayers leave off and their spells begin. Let's get cracking before something happens. I don't like the smell of the time stream tonight."

I nodded and steered for the principal building. The Johnny didn't fret me too much. Chances were he was just holding one of his esoteric masses to encourage the demonstrators. Didn't the claim go that his church was the church of universal benevolence? That it actually had no need of violence, being above the things of this earth? "The day of the Old Testament, of the Father, was the day of power and fear; the day of the New Testament, of the Son, has been the day of expiation; the day of the Johannine Gospel, of the Holy Spirit, will be the day of love and unveiled mysteries." No matter now.

The police were interdicting airborne traffic in the immediate vicinity except for whoever chose to leave it. That was a common-sense move. None but a minority of the mob were Johnnies. To a number of them, the idea of despising and renouncing a sinful material world suggested nothing more than that it was fashionable to wreck that world. The temptation to flit overhead and drop a few Molotov cocktails could get excessive.

Naturally, Ginny and I might have insisted on our right to come here, with an escort if need be. But that could provoke the explosion we wanted to avoid. Altogether, the best idea was to slip in, unnoticed by friend and foe alike. Our commando-type skills were somewhat rusty, though; the maneuver demanded our full attention.

We succeeded. Our stick ghosted through a skylight left open, into the garage. To help ventilate the rest of the place, this was actually a well from roof to ground floor. Normally our employees came and went by the doors. Tonight, however, those were barred on two sides—by the bodies of the opposition, and by protective force-fields of our own which it would take an expert wizard to break.

The Pinkerton technician hadn't conjured quite fast enough for us. Every first-story window was shattered. Through the holes drifted mumbled talk, background chant. Racking the broom, I murmured in Ginny's ear—her hair tickled my lips and was fragrant—"You know, I'm glad they did get a priest. During the day, they had folk singers."

"Poor darling." She squeezed my hand. "Watch out for busted glass." We picked our way in the murk to a hall and upstairs to the R & D section. It was defiantly lighted. But our footfalls rang too loud in its emptiness. It was a relief to enter Barney Sturlason's office.

His huge form rose behind the desk. "Virginia!" he rumbled. "What an unexpected pleasure." Hesitating: "But, uh, the hazard—"

"Shouldn't be noticeable, Steve tells me," she said. "And I gather you could use an extra thaumaturgist."

"Sure could." I saw how his homely features sagged with exhaustion. He'd insisted that I go home and rest. This was for the practical reason that, if things went sour and we found ourselves attacked, I'd have to turn wolf and be the main line of defense until the police could act. But he'd stayed on, helping his few volunteers make ready. That, far more than his great competence as a research man, was his mark of bosshood.

"Steve's explained our scheme?" he went on. His decision to accept her offer had been instantaneous. "Well, we need to make sure the most delicate and expensive equipment doesn't suffer. Quite apart from stuff being ruined, imagine the time and cost of recalibrating every instrument we've got, from dowsers to tarots! I think everything's adequately shielded, but I'd certainly appreciate an independent check by a fresh mind. Afterward you might cruise around the different shops and labs, see what I've overlooked and arrange its protection."

"Okay." She'd visited sufficiently often to be familiar with the layout. "I'll help myself to what I need from the stockroom, and ask the boys in—in the alchemistry section, did you say, dear?—for help if necessary." She paused. "I expect you two'll be busy for a while."

"Yes, I'm going to give them one last chance out there," Barney said, "and in case somebody gets overexcited, I'd better have Steve along for a bodyguard."

"And *I* still believe you might as well save your breath," I snorted.

"No doubt you're right, as far as you go," Barney said; "but don't forget the legal aspect. I don't own this place, I only head up a department. We're acting on our personal initiative after the directors agreed to suspend operations. Jack Roberts' approval of our plan was strictly *sub rosa*. Besides, ownership or not, we can no more use spells offensively against trespassers than we could use shotguns. The most we're allowed is harmless defensive forces to preserve life, limb, and property."

"Unless we're directly endangered," I said.

"Which is what we're trying to prevent," he reminded me. "Anyhow, because of the law, I have to make perfectly clear before plenty of witnesses that we intend to stay within it."

I shrugged and shed my outer garments. Underneath was the elastic knit one-piecer that would keep me from arrest for indecent exposure as a human, and not hamper me as a wolf. The moonflash already hung around my neck like a thick round amulet. Ginny kissed me hard. "Take care of yourself, tiger," she whispered.

She had no strong cause to worry. The besiegers were unarmed, except for fists and feet and possibly some smuggled billies or the like—nothing I need fear after Skinturning. Even knives and bullets and fangs could only inflict permanent harm under rare and special conditions, like those which had cost me my tail during the war. Besides, the likelihood of a fight was very small. Why should the opposition set on us? That would launch the police against them; and, while martyrdom has its uses, closing down our plant was worth more. Nonetheless, Ginny's tone was not completely level, and she watched us go down the hall till we had rounded a corner.

At that time, Barney said, "Wait a tick," opened a closet, and extracted a blanket that he hung on his arm. "If you should have to change shape," he said, "I'll throw this over you."

"Whatever for?" I exclaimed. "That's not sunlight outside, it's elflight. It won't inhibit transformation."

"It's changed character since that priest set up shot. I used a spectroscope to make certain. The glow's acquired enough ultraviolet—3500 angströms to be exact—that you'd have trouble. By-product of a guardian spell against any that we might try to use offensively."

"But we *won't!*"

"Of course not, It's pure ostentation on his part. Clever, though. When they saw a shieldfield established around them, the fanatics and naive children in the mob leaped to the conclusion that it was necessary; and thus Nornwell gets reconfirmed as the Enemy." He shook his head. "Believe me, Steve, these demonstrators are being operated like gloves, by some mighty shrewd characters."

"You sure the priest himself raised the field?"

"Yeah. They're all Magnuses in that clergy, remember—part of their training—and I wonder what else they learn in those lonesome seminaries. Let's try talking with him."

"Is he in charge?" I wondered. "The Johannine hierarchy does claim that when its members mix in politics, they do it strictly as private citizens."

"I know," Barney said. "And I am the Emperor Norton."

"No, really," I persisted. "These conspiracy theories are too bloody simple to be true. What you've got is a, uh, general movement, something in the air, people disaffected—"

But then, walking, we'd reached one of the ornamental glass panels that flanked the main entrance. It was smashed like the windows, but no one had thought to barricade it, and our protective spell forestalled entry. Of course, it did not affect us. We stepped through, onto the landing, right alongside the line of bodies that was supposed to keep us in.

We couldn't go further. The stairs down to the ground were packed solid. For a moment we weren't noticed. Barney tapped one scraggle-bearded adolescent on the shoulder. "Excuse me," he said from his towering height. "May I?" He plucked a sign out of the unwashed hand, hung the blanket over the placard, and waved his improvised flag of truce aloft. The color was bilious green.

A kind of gasp, like the puff of wind before a storm, went through the crowd. I saw faces and faces and faces next to me, below me, dwindling off into the dusk beyond the flickering elflight. I don't think it was only my haste and my prejudice that made them look eerily alike.

You hear a lot about long-haired men and short-haired women, bathless bodies and raggedy clothes. Those were certainly present in force. Likewise I identified the usual graybeard radicals and campus hangers-on, hoodlums, unemployables, vandals, True Believers, and the rest. But there were plenty of clean, well-dressed, terribly earnest boys and girls. There were the merely curious, too, who had somehow suddenly found themselves involved. And everyone was tall, short, or medium, fat, thin, or average, rich, poor, or middleclass, bright, dull, or normal, heterosexual, homosexual, or I know not what, able in some fields, inept in others, interested in some things, bored by others, each with an infinite set of memories, dreams, hopes, terrors, loves—each with a soul.

No, the sameness appeared first in the signs they carried. I didn't count how many displayed ST. JOHN 13:34 or I JOHN 2:9-11 or another of those passages; how many more carried the texts, or some variation like LOVE THY NEIGHBOR or plain LOVE: quite a few, anyway, repeating and repeating. Others were less amiable:

DEMATERIALIZE THE MATERIALISTS!

WEAPONMAKERS, WEEP!

STOP GIVING POLICE DEVILS HORNS

KILL THE KILLERS, HATE THE HATERS, DESTROY THE DESTROYERS!

SHUT DOWN THIS SHOP

And so it was as if the faces—worse, the brains behind them—had become nothing but placards with slogans written across.

Don't misunderstand me. I wouldn't think much of a youngster who never felt an urge to kick the God of Things As They Are in his fat belly. It's too bad that most people lose it as they get old and fat themselves. The Establishment is often unendurably smug and stupid; the hands it folds so piously are often bloodstained.

And yet . . . and yet . . . it's the only thing between us and the Dark Ages that'd have to intervene before another and probably worse Establishment could arise to restore order. And don't kid yourself that none would. Freedom is a fine thing until it becomes somebody else's freedom to enter your house, kill, rob, rape, and enslave the people you care about. Then you'll accept any man on horseback who promises to bring some predictability back into life, and you yourself will give him his saber and knout.

Therefore isn't our best bet to preserve this thing we've got? However imperfectly, it does function; and it's ours, it shaped us, we may not understand it any too well but surely we understand it better than something untried and alien. With a lot of hard work, hard thinking, hard-nosed good will, we can improve it.

You will not, repeat not, get improvement from wild-blue-yonder theorists who'd take us in one leap outside the whole realm of our painfully acquired experience; or from dogmatists mouthing the catchwords of reform movements that accomplished something two generations or two centuries ago; or from college sophomores convinced they have the answer to every social problem over which men like Hammurabi, Moses, Confucius, Aristotle, Plato, Marcus Aurelius, Thomas Aquinas, Hobbes, Locke, Voltaire, Jefferson, Burke, Lincoln, a thousand others broke their heads and their hearts.

But enough of that. I'm no intellectual; I try to think for myself. It depressed me to see these mostly well-meaning people made tools of the few whose aim was to bring the whole shebang down around their ears.

XXII

THE INDRAWN BREATH returned as a guttural sigh that edged toward a growl. The nearest males took a step or two in our direction. Barney waved his flag. "Wait!" he called, a thunderous basso overriding any other sound. "Truce! Let's talk this over! Take your leader to me!"

"Nothing *to* talk about, you murderers!" screamed a pimply girl. She swung her sign at me. I glimpsed upon it PEACE AND BROTHERHOOD before I had to get busy protecting my scalp. Someone began a chant that was quickly taken up by more and more: "Down with Diotrephes, down with Diotrephes, down with Diotrephes—"

Alarm stabbed through me. Though Diotrephes is barely mentioned in John's third epistle, the Johannines of today made him a symbol of the churches that opposed their movement. (No doubt he also meant other things to their initiates and adepts.) The unbelieving majority of the purely rebellious hadn't bothered to understand this. To them, Diotrephes became a name for the hated secular authority, or anyone else that got in their way. Those words had hypnotized more than one crowd into destructive frenzy.

I took her sign away from the girl, defended my eyes from her fingernails, and reached for my flash. But abruptly everything changed. A bell sounded. A voice cried. Both were low, both somehow penetrated the rising racket.

"Peace. Hold love in your hearts, children. Be still in the presence of the Holy Spirit."

My attacker retreated. The others who hemmed us in withdrew. Individuals started falling on their knees. A moan went through the mob, growing almost orgasmic before it died away into silence. Looking up, I saw the priest approach.

He traveled with bell in one hand, holding onto the upright of his tau crucifix while standing on its pedestal. Thus Christ nailed to the Cross of Mystery went before him. Nothing strange about that, I thought wildly, except that other churches would call it sacrilegious to give the central sign of their faith yonder shape, put an antigrav spell on it and use it like any broomstick. Yet the spectacle was weirdly impressive. It was like an embodiment of that Something Else on which Gnosticism is focused.

I'd regarded the Johnnies' "ineffable secrets" as unspeakable twaddle. Tonight I knew better. More was here than the ordinary paranatural emanations. Every nerve of my werewolf heritage sensed it. I didn't think the Power was of the Highest. But whence, then?

As the priest landed in front of us, though, he looked entirely human. He was short and skinny, his robe didn't fit too well, glasses perched precariously on his button nose, his graying hair was so thin I could hardly follow the course of his tonsure—the strip shaven from ear to ear, across the top of the head, that was said to have originated with Simon Magus.

He turned to the crowd first. "Let me speak with these gentlemen out of love, not hatred, and righteousness may prevail," he said in his oddly carrying tone. " 'He that loveth not knoweth not God; for God is love.' "

"Amen," mumbled across the grounds.

As the little man faced back toward us, I had a sudden belief that he really meant that dear quotation. It didn't drive away the miasma. The Adversary knows well how to use single-minded sincerity. But I felt less hostile to this priest as a person.

He smiled at us and bobbed his head. "Good evening," he said. "I am Initiate Fifth Class Marmiadon, at your service."

"Your, uh, ecclesiastical name?" Barney asked.

"Why, of course. The old name is the first of the things of this world that must be left behind at the Gate of Passage. I'm not afraid of a hex, if that is what you mean, sir."

"No, I suppose not." Barney introduced us, a cheap token of amity since we were both easily identifiable. "We came out hoping to negotiate a settlement."

Marmiadon beamed. "Wonderful! Blessings! I'm not an official spokesman, you realize. The Committee for National Righteousness called for this demonstration. However, I'll be glad to use my good offices."

"The trouble is," Barney said, "we can't do much about their basic demands. We're not against world peace and universal disarmament ourselves, you understand; but those are matters for international diplomacy. In the same way, the President and Congress have to decide whether to end the occupation of formerly hostile countries and spend the money on social uplift at home. Amnesty for rioters is up to state or city governments. School courses in Gnostic philosophy and history have to be decided on by elected authorities. As for total income equalization and the phasing out of materialism, hypocrisy, injustice—'' He shrugged. "That needs a Constitutional amendment at least.''

"You can, however, lend your not inconsiderable influence to forwarding those ends,'' Marmiadon said. "For example, you can contribute to the Committee's public education fund. You can urge the election of the proper candidates and help finance their campaigns. You can allow proselytizers to circulate among your employees. You can stop doing business with merchants who remain obstinate.'' He spread his arms. "In the course of so doing, my children, you can rescue yourselves from eternal damnation!''

"Well, maybe; though Pastor Karlslund over at St. Olaf's Lutheran might give me a different opinion on that,'' Barney said. "In any case, it's too big a list to check off in one day.''

"Granted, granted.'' Marmiadon quivered with eagerness. "We reach our ends a step at a time. 'While ye have light, believe in the light, that ye may be the children of light.' The present dispute is over a single issue.''

"The trouble is,'' Barney said, "you want us to cancel contracts we've signed and taken money for. You want us to break our word and let down those who trust us.''

His joy dropped from Marmiadon. He drew himself to his full meager height, looked hard and straight at us, and stated: "These soldiers of the Holy Spirit demand that you stop making equipment for the armed forces, oppressors abroad, and for the police, oppressors at home. Nothing more is asked of you at this time, and nothing less. The question is not negotiable.''

"I see. I didn't expect anything else,'' Barney said. "But I wanted to put the situation in plain language before witnesses. Now I'm going to warn you.''

Those who heard whispered to the rest, a hissing from mouth to mouth. I saw tension mount anew.

"If you employ violence upon those who came simply to remonstrate,'' Marmiadon declared, "they will either have the law upon you, or see final proof that the law is a creature of the vested interests . . . which I tell you in turn are the creatures of Satan.''

"Oh, no, no,'' Barney answered. "We're mild sorts, whether

you believe it or not. But you are trespassing. You have interfered with our work to the point where we're delayed and shorthanded. We must carry on as best we can, trying to meet our contractual obligations. We're about to run an experiment. You could be endangered. Please clear the grounds for your own saftey.''

Marmiadon grew rigid. ''If you think you can get away with a deadly spell—''

''Nothing like. I'll tell you precisely what we have in mind. We're thinking about a new method of transporting liquid freight. Before going further, we have to run a safety check on it. If the system fails, unprotected persons could be hurt.'' Barney raised his volume, though we knew some of the police officers would have owls' ears tuned in. ''I order you, I warn you, I beg you to stop trespassing and get off company property. You have half an hour.''

We wheeled and were back inside before the noise broke loose. Curses, taunts, obscenities, and animal howls followed us down the halls until we reached the blessed isolation of the main alchem lab.

The dozen scientists, technicians, and blue-collar men whom Barney had picked out of the volunteers to stay with him, were gathered there. They sat smoking, drinking coffee brewed on Bunsen burners, talking in low voices. When we entered, a small cheer came from them. They'd watched the confrontation on a closed-loop ball. I sought out Ike Abrams, the warehouse foreman. Ever since we soldiered together, I'd known him as a good man, and had gotten him his job here. ''All in order?'' I asked.

He made a swab-O sign. ''By me, Cap'n, she's clear and on green. I can't wait.''

I considered him for a second. ''You really have it in for those characters, don't you?''

''In my position, wouldn't you?'' He looked as if he were about to spit.

In your position, I thought, or in any of a lot of other positions, but especially in yours, Ike—yes.

As a rationalist, I detested the irrationality at the heart of Gnosticism. Were I a devout Christian, I'd have more counts against the Johannine Church: its claim to be the successor of all others, denying them any further right to exist; worse, probably, its esotericism, that would deny God's grace to nearly the whole of mankind. Rationalist and religionist alike could revolt against its perversion of the Gospel According to St. John, perhaps the most beautiful and gentle if the most mystical book in Holy Writ.

But if you were Jewish, the Johnnies would pluck out of context and throw at you texts like "For many deceivers are entered into the world, who confess not that Jesus Christ is come in the flesh. This is a deceiver and an antichrist." You would see reviving around you the ancient nightmare of anti-Semitism.

A little embarrassed, I turned to Bill Hardy, our chief paracelsus, who sat swinging his legs from a lab bench. "How much stuff did you produce?" I asked.

"About fifty gallons," he said, pointing.

"Wow! With no alchemy?"

"Absolutely not. Pure, honest-to-Berzelius molecular interaction. I admit we were lucky to have a large supply of the basic ingredients on hand."

I winced, recalling the awful sample he'd whipped up when our scheme was first discussed. "How on Midgard did that happen?"

"Well, the production department is—was—filling some big orders," he said. "For instance, a dairy chain wanted a lot of rancidity preventers. You know the process, inhibit the reaction you don't want in a test tube, and cast a sympathetic spell to get the same effect in ton lots of your product. Then the government is trying to control the skunk population in the Western states, and—" He broke off as Ginny came in.

Her eyes glistened. She held her wand like a Valkyrie's sword. "We're set, boys." The words clanged.

"Let's go." Barney heaved his bulk erect. We followed him to the containers. They were ordinary flat one-gallon cans such as you buy paint thinner in, but Solomon's seal marked the wax that closed each screw top and I could subliminally feel the paranatural forces straining around them. It seemed out of keeping for the scientists to load them on a cart and trundle them off.

Ike and his gang went with me to my section. The apparatus I'd thrown together didn't look especially impressive either. In fact, it was a haywire monstrosity, coils and wires enclosing a big gasoline-driven electric generator. Sometimes you need more juice for an experiment than the carefully screened public power lines can deliver.

To cobble that stuff on, I'd have to remove the generator's own magnetic screens. What we had, therefore, was a mass of free cold iron; no spell would work in its immediate vicinity. Ike had been in his element this afternoon, mounting the huge weight and awkward bulk on wheels for me. He was again, now, as he directed it along the halls and skidded it over the stairs.

No doubt he sometimes wished people had never found how to degauss the influences that had held paranatural forces in check since the Bronze Age ended. He wasn't Orthodox; his faith didn't prohibit him having anything whatsoever to do with goetics. But neither was he Reform or Neo-Chassidic. He was a Conservative Jew, who could make use of objects that others had put under obedience but who mustn't originate any cantrips himself. It's a tribute to him that he was nonetheless a successful and popular foreman.

He'd rigged a husky block-and-tackle arrangement in the garage. The others had already flitted to the flat roof. Ginny had launched the canisters from there. They bobbed about in the air, out of range of the magnetic distortions caused by the generator when we hoisted its iron to their level. Barney swung the machine around until we could ease it down beside the skylight. That made it impossible for us to rise on brooms or a word. We joined our friends via rope ladder.

"Ready?" Barney asked. In the restless pale glow, I saw sweat gleam on his face. If this failed, he'd be responsible for unforeseeable consequences.

I checked the connections. "Yeah, nothing's come loose. But let me first have a look around."

I joined Ginny at the parapet. Beneath us roiled the mob, faces and placards turned upward to hate us. They had spied the floating containers and knew a climax was at hand. Behind his altar, Initiate Marmiadon worked at what I took to be reinforcement of his defensive field. Unknown phrases drifted to me: ". . . *Heliphomar Mabon Saruth Gefutha Enunnas Sacinos . . .*" above the sullen mumble of our besiegers. The elflight flickered brighter. The air seethed and crackled with energies. I caught a thunderstorm whiff of ozone.

My darling wore a slight, wistful smile. "How Svartalf would love this," she said.

Barney lumbered to our side. "Might as well start," he said. "I'll give them one last chance." He shouted the same warning as before. Yells drowned him out. Rocks and offal flew against our walls. "Okay," he growled. "Let 'er rip!"

I went back to the generator and started the motor, leaving the circuits open. It stuttered and shivered. The vile fumes made me glad we'd escaped depending on internal combustion engines. I've seen automobiles, as they were called, built around 1900, shortly before the first broomstick flights. Believe me, museums are where they belong—a chamber of horrors, to be exact.

Ginny's clear call snapped my attention back. She'd directed the canisters into position. I could no longer see them, for they floated ten feet over the heads of the crowd, evenly spaced. She made a chopping gesture with her wand. I threw the main switch.

No, we didn't use spells to clear Nornwell's property. We used the absence of spells. The surge of current through the coils on the generator threw out enough magnetism to cancel every charm, ours and theirs alike, within a hundred-yard radius.

We'd stowed whatever gear might be damaged in safe conductive-shell rooms. We'd repeatedly cautioned the mob that we were about to experiment with the transportation of possibly dangerous liquids. No law required us to add that these liquids were in super-pressurized cans which were bound to explode and spray their contents the moment that the wall-strengthening force was annulled.

We'd actually exaggerated the hazard . . . in an attempt to avoid any slightest harm to trespassers. Nothing vicious was in those containers. Whatever might be slightly toxic was present in concentrations too small to matter, although a normal sense of smell would give ample warning regardless. Just a harmless mixture of materials like butyl mercaptan, butyric acid, methanethiol, skatole, cadaverine, putrescine . . . well, yes, the organic binder did have penetrative properties; if you got a few drops on your skin, the odor wouldn't disappear for a week or two. . . .

The screams reached me first. I had a moment to gloat. Then the stench arrived. I'd forgotten to don my gas mask, and even when I'm human my nose is quite sensitive. The slight whiff I got sent me gasping and retching backward across the roof. It was skunk, it was spoiled butter, it was used asparagus, it was corruption and doom and the wheels of Juggernaut lubricated with Limburger cheese, it was beyond imagining. I barely got my protection on in time.

"Poor dear. Poor Steve." Ginny held me close.

"Are they gone?" I sputtered.

"Yes. Along with the policemen and, if we don't get busy, half this postal district."

I relaxed. The uncertain point in our plan had been whether the opposition would break or would come through our now undefended doors in search of our lives. After my experience I didn't see how the latter would have been possible. Our chemists had builded better than they knew.

We need hardly expect a return visit, I thought in rising glee. If you suffer arrest or a broken head for the Cause, you're a hero who inspires others. But if you merely acquire for a while a condition your best friends won't tell you about because they can't come within earshot of you—hasn't the Cause taken a setback?

I grabbed Ginny to me and started to kiss her. Damn, I'd forgotten my gas mask again! She disentagled our snouts. "I'd better help Barney and the rest hex away those molecules before they spread," she told me. "Switch off your machine and screen it."

"Uh, yes," I must agree. "We want our staff returning to work in the morning."

What with one thing and another, we were busy for a couple of hours. After we finished, Barney produced some bottles, and the celebration lasted till well-nigh dawn. The eastern sky blushed pink when Ginny and I wobbled aboard our broom and hiccoughed, "Home, James."

The air blew cool, heaven reached high. "Know something?" I said over my shoulder. "I love you."

"Purr-rr-rr." She leaned forward to rub her cheek against mine. Her hands wandered.

"Shameless hussy," I said.

"You prefer some other kind?" she asked.

"Well, no," I said, "but you might wait a while. Here I am in front of you, feeling more lecherous every minute but without any way to lech."

"Oh, there are ways," she murmured dreamily. "On a broomstick yet. Have you forgotten?"

"No. But dammit, the local airlanes are going to be crowded with commuter traffic pretty soon, and I'd rather not fly several miles looking for solitude when we've got a perfectly good bedroom nearby."

"Right. I like that thought. Only fifteen minutes a day, in the privacy of your own home— Pour on the coal, James."

The stick accelerated.

I was full of glory and the glory that was her. She caught the paranatural traces first. My indication was that her head lifted from between my shoulder blades, her arms loosened around my waist while the fingernails bit through my shirt. "What the Moloch?" I exclaimed.

"Hsh!" she breathed. We flew in silence through the thin chill dawn wind. The city spread darkling beneath us. Her voice came at last, tense, but somehow dwindled and lost: "I said I didn't like the scent of the time-stream. In the excitement and everything, I forgot."

My guts crawled, as if I were about to turn wolf. Senses and extrasenses strained forth. I've scant thaumaturgic skill—the standard cantrips, plus a few from the Army and more from engineering training—but a lycanthrope has inborn instincts and awarenesses. Presently I also knew.

Dreadfulness was about.

As we flitted downward, we knew that it was in our house.

We left the broomstick on the front lawn. I turned my key in the door and hurled myself through. "Val!" I yelled into the dim rooms. "Svartalf!"

No lock had been forced or picked, no glass had been broken, the steel and stone guarding every paranatural entry were unmoved. But chairs lay tumbled, vases smashed where they had fallen off shaken tables, blood was spattered over walls, floors, carpets, from end to end of the building.

We stormed into Valeria's room. When we saw that little shape quietly asleep in her crib, we held each other and wept.

Finally Ginny could ask, "Where's Svartalf? What happened?"

"I'll look around," I said. "He gave an epic account of himself, at least."

"Yes—" She wiped her eyes. As she looked around the wreckage in the nursery, that green gaze hardened. She stared down into the crib. "Why didn't you wake up?" she said in a tone I'd never heard before.

I was already on my way to search. I found Svartalf in the kitchen. His blood had about covered the linoleum. In spite of broken bones, tattered hide, belly gashed open, the breath rattled faintly in and out of him. Before I could examine the damage further, a shriek brought me galloping back to Ginny.

She held the child. Blue eyes gazed dully at me from under tangled gold curls. Ginny's face, above, was drawn so tight it seemed the skin must rip on the cheekbones. "Something's wrong with her," she told me. "I can't tell what, but something's wrong."

I stood for an instant feeling my universe break apart. Then I went into the closet. Dusk was giving place to day, and I needed darkness. I shucked my outer clothes and used my flash. Emerging, I went to those two female figures. My wolf nose drank their odors.

I sat on my haunches and howled.

Ginny laid down what she was holding. She stayed completely motionless by the crib while I changed back.

"I'll call the police," I heard my voice say to her. "That thing isn't Val. It isn't even human."

XXIII

I TAKE CARE not to remember the next several hours in detail.

At noon we were in my study. Our local chief had seen almost at once that the matter was beyond him and urged us to call in the FBI. Their technicians were still busy checking the house and grounds, inch by inch. Our best service was to stay out of their way. I sat on the day bed, Ginny on the edge of my swivel chair. From time to time one of us jumped up, paced around, made an inane remark, and slumped back down. The air was fogged with smoke from ashtray-overflowing cigarets. My skull felt scooped out. Her eyes had retreated far back into her head. Sunlight, grass, trees were unreal in the windows.

"You really ought to eat," I said for the ?-th time. "Keep your strength."

"Same to you," she answered, not looking at me or at anything I could tell.

"I'm not hungry."

"Nor I."

We returned to the horror.

The extension phone yanked us erect. "A call from Dr. Ashman," it said. "Do you wish to answer?"

"For God's sake yes!" ripped from me. "Visual." Momentarily, crazily, I couldn't concentrate on our first message from the man who brought Valeria into the world. My mind spun off into the principles of telephony. Sympathetic vibrations, when sender and receiver are spelled to the same number; a scrying unit for video when desired; a partial animation to operate the assembly—Ginny's hand seized mine. Its cold shocked me into sanity.

Ashman's face looked well-nigh as exhausted as hers. "Virginia," he said. "Steve. We have the report."

I tried to respond and couldn't.

"You were right," he went on. "It's a homunculus."

"What took you so long?" Ginny asked. Her voice wasn't husky any more, just hoarse and harsh.

"Unprecedented case," Ashman said. "Fairy changelings have always been considered a legend. Nothing in our data suggests any motive for nonhuman intelligences to steal a child . . . nor any method by which they could if they wanted to, assuming the parents take normal care . . . and certainly no reason for such hypothetical kidnapers to leave a sort of golem in its place." He sighed. "Apparently we know less than we believed."

"What are your findings?" The restored determination in Ginny's words brought my gaze to her.

"The police chirurgeon, the crime lab staff, and later a pathologist from the University hospital worked with me," Ashman told us. "Or I with them. I was merely the family doctor. We lost hours on the assumption Valeria was bewitched. The simulacrum is excellent, understand. It's mindless—the EEG is practically flat—but it resembles your daughter down to fingerprints. Not till she . . . it . . . had failed to respond to every therapeutic spell we commanded between us, did we think the body might be an imitation. You told us so at the outset, Steve, but we discounted that as hysteria. I'm sorry. Proof required a whole battery of tests. For instance, the saline content and PBI suggest the makers of the homunculus had no access to oceans. We clinched the matter when we injected some radioactivated holy water; that metabolism is not remotely human."

His dry tone was valuable. The horror began to have some shadowy outline; my brain creaked into motion, searching for ways to grapple it. "What'll they do with the changeling?" I asked.

"I suppose the authorities will keep it in the hope of—of learning something, doing something through it," Ashman said. "In the end, if nothing else happens, it'll doubtless be in-stitutionalized. Don't hate the poor thing. That's all it is, a poor thing, manufactured for some evil reason but not to blame."

"Not to waste time on, you mean," Ginny rasped. "Doctor, have you any ideas about rescuing Val?"

"No. It hurts me." He looked it. "I'm only a medicine man, though. What further can I do? Tell me and I'll come flying."

"You can start right away," Ginny said. "You've heard, haven't you, my familiar was critically wounded defending her? He's at the vet's, but I want you to take over."

Ashman was startled. "What? Really— Look, I can't save an animal's life when a specialist isn't able."

"That's not the problem. Svartalf will get well. But vets don't have the expensive training and equipment used on people. I want him rammed back to health overnight. What runes and potions you don't have, you'll know how to obtain. Money's no object."

"Wait," I started to say, recalling what leechcraft costs are like.

She cut me off short. "Nornwell will foot the bill, unless a government agency does. They'd better. This isn't like anything else they've encountered. Could be a major emergency shaping up." She stood straight. Despite the sooted eyes, hair hanging lank, unchanged black garb of last night, she was once more Captain Graylock of the 14th United States Cavalry. "I am not being silly, Doctor. Consider the implications of your discoveries. Svartalf may or may not be able to convey a little information to me about what he encountered. He certainly can't when he's unconscious. At the least, he's always been a good helper, and we need whatever help we can get."

Ashman reflected a minute. "All right," he said.

He was about to sign off when the study door opened. "Hold it," a voice ordered. I turned on my heel, jerkily, uselessly fast.

The hard brown face and hard rangy frame of Robert Shining Knife confronted me. The head of the local FBI office had discarded the conservative business suit of his organization for working clothes. His feather bonnet seemed to brush the ceiling; a gourd stuck into his breechclout rattled dryly to his steps; the blanket around his shoulders and the paint on his skin were patterned in thunderbirds, sun discs, and I know not what else.

"You listened in," I accused.

He nodded. "Couldn't take chances, Mr. Matuchek. Dr. Ashman, you'll observe absolute secrecy. No running off to any blabbermouth shaman or goodwife you think should be brought in consultation."

Ginny blazed up. "See here—"

"Your cat'll be repaired for you," Shining Knife promised in the same blunt tone. "I doubt he'll prove of assistance, but we can't pass by the smallest possibility. Uncle Sam will pick up the tab—on the QT—and Dr. Ashman may as well head the team. But I want to clear the other members of it, and make damn sure they aren't told more than necessary. Wait in your office, Doctor. An operative will join you inside an hour."

The physician bristled. "And how long will he then take to certify each specialist I may propose is an All-American Boy?"

"Very little time. You'll be surprised how much he'll know about them already. You'd also be surprised how much trouble someone would have who stood on his rights to tell the press or even his friends what's been going on." Shining Knife smiled sardonically. "I'm certain that's a superfluous warning, sir. You're a man of patriotism and discretion. Good-bye."

The phone understood him and broke the spell.

"Mind if I close the windows?" Shining Knife asked as he did. "Eavesdroppers have sophisticated gadgets these days." He had left the door ajar; we heard his men move around in the house, caught faint pungencies and mutterings. "Please sit down." He leaned back against a bookshelf and watched us.

Ginny controlled herself with an effort I could feel. "Aren't you acting rather high-handed?"

"The circumstances require it, Mrs. Matuchek," he said.

She bit her lip and nodded.

"What's this about?" I begged.

The hardness departed from Shining Knife. "We're confirming what your wife evidently suspects," he said with a compassion that made me wonder if he had a daughter of his own. "She's a witch and would know, but wouldn't care to admit it till every hope of a less terrible answer was gone. This is no ordinary kidnaping."

"Well, of course—!"

"Wait. I doubt if it's technically any kind of kidnaping. My bureau may have no jurisdiction. However, as your wife said, the case may well involve the national security. I'll have to communicate with Washington and let them decide. In the last analysis, the President will. Meanwhile, we don't dare rock the boat."

I looked from him to Ginny to the horror that was again without form, not a thing to be fought but a condition of nightmare. "Please," I whispered.

Shining Knife's mouth contorted too for an instant. He spoke flatly and fast:

"We've ascertained the blood is entirely the cat's. There are some faint indications of ichor, chemical stains which may have been caused by it, but none of the stuff itself. We got better clues from scratches and gouges in floor and furnishings. Those marks weren't left by anything we can identify, natural or paranatural; and believe me, our gang is good at identifications.

"The biggest fact is that the house was never entered. Not in any way we can check for—and, again, we know a lot of different ones. Nothing was broken, forced, or picked. Nothing had affected the guardian signs and objects; their fields were at full strength, properly meshed and aligned, completely undisturbed. Therefore nothing flew down the chimney, or oozed through a crack, or dematerialized past the walls, or compelled the babysitter to let it in.

"The fact that no one in the neighborhood was alerted is equally significant. Remember how common hex alarms and second-sighted watchdogs are. Something paranatural and hostile in the street would've touched off a racket to wake everybody for three blocks around. Instead, we've only got the Delacortes next door, who heard what they thought was a catfight."

He paused. "Sure," he finished, "we don't know everything about goetics. But we do know enough about its felonious uses to be sure this was no forced entry."

"What, then?" I cried.

Ginny said it for him: "It came in from the hell universe."

"Theoretically, could have been an entity from Heaven." Shining Knife's grin was brief and stiff. "But that's psychologically—spiritually—impossible. The M.O. is diabolic."

Ginny sat forward. Her features were emptied of expression, her chin rested on a fist, her eyes were half-shut, the other hand drooped loosely over a knee. She murmured as if in a dream:

"The changeling fits your theory quite well, doesn't it? To the best of our knowledge, matter can't be transferred from one space-time plenum to another in violation of the conservation laws of physics. Psychic influences can go, yes. Visions, temptations, inspirations, that sort of thing. The uncertainty principle allows them. But not an actual object. If you want to take it from its proper universe to your own, you have to replace it with an identical amount of matter, whose configuration has to be fairly similar to preserve momentum. You may remember Villegas suggested this was the reason angels take more or less anthropomorphic shapes on earth."

Shining Knife looked uneasy. "This is no time to be unfriends with the Most High," he muttered.

"I've no such intention," Ginny said in her sleepwalker's tone. "He can do all things. But His servants are finite. They must often find it easier to let transferred matter fall into the shape it naturally wants to, rather than solve a problem involving the velocities of ten to the umpteenth atoms in order to give it another form. And the inhabitants of the Low Continuum probably can't. They aren't creative. Or so the Petrine churches claim. I understand the Johannine doctrine includes Manichaean elements.

"A demon could go from his universe to a point in ours that was inside this house. Because his own natural form is chaotic, he wouldn't have to counter-transfer anything but dirt, dust, trash, rubbish, stuff in a high-entropy condition. After he finished his task, he'd presumably return that material in the course of returning himself. It'd presumably show effects. I know things got generally upset in the fight, Mr. Shining Knife, but you might run a lab check on what was in the garbage can, the catbox, and so forth."

The FBI man bowed. "We thought of that, and noticed its homogenized condition," he said. "If *you* could think of it, under these circumstances—"

Her eyes opened fully. Her speech became like slowly drawn steel: "Our daughter is in hell, sir. We mean to get her back."

I thought of Valeria, alone amidst cruelty and clamor and unnamable distortions, screaming for a Daddy and a Mother who did not come. I sat there on the bed, in the night which has no ending, and heard my lady speak as if she were across a light-years-wide abyss:

"Let's not waste time on emotions. I'll continue outlining the event as I reconstruct it; check me out. The demon—could have been more than one, but I'll assume a singleton—entered our cosmos as a scattered mass of material but pulled it together at once. By simple transformation, he assumed the shape he wanted. The fact that neither the Adversary nor any of his minions can create—if the Petrine tradition is correct—wouldn't handicap him. He could borrow an existing shape. The fact that you can't identify it means nothing. It could be a creature of some obscure human mythology, or some imaginative drawing somewhere, or even another planet.

"This is not a devout household. It'd be hypocrisy, and therefore useless, for us to keep religious symbols around that we don't love. Besides, in spite of previous experience with a demon or two, we didn't expect one to invade a middle-class suburban home. No authenticated case of that was on record. So the final possible barrier to his appearance was absent.

"He had only a few pounds of mass available to him. Any human who kept his or her head could have coped with him—if nothing else, kept him on the run, too busy to do his dirty work, while phoning for an exorcist. But on this one night, no human was here. Svartalf can't talk, and he obviously never got the chance to call in help by different means. He may have outweighed the demon, but not by enough to prevail against a thing all teeth, claws, spines, and armor plate. In the end, when Svartalf lay beaten, the demon took our Val to the Low Continuum. The counter-transferred mass was necessarily in her form.

"Am I right?"

Shining Knife nodded. "I expect you are."

"What do you plan to do about it?"

"Frankly, at the moment there's little or nothing we can do. We haven't so much as a clue to motive."

"You've been told about last night. We made bad enemies. I'm inclined to take at face value the Johnnies' claim that their adepts have secret knowledge. Esotericism has always been associated more with the Low than the High. I'd say their cathedral is the place to start investigating."

Behind his mask of paint, Shining Knife registered unhappiness. "I explained to you before, Mrs. Matuchek, when we first inquired who might be responsible, that's an extremely serious charge to make on no genuine evidence. The public situation is delicately balanced. Who realizes that better than you? We can't afford fresh riots. Besides, more to the point, this invasion could be the start of something far bigger, far worse than a kidnaping."

I stirred. "Nothing's worse," I mumbled.

He ignored me, sensing that at present Ginny was more formidable. "We know practically zero about the hell universe. I'll stretch a point of security, because I suspect you've figured the truth out already on the basis of unclassified information; quite a few civilian wizards have. The Army's made several attempts to probe it, with no better success than the Faustus Institute had thirty years ago. Men returned in states of acute psychic shock, after mere minutes there, unable to describe what'd happened. Instruments recorded data that didn't make sense."

"Unless you adopt Nickelsohn's hypothesis," she said.

"What's it?"

"That space-time in that cosmos is non-Euclidean, violently

so compared to ours, and the geometry changes from place to place.'' Her tone was matter-of-fact.

''Well, yes, I'm told the Army researchers did decide—'' He saw the triumph in her eyes. ''Damn! What a neat trap you set for me!'' With renewed starkness: ''Okay. You'll understand we dare not go blundering around when forces we can't calculate are involved for reasons we can scarcely guess. The consequences could be disastrous. I'm going to report straight to the Director, who I'm sure will report straight to the President, who I'm equally sure will have us keep alert but sit tight till we've learned more.''

''What about Steve and me?''

''You too. You might get contacted, remember.''

''I doubt it. What ransom could a demon want?''

''The demon's master—''

''I told you to check on the Johnnies.''

''We will. We'll check on everything in sight, reasonable or not. But it'll take time.''

''Meanwhile Valeria is in hell.''

''If you want a priest—we've clergy of most faiths cleared to serve our personnel. I can bring one here if you like.''

The red head shook. ''No, thanks. Ask them to pray for her. It can't hurt. I doubt it'll help much, either. Certainly none of them can help us two. What we want is a chance to go after our daughter.''

My heart sprang. The numbness tingled out of me. I rose.

Shining Knife braced himself. ''I can't permit that. Sure, you've both accomplished remarkable things in the past, but the stakes are too high now for amateurs to play. Hate me all you want. If it's any consolation, that'll pain me. But I can't let you jeopardize yourselves and the public interest. You'll stay put. Under guard.''

''You—'' I nearly jumped him. Ginny drew me back.

''Hold on, Steve,'' she said crisply. ''Don't make trouble. What we'll do, you and I, if it won't interfere with the investigation, is choke down some food and a sleeping potion and cork off till we're fit to think again.''

Shining Knife smiled. ''Thanks,'' he said. ''I was certain you'd be sensible. I'll go hurry 'em along in the kitchen so you can get that meal soon.''

I closed the door behind him. Rage shivered me. ''What the

blue deuce is this farce?'' I stormed. ''If he thinks we'll sit and
wait on a gaggle of bureaucrats—''

''Whoa.'' She pulled my ear down to her lips. ''What he
thinks,'' she whispered, ''is that his wretched guard will make
any particular difference to us.''

''Oh-ho!'' For the first time I laughed. It wasn't a merry or
musical noise, but it was a laugh of sorts.

XXIV

WE WEREN'T EXACTLY under house arrest. The well-behaved young man who stayed with us was to give us what protection and assistance we might need. He made it clear, though, that if we tried to leave home or pass word outside, he'd suddenly and regretfully discover reason to hold us for investigation of conspiracy to overthrow the Interstate Commerce Commission.

He was a good warlock, too. An FBI agent must have a degree in either sorcery or accounting; and his boss wanted to be sure we didn't try anything desperate. But at supper Ginny magicked out of him the information she required. How she did that, I'll never understand. I don't mean she cast a spell in the technical sense. Rather, the charm she employed is the kind against which the only male protection is defective glands. What still seems impossible to me is that she could sit talking, smiling, flashing sparks of wit across a surface of controlled feminine sorrow, waggling her eyelashes and leading him on to relate his past exploits . . . when each corner of the place screamed that Valeria was gone.

We retired early, pleading exhaustion. Actually we were well rested and wire-taut. "He's sharp on thaumaturgy," my sweetheart murmured in the darkness of our bedroom, "but out of practice on mantics. A smoothly wrought Seeming ought to sucker him. Use the cape."

I saw her intent. A cold joy, after these past hours in chains, beat through me. I scrambled out of my regular clothes, into my wolf suit, and put the civvies back on top. As I reached for the Tarnkappe—unused for years, little more than a war souvenir—she came to me and pressed herself close. "Darling, be careful!" Her voice was not steady and I tasted salt on her lips.

She had to stay, allaying possible suspicion, ready to take the ransom demand that *might* come. Hers was the hard part.

I donned the cloak. The hood smelled musty across my face, and small patches of visibility showed where moths had gotten at the fabric. But what the nuts, it was merely to escape and later (we hoped) return here in. There are too many counter-agents these days for Tarnkappen to be effective for serious work, ranging from infrared detectors to spray cans of paint triggered by an unwary foot. Our friendly Fed no doubt had instruments ready to buzz him if an invisibilizing field moved in his vicinity.

Ginny went into her passes, *sotto voce* incantations, and the rest. She'd brought what was necessary into this room during the day. Her excuse was that she wanted to give us both as strong a protection against hostile influences as she was able. She'd done it, too, with the FBI man's admiring approval. In particular, while the spell lasted, I'd be nearly impossible to locate by paranatural means alone.

The next stage of her scheme was equally straightforward. While terrestrial magnetism is too weak to cancel paranatural forces, it does of course affect them, and so do its fluctuations. Therefore ordinary goetic sensor devices aren't designed to register minor quantitative changes. Ginny would establish a Seeming. The feeble Tarnkappe field would appear gradually to double in intensity, then, as I departed, oscillate back to its former value. On my return, she'd phase out the deception.

Simple in theory. In practice it took greater skill to pull off without triggering an alarm than her record showed she could possess. What the poor old FBI didn't know was that she had what went beyond training and equipment, she had a Gift.

At her signal, I slipped through the window. The night air was chill and moist; dew glistened on the lawn in the goblin glow of street lamps; I heard a dog howl. It had probably caught a whiff of my cloak. And no doubt the grounds were under surveillance . . . yes, my witch-sight picked out a man in the shadows beneath the elms across the way. . . . I padded fast and softly down the middle of the pavement, where I'd be least likely to affect some watchbeast or sentry field. When it comes to that sort of business, I'm pretty good myself.

After several blocks, safely distant, I reached the local grade school and stowed my Tarnkappe in a playground trash can. Thereafter I walked openly, an unremarkable citizen on his lawful occasions. The night being new, I did have to be careful that no passer-by recognized me. At the first phone booth I called Barney Sturlason's home. He said to come right on over. Rather than a taxi, I took a crosstown carpet, reasoning I'd be more anonymous as one of a crowd of passengers. I was.

Barney opened the door. Hallway light that got past his

shoulders spilled yellow across me. He let out a soft whistle. "I figured you'd be too bushed to work today, Steve, but not that you'd look like Monday after Ragnarök. What's wrong?"

"Your family mustn't hear," I said.

He turned immediately and led me to his study. Waving me to one of the leather armchairs, he relocked the door, poured two hefty Scotches, and settled down opposite me. "Okay," he invited.

I told him. Never before had I seen anguish on those features. "Oh, no," he whispered.

Shaking himself, like a bear making ready to charge, he asked: "What can I do?"

"First off, lend me a broom," I answered.

"Hold on," he said. "I do feel you've been rash already. Tell me your next move."

"I'm going to Siloam and learn what I can."

"I thought so." The chair screaked under Barney's shifting weight. "Steve, it won't wash. Burgling the Johnny cathedral, maybe trying to beat an admission out of some priest— No. You'd only make trouble for yourself and Ginny at a time when she needs every bit of your resources. The FBI will investigate, with professionals. You could wreck the very clues you're after, assuming they exist. Face it, you are jumping to conclusions." He considered me. "A moral point in addition. You didn't agree that mob yesterday had the right to make its own laws. Are you claiming the right for yourself?"

I took a sip and let the whisky burn its loving way down my gullet. "Ginny and I've had a while to think," I said. "We expected you'd raise the objections you do. Let me take them in order. I don't want to sound dramatic, but how can we be in worse trouble? Add anything to infinity and, and, and"—I must stop for another belt of booze—"you've got the same infinity.

"About the FBI being more capable. We don't aim to bull around just to be doing something; give us credit for some brains. Sure, the Bureau must've had agents in the Johannine Church for a long while, dossiers on its leaders, the standard stuff. But you'll remember how at the HCUA hearings a few years back, no evidence could be produced to warrant putting the Church on the Attorney General's list, in spite of its disavowal of American traditions."

"The Johnnies are entitled to their opinions," Barney said. "Shucks, I'll agree with certain claims of theirs. This society has gotten too worldly, too busy chasing dollars and fun, too preoccupied with sex and not enough with love, too callous about the unfortunate—''

''Barney,'' I snapped, ''you're trying to sidetrack me and cool me off, but it's no go. Either I get your help soon or I take my marbles elsewhere.''

He sighed, fumbled a pipe from his tweed jacket and began stuffing it. ''Okay, continue. If the Feds can't find proof that the Johannine hierarchy is engaged in activities illegal or subversive, does that prove the hierarchy is diabolically clever . . . or simply innocent?''

''Well, the Gnostics brag of having information and powers that nobody else does,'' I said, ''and they do get involved one way or another in more and more of the social unrest going on— and mainly, who else, what else might be connected with this thing that's happened? Maybe even unwittingly; that's imaginable; but connected.''

I leaned forward. ''Look, Barney,'' I went on, ''Shining Knife admits he'll have to move slow. And Washington's bound to keep him on tighter leash than he wants personally. Tomorrow, no doubt, he'll have agents interviewing various Johnnies. In the nature of the case, they'll learn nothing. You'd need mighty strong presumptive evidence to get a search warrant against a church, especially one that so many people are convinced bears the final Word of God, and most especially when the temple's a labyrinth of places that none but initiates in the various degrees are supposed to enter.

''Well, if and when you got your warrant, what could you uncover? This was no ordinary job. The usual tests for nigromancy and so forth aren't applicable. Why, if I were High Adept Zarathra, I'd invite the G-men to come inspect everything that's religiously permissible. What could he lose?''

''What could you gain?'' Barney replied.

''Perhaps nothing,'' I said. ''But I mean to act now, not a week from now; and I won't be handicapped by legal rules and public opinion; and I do have special abilities and experience in dark matters; and they won't expect me; and in short, if anything's there to find, I've the best chance in sight of finding it.''

He scowled past me.

''As for the moral issue,'' I said, ''you may be right. On the other hand, I'm not about to commit brutalities like some imaginary Special Agent Vee Eye Eye. And in spite of Shining Knife's fear, I honestly don't see what could provoke a major invasion from the Low World. That'd bring in the Highest, and the Adversary can't afford such a confrontation.

"Which is worse, Barney, an invasion of property and privacy, maybe a profanation of a few shrines . . . or a child in hell?"

He set his glass down on an end table. "You win!" exploded from him. Blinking in surprise: "I seem to've smashed the bottom out of this tumbler."

"Finish mine," I said. "I'm on my way."

We rose together. "How about a weapon?" he offered.

I shook my head. "Let's not compound the felony. Whatever I meet, probably a gun won't handle." It seemed needless to add that I carried a hunting knife under my civvies and, in wolf-shape, a whole mouthful of armament. "Uh, we'll fix it so you're in the clear. I visited you; that can no doubt be proven if they try hard. But I sneaked back after I left and boosted your broom."

He nodded. "I suggest you take the Plymouth," he said. "It's not as fast as either sports job, but the spell runs quieter and the besom was tuned only the other day." He stood for a bit, thinking. Stillness and blackness pressed on the windowpanes. "Meanwhile I'll start research on the matter. Bill Hardy . . . Janice Wenzel from our library staff . . . hm, we could co-opt your Dr. Ashman, and how about Prof Griswold from the University? . . . and more, able close-mouthed people, who'll be glad to help and hang any consequences. If nothing else, we can assemble all unclassified data regarding the Low Continuum, and maybe some that aren't. We can set up equations delimiting various conceivable approaches to the rescue problem, and crank 'em through the computator, and eliminate unworkable ideas. Yeah, I'll get busy right off."

What can you say to a guy like that except thanks?

XXV

IT SEEMED IN character for the Johannine Church to put its cathedral for the whole Upper Midwest not in Chicago, Milwaukee, or any other city, but off alone, a hundred miles even from our modest town. The placing symbolized and emphasized the Gnostic rejection of this world as evil, the idea of salvation through secret rites and occult knowledge. Unlike Petrine Christianity, this kind didn't come to you; aside from dismal little chapels here and there, scarcely more than recruiting stations, you came to it.

Obvious, yes. And therefore, I thought, probably false. Nothing about Gnosticism was ever quite what it seemed. That lay in its very nature.

Perhaps its enigmas, veils behind veils and mazes within mazes, were one thing that drew so many people these days. The regular churches made their theologies plain. They clearly described and delimited the mysteries as such, with the commonsense remark that we mortals aren't able to understand every aspect of the Highest. They declared that this world was given us to live in by the Creator, and hence must be fundamentally good; a lot of the imperfections are due to human bollixing, and it's our job to improve matters.

Was that overly unromantic? Did the Johannines appeal to the daydream, childish but always alive in us, of becoming omnipotent by learning a secret denied the common herd? I'd made that scornful assumption, and still believed it held a lot of truth. But the more I thought, the less it felt like the whole explanation.

I had plenty of time and chance and need for thought, flitting above the night land, where scattered lights of farms and villages looked nearly as remote as the stars overhead. The air that slid around the windfield was turning cold. Its breath went through and through me, disrupting cobwebs in my head until I saw how little I'd really studied, how much I'd lazily taken for granted. But I saw, too, facts I'd forgotten, and how they might be fitted together in a larger understanding. Grimly, as I traveled, I set myself to review what I could about the Johannine Church, from the ground up.

Was it merely a thing of the past two or three generations, a nut cult that happened to appeal to something buried deep in Western man? Or was it in truth as old as it maintained—founded by Christ himself?

The other churches said No. Doubtless Catholic, Orthodox, and Protestant should not be lumped together as Petrine. But the popular word made a rough kind of sense. They did have a mutual interpretation of Jesus' charge to his disciples. They agreed on the special importance of Peter. No matter what differences had arisen since, including the question of apostolic succession, they all derived from the Twelve in a perfectly straightforward way.

And yet . . . and yet . . . there is that strange passage at the close of the Gospel According to St. John. "Then Peter, turning about, seeth the disciple whom Jesus loved following; which also leaned on his breast at supper, and said, Lord, which is he that betrayeth thee? Peter seeing him saith to Jesus, Lord, and what shall this man do? Jesus saith unto him, If I will that he tarry till I come, what is that to thee? follow thou me. Then went this saying abroad among the brethren, that that disciple should not die: yet Jesus said not unto him, He shall not die; but, If I will that he tarry till I come, what is that to thee? This is the disciple which testifieth of these things, and wrote these things: and we know that his testimony is true."

I don't understand it, and I'm not sure Biblical scholars do either, regardless of what they say. Certainly it gave rise to a fugitive tradition that here Our Lord was creating something more than any of them but John ever knew—some unproclaimed other Church, within or parallel to the Church of Peter, which would at the end manifest itself and guide man to a new dispensation. Today's cult might have originated entirely in this century. But the claim it trumpeted had been whispered for two thousand years.

The association of such a claim with otherworldliness was almost inevitable. Under many labels, Gnosticism has been a recurring heresy. The original form, or rather forms, were an attempt to fuse Christianity with a mishmash of Oriental mystery cults, Neoplatonism, and sorcery. Legend traced it back to the Simon Magus who appears in the eighth chapter of Acts, whose memory was accordingly held in horror by the orthodox. Modern Johanninism was doubly bold in reviving that dawn-age movement by name, in proclaiming it not error but a higher truth and Simon Magus not a corrupter but a prophet.

Could that possibly be right? Might the world actually be at the morning of the Reign of Love? I didn't know; how could I? But by using my brains, as the Petrine tradition held we should, rather than my emotions, I'd decided the Johanine dogma was false. Its spreading acceptance I found due to plain human irrationality.

So you got communities of Truth Seekers, settling down to practice their rites and meditations where nobody would interfere. They drew pilgrims, who needed housing, food, services. The priests, priestesses, acolytes, and lay associates did too. A temple (more accurate than "cathedral," but the Johnnies insisted on the latter word to emphasize that they were Christians) needed income; and as a rule it had a substantial endowment, shrewdly managed. Thus a town often grew up around the original foundation—like Siloam, where I was headed.

Simple. Banal. Why did I bother marshaling information that any reader of the daily papers had? Merely to escape thinking about Valeria? No. To get as much as possible straight in my head, when most was tangled and ghostly.

The Something Else, the Thing Beyond . . . was it no illusion, but a deeper insight? And if so, an insight into what? I thought of the Johannines' intolerance and troublemaking. I thought of the frank assertion that their adepts held powers no one else imagined, and that more was revealed to them every year. I thought of stories told by certain apostates, who hadn't advanced far in their degrees when they experienced that which scared them off: nothing illegal, immoral, or otherwise titillating; merely ugly, hateful, sorrowful, and hence not very newsworthy; deniable or ignorable by those who didn't want to believe them. I thought of the Gnostic theology, what part of it was made public: terrible amidst every twist of revelation and logic, the identification of their Demiurge with the God of the Old Testament with Satan.

I thought of Antichrist.

But there I shied off, being agnostic about such matters, as I've said. I took my stand on the simple feeling that it didn't make sense the Almighty would operate in any such fashion.

Light glimmered into view, far off across the prairie. I was glad of journey's end, no matter what happened next. I didn't care to ride further with those reflections of mine.

Siloam was ordinary frame houses in ordinary yards along ordinary streets. A sign beneath the main airlane, as you neared, said POP. 5240; another announced that the Lions Club met every Thursday at the Kobold Kettle Restaurant. There were a couple of small manufacturing enterprises, a city hall, an elementary school, a high school, a firehouse, a bedraggled park, a hotel, more service stations than needed. The business district held stores, a cafe or two, a bank, chirurgeon's and dentist's offices above a Rexall apothecary . . . the American works.

That homeliness made the rest freezingly alien. Though the hour lacked of midnight, downtown was a tomb. The residential streets were nearly as deserted—nobody out for a stroll, no teen-agers holding hands, scarcely a stick or a wagon moving, be-neath the rare lamps—once in a while a robed and hooded figure slowly pacing. Each home lay drawn into itself, behind drawn shades. Where the inhabitants weren't asleep, they were prob-ably not watching crystal or playing cards or having a drink or making love, they were most likely at the devotions and studies they hoped would qualify them for a higher religious degree, more knowlege and power and surety of salvation.

And everything centered on the cathedral. It soared above the complex of boxlike ancillary buildings that surrounded it, above town and plain. The pictures I'd seen of it had not conveyed the enormity. Those flat, bone-white walls went up and up and *up*, till the roof climbed further yet to make the vast central cupola. From afar, the windows looked like nailheads, one row to a story; but then I saw the stained-glass pair, each filling half the façade it occupied with murky colors and bewildering patterns, Mandala at the west end and Eye of God at the east. From the west, also, rose the single tower, which in a photograph only looked austere, but now became one leap into the stars.

Light played across the outside of the cathedral and shone dimly from its glass. I heard a chant, men's voices marching deep beneath the wild icy sweepings and soarings of women who sang on no scale I could identify, in no language of earth.

". . . Helfioth Alaritha arbar Neniotho Melitho Tarasunt Chanados Umia Theirura Marada Seliso . . ."

The music was so amplified as to be audible to the very outskirts of town. And it never ended. This was a perpetual choir. Priests, acolytes, pilgrims were always on hand to step in when any of the six hundred and one wearied. I failed to imagine how it must be to live in that day-and-night haze of canticle. If you were a dweller in Siloam, perhaps not even a Johnny, you'd soon stop noticing on a conscious level. But wouldn't the sound weave into your thoughts, dreams, bones, finally into your soul?

I couldn't interpret the extrasensation I felt, either, more powerful for every yard I approached. Wrongness—or rightness of a kind that I was simply unable to fathom?

After all, the attendant at the gate was a pleasant young man, his tow hair and blue eyes right out of the folk who'd been hereabouts for more than a hundred years, his friendliness out of Walt Whitman's own America. When I had parked my broom in the lot that stretched wide and bare into the dark, approached him, and asked, ''Okay to go in?'' he regarded me for a moment before answering lightly, ''You're not a communicant, are you?''

''N-no,'' I said, a bit taken aback.

He chuckled. ''Wanna know how I can tell? They've got to the Elphuë. We'd wait till Mary's invocation was finished before we entered.''

''I'm sorry, I—''

'' 'S okay. Nobody minds, long's you're quiet. In theory, you're damned anyway. I don't buy that myself, know what I mean? My girl's a Methodist. I'll go along with the red tape the priests want before they'll let me marry her, but I can't believe she'll burn.'' He realized he might have spoken too freely and added in haste: ''How come you're this late? The tourists arrive in the daytime.''

I decided he wasn't a lay brother, just an employee, and no more fanatical than the average Christian of any type—in short, one of the decent majority you find in all organizations, all countries. I was prepared for his question. ''I travel in ankhs,'' I said. ''Got an appointment in town early tormorrow morning before moving on. Got hung up today and didn't reach here till now. Your choir is so famous I didn't want to miss it.''

''Thanks.'' He handed me a leaflet. ''You know the rules? Use the main door. Take a seat in the Heath—uh, the Spectators' Corner. No noise, no picture-taking. When you want to leave, do it quietly, same way as you came.''

I nodded and walked through the gate. The auxiliary buildings formed a square around a paved yard centered on the cathedral. Where they did not butt directly on each other, walls had been raised between, making the only entrances three portals closable by wire gates. The offices, storerooms, living quarters were plain, in fact drab. A few cenobites moved about, male scarcely distinguishable from female in their robes and overshadowing cowls. I remembered the complete absence of any scandals, anywhere in the world, though the Johannines mingled the sexes in celibacy. Well, of course their monks and nuns weren't simply consecrated; they were initiates. They had gone beyond baptism, beyond the elementary mystery rites and name-changing (with the old public name retained for secular use) that corresponded to a Petrine confirmation. For years they had mortified the flesh, disciplined the soul, bent the mind to mastering what their holy books called divine revelation, and unbelievers called pretentious nonsense, and some believers in a different faith called unrecognized diabolism. . . .

Blast it, I thought, I've got to concentrate on my job. Never mind those silent sad figures rustling past. Ignore, if you can, the overwhelmingness of the cathedral you are nearing and the chant that now swells from it to fill the whole night. Deny that your werewolf heritage senses things it fears to a degree that is making you ill. Sweat prickles forth on your skin, runs cold down your ribs and reeks in your nostrils. You see the world through a haze of dream and relentless music. But Valeria is in hell.

I stopped where the vague shifty light was strongest and read the leaflet. It bade me a courteous welcome and listed the same regulations as the gatekeeper had. On the flip side was a floor plan of the basilica section of the main building. The rest was left blank. Everybody realized that an abundance of rooms existed in the levels of the north and south sides, the tower, and even the cupola. It was no secret that great crypts ran beneath. They were used for certain ceremonies—parts of them, anyhow. Beyond this information: nothing. The higher in degree you advanced, the more you were shown. Only adepts might enter the final sanctums, and only they knew what went on there.

I mounted the cathedral steps. A couple of husky monks stood on either side of the immense, open door. They didn't move, but their eyes frisked me. The vestibule was long, low-ceilinged, whitewashed, bare except for a holy water font. Here was no cheerful clutter of bulletin board, parish newsletter, crayon drawings from the Sunday school. A nun standing at the middle pointed me to a left entrance. Another one at that position looked from me to a box marked Offerings and back until I had to stuff in a couple of dollars. It might have been funny except for the singing, the incense, the gazes, the awareness of impalpable forces which drew my belly muscles taut.

I entered an aisle and found myself alone in a roped-off section of pews, obviously for outsiders. It took me a minute to get over the impact of the stupendous interior and sit down. Then I spent several more minutes trying to comprehend it, and failing.

The effect went beyond size. When everything was undecorated, naked white geometry of walls and pillars and vaulting, you had nothing to scale by; you were in a cavern that reached endlessly on. God's Eye above the altar, Mandala above the choir loft, dominated a thick dusk. But they were unreal too, more remote than the moon, just as the candles glimmering from place to place could have been stars. Proportions, curves, intersections, all helped create the illusion of illimitable labyrinthine spaces. Half a dozen worshipers, scattered along the edge of the nave, were lost. But so would any possible congregation be. This church was *meant* to diminish its people.

A priest stood at the altar with two attendants. I recognized them by their white robes as initiates. At their distance they were dwarfed nearly to nothing. Somehow the priest was not. In the midnight-blue drapery and white beard of an adept, he stood tall, arms outspread, and I feared him. Yet he wasn't moving, praying, anything. . . . Smoke from the hanging censers drugged my lungs. The choir droned and shrilled above me. I had never felt more daunted.

Hauling my glance away, I forced myself to study the layout as if this were an enemy fortress to be penetrated: which it was, for me tonight, whether or not it bore any guilt for what had happened to my little girl. The thought of her started a rage brewing that soon got strong enough to serve for courage. My witch-sight didn't operate here; counterspells against such things must have been laid. Normal night vision was adapting, though, stretched to the same ultimate as every other faculty I had.

The noncommunicants' section was as far as could be from the altar, at the end of the extreme left side aisle. So on my right hand were pews reaching to the nave, on my left a passage along the north wall. The choir loft hung over me like a thundercloud. Directly ahead, at the end of a field of empty benches, rose one of the screens that cut off most of the transept from view, ornamented with a black crux ansata.

This isn't helping me figure out how to burgle the joint, I thought.

A monk went past me on soft-sandaled feet. Over his robe he wore a long surplice embroidered with cabalistic symbols. Halfway to the transept he halted before a many-branched sconce, lit a candle, and prostrated himself for minutes. Rising, bowing, and backing off seven steps, he returned in my direction.

From pictures, I recognized his outer garment as the one donned by choristers. Evidently he'd been relieved and, instead of taking straight off to shuck the uniform, had acquired a bit of merit first. When he'd gone by, I twisted around to follow his course. The pews did not extend the whole way back to the vestibule wall. They left some clear space at the rear end. The choral balcony threw it into such gloom that I could barely see the monk pass through a door in the corner nearest me.

The idea burst forth like a pistol from the holster. I sat outwardly still, inwardly crouched, and probed from side to side of the basilica. Nobody was paying attention to me. Probably I wasn't even visible to celebrants or worshipers; this placement was designed to minimize the obtrusiveness of infidels. My ears, which beneath the clamant song picked out the monk's footfalls, had detected no snick of key in lock. I could follow him.

Then what? I didn't know and didn't greatly care. If they nailed me at once, I'd be a Nosy Parker. They'd scold me and kick me out, and I'd try some different approach. If I got caught deeper in the building—well, that was the risk I'd come courting.

I waited another three hundred million microseconds, feeling each one. The monk needed ample time to get out of this area. During the interval I knelt, gradually hunching lower and lower until I'd sunk out of sight. It drew no stares or inquiries. Finally I was on all fours.

Now! I scuttled, not too fast, across to that shadowy corner. Risen, I looked behind me. The adept stood like a gaunt eidolon, the initiates handled the four sacred objects in complicated ways, the choir sang, a man signed himself and left via the south aisle. I waited till he had exited before gripping the doorknob. It felt odd. I turned it most slowly and drew the door open a crack. Nothing happened. Peering in, I saw dim blue lights.

I went through.

Beyond was an anteroom. A drapery separated it from a larger chamber, which was also deserted. That condition wouldn't last long. The second of the three curtained openings gave on a spiral staircase down which the hymn came pouring. The third led to a corridor. Most of the space was occupied by racks on which hung surplices. Obviously you borrowed one after receiving your instructions elsewhere, and proceeded to the choir loft. At the end of your period, you came back this way. Given six hundred and one singers, reliefs must show quite often. Maybe they weren't so frequent at night, when the personnel were mostly clergy with more training and endurance than eager-beaver laymen. But I'd best not stick around.

I could ditch my outer garments, that'd hamper a wolf, under one of those pullovers. However, somebody who happened to spy me barefoot, in skin-tight briefs, would be hard to convince of my bona fides. I settled for unsnapping the sheath from my inner belt and stuffing my knife in a jacket pocket before I stepped into the hall.

XXVI

LINED WITH DOORS for the length of the building, the corridor might have been occupied by any set of prosaic offices. Mostly they were closed, and the light overhead was turned low. Names on the frosted glass ran to such as "I-2 Saktinos, Postal Propaganda." Well, a lot of territory was controlled from here. A few panels glowed yellow. Passing by one, I heard a typewriter. Within the endless chant, that startled me as if it'd been the click of a skeleton's jaws.

My plans were vague. Presumably Marmiadon, the priest at the Nornwell demonstration, operated out of this centrum. He'd have returned and asked his brethren to get the stench off him. An elaborate spell, too expensive for the average person, would clean him up sooner than nature was able. At least, he was my only lead. Otherwise I could ransack this warren for a fruitless decade.

Where staircases ran up and down, a directory was posted on the wall. I'd expected that. A lot of civilians and outside clergy had business in the nonreserved sections. Marmiadon's office was listed as 413. Because an initiate in the fifth degree ranked fairly high—two more and he'd be a candidate for first-degree adept status—I'd assumed he was based in the cathedral rather than serving as a mere chaplain or missionary. But it occurred to me that I didn't know what his regular job was.

I took the steps quietly, by twos. At the third-floor landing, a locked wrought-iron gate barred further passage. Not surprising, I thought; I'm getting into officer country. It wasn't too big for an agile man to climb over. What I glimpsed of that hall looked no different from below, but my skin prickled at a strengthened sense of abnormal energies.

The fourth floor didn't try for any resemblances to Madison Avenue. Its corridor was brick, barrel-vaulted, lit by Grail-shaped oil lamps hung in chains from above, so that shadows flickered huge. The chant echoed from wall to wall. The atmosphere smelled of curious, acrid musks and smokes. Rooms must be large, for the pointed-arch doors stood well apart. They weren't numbered, but they bore nameplates and I guessed the sequence was the same as elsewhere.

One door stood open between me and my goal. Incongruously bright light spilled forth. I halted and stared in slantwise at shelves upon shelves of books. Some few appeared ancient, but mostly they were modern—yes, that squat one must be the *Handbook of Alchemy and Metaphysics,* and yonder set the *Encyclopaedia Arcanorum,* and there was a bound file of *Mind*—well, scientists need reference libraries, and surely very strange research was conducted here. It was my hard luck that someone kept busy this late at night.

I glided to the jamb and risked a closer peek. One man sat alone. He was huge, bigger than Barney Sturlason, but old, old; hair and beard were gone, the face might have belonged to Rameses' mummy. An adept's robe swathed him. He had a book open on his table, but wasn't looking at it. Deep-sunken, his eyes stared before him while a hand walked across the pages. I realized he was blind. That book, though, was not in Braille.

The lights could be automatic, or for another worker in the stacks. I slipped on by.

Marmiadon's place lay several yards further. Beneath his name and rank, the brass plate read "Fourth Assistant Toller." Not a bell ringer, for God's sake, that runt . . . was he? The door was locked. I should be able to unscrew the latch or push out the hinge pins with my knife. Better wait till I was quite alone, however. Meanwhile I could snoop—

"What walks?"

I whipped about. The adept stood in the hall at the library entrance. He leaned on a pastoral staff; but his voice reverberated so terribly that I didn't believe he needed support. Dismay poured through me. I'd forgotten how strong a Magus he must be.

"Stranger, what are you?" the bass cry bayed.

I tried to wet my sandpapery lips. "Sir—your Enlightenment—"

The staff lifted to point at me. It bore a Johannine capital, the crook crossed by a tau. I knew it was more than a badge, it was a wand. "Menace encircles you," the adept called. "I felt you in my darkness. Declare yourself."

I reached for the knife in my pocket, the wereflash under my shirt. Forlorn things; but when my fingers closed on them, they became talismans. Will and reason woke again in me. I thought beneath the hammering:

It'd have been more luck than I could count on, not to get accosted. I meant to try and use the circumstance if it happened. Okay, it has. That's a scary old son of a bitch, but he's mortal. Whatever his powers are, they don't reach to seeing me as I see him, or he'd do so.

Nonetheless I must clear my throat a time or two before speaking, and the words rang odd in my ears. "I—I beg your Enlightenment's pardon. He took me by surprise. Would he please tell me . . . where Initiate Marmiadon is?"

The adept lowered his staff. Otherwise he didn't move. The dead eyes almost rested on me, unwavering: which was worse than if they actually had. "What have you with him to do?"

"I'm sorry, your Enlightenment. Secret and urgent. As your Enlightenment recognizes, I'm a, uh, rather unusual messenger. I can tell him I'm supposed to get together with Initiate Marmiadon in connection with the, uh, trouble at the Nornwell company. It turns out to be a lot more important than it looks."

"That I know, and knew from the hour when he came back. I summoned—I learned— Enough. It is the falling stone that may loose an avalanche."

I had the eldritch feeling his words weren't for me but for someone else. And what was this about the affair worrying him also? I dared not stop to ponder. "Your Enlightenment will understand, then, why I'm in a hurry and why I can't break my oath of secrecy, even to him. If he'd let me know where Marmiadon's cell is—"

"The failed one sleeps not with his brothers. The anger of the Light-Bearer is upon him for his mismanagement, and he does penance alone. You may not seek him before he has been purified." An abrupt snap: "Answer me! Whence came you, what will you, how can it be that your presence shrills to me of danger?"

"I . . . I don't know either," I stammered.

"You are no consecrate—"

"Look, your Enlightenment, if you, if he would— Well, maybe there's been a misunderstanding. My, uh, superior ordered me to get in touch with Marmiadon. They said at the entrance I might find him here, and lent me a gate key." That unobtrusive sentence was the most glorious whopper I ever hope to tell. Consider its implications. Let them ramify. Extrapolate, extrapolate. Sit back in wonder. "I guess they were mistaken."

"Yes. The lower clerics have naturally not been told. However—"

The Magus brooded.

"If your Enlightenment 'ud tell me where to go, who to see, I could stop bothering him."

Decision. "The night abbot's secretariat, Room 107. Ask for Initiate-Six Hesathouba. Of those on duty at the present hour, he alone has been given sufficient facts about the Matuchek case to advise you."

Matuchek case?

I mumbled my thanks and got away at just short of a run, feeling the sightless gaze between my shoulder blades the whole distance to the stairs. Before climbing back over the gate, I stopped to indulge in the shakes.

I knew I'd scant time for that. The adept might suffer from a touch of senility, but only a touch. He could well fret about me until he decided to set inquiries afoot, which might not end with a phone call to Brother Hesathouba. If I was to have any chance of learning something real, I must keep moving.

Where to, though, in this Gormenghast house? How? What hope? I ought to admit my venture was sheer quixotry and slink home.

No! While the possibility remained, I'd go after the biggest windmills in sight. My mind got into gear. No doubt the heights as well as the depths of the cathedral were reserved for the ranking priests. But the ancient mystery religions had held their major rites underground. Weren't the crypts my best bet for locating Marmiadon?

I felt a grin jerk of itself across my face. They wouldn't lighten his ordeal by spelling the smell off him. Which was another reason to suppose he was tucked away below, out of nose range.

Human noses, that is.

I retraced my steps to the first level. From there I hastened downward. No one happened by. The night was far along; sorcerers might be at work, but few people else.

I descended past a couple of sublevels apparently devoted to storage, janitorial equipment, and the like. In one I glimpsed a sister hand-scrubbing the hall floor. Duty? Expiation? Self-abasement? It was a lonely sight. She didn't see me.

A ways beyond, I encountered another locked gate. On its far side the stairway steepened, concrete no longer but rough-hewn stone. I was down into bedrock. The well was chilly and wet to touch, the air to breathe. Modern illumination fell behind. My sole lights were candles, set in iron sconces far apart. They guttered in the draft from below. My shadow flapped misshapen around them. Finally I could not hear the mass. And still the path led downward.

And downward, until after some part of eternity it ended.

I stepped onto the floor of a natural cave. Widely spaced blue flames picked stalactites and stalagmites out of dense, unrestful murk. These burned from otherwise inactivated Hands of Glory fastened over the entrances to several tunnels. I knew that the Johannine hierarchy had used its influence to get special police licenses for such devices. Was that really for research? From one tunnel I heard the rushing of an underground river; from another glowed wan lights, drifted incense and a single quavering voice. Prayer, vigil, theurgy, or what? I didn't stop to investigate. Quickly I peeled off suit, socks, shoes, and hid them behind a rock. The knife I clipped back onto my elastic shorts.

Turning the lens on myself, I transformed, trying not to let the quasi-sexual sensation get to me, much. Instead I held tight in my diminished cerebral cortex the purpose I had, to use animal senses and sinews for my human end.

Therefore I noted a resistance to the change. I needed twice as long as normal to complete it. More counterspells, no doubt. I probably couldn't have lycoed if I'd not had the right chromosomes, unless I were a most powerful thaumaturge.

Never mind. I was wolf again!

The feeble illumination ceased being a handicap. Wolves don't depend on their eyes the way men do. Ears, feet, tongue, every hair on my body, before all else my nose, drank a flood of data. The cave was not now a hole to stumble in, it was a place that I understood.

And . . . yes, faint but unmistakable from one tunnel came a gust of unforgettable nastiness. I checked a hunter's yelp barely in time and trotted off in that direction.

XXVII

THE PASSAGE WAS LENGTHY, twisting, intersected by many others. Without my sense of smell for a guide, I'd soon have been lost. The lighting was from Hands, above the cells dug out of the rock at rare intervals. It was public knowledge that every candidate for primary initiation spent a day and night alone here, and the devout went back on occasion. Allegedly the soul benefited from undisturbed prayers and meditations. But I wasn't sure what extra influences crept in subliminally as well. Certain odors, at the edge of my lupine perception, raised the fur on my neck.

After a while they were drowned out by the one I was tracing. Wolves have stronger stomachs than people, but I began to gag. When finally I reached the source, I held my breath while looking in.

The dull blue glow from the fingers over the entrance picked out little more than highlights in the cubicle. Marmiadon was asleep on a straw pallet. He wore his robe for warmth; it was grubby as his skin. Otherwise he had some hardtack, a jerry can of water, a cup, a Johannine Bible, and a candle to read it by. He must only have been leaving his cell to visit an oubliette down the tunnel. Not that it would have made any large difference if he didn't. Phew!

I backed off and humanized. The effluvium didn't strike me too hard in that shape, especially after my restored reasoning powers took charge. No doubt Marmiadon wasn't even noticing it any more.

I entered his quarters, hunkered, and shook him. My free hand drew the knife. "Wake up, you."

He floundered to awareness, saw me, and gasped. I must have been a pretty grim sight, black-clad where I wasn't nude and with no mercy in my face. He looked as bad, hollow-eyed in that corpse-light. Before he could yell, I clapped my palm over his mouth. The bristles of unshavenness felt scratchy, the flesh doughlike. "Be quiet," I said without emphasis, "or I'll cut your guts out."

He gestured agreement and I let go. "M-m-mister Matuchek," he whispered, huddling away from me till the wall stopped him.

I nodded. "Want to talk with you."

"I— How— In God's name, what about?"

"Getting my daughter home unharmed."

Marmiadon traced crosses and other symbols in the air. "Are you possessed?" He became able to look at me and answer his own question. "No. I could tell—"

"I'm not being puppeted by a demon," I grunted, "and I haven't got a psychosis. Talk."

"Bu-bu-but I haven't anything to say. Your daughter? What's wrong? I didn't know you had one."

That rocked me back. He wasn't lying, not in his state. "Huh?" I could only say. He grew a trifle calmer, fumbled around after his glasses and put them on, settled down on the pallet and watched me.

"It's holy truth," he insisted. "Why should I have information about your family? Why should anyone here?"

"Because you've appointed yourselves my enemies," I said in renewed rage.

He shook his head. "We're no man's foe. How can we be? We hold to the Gospel of Love." I sneered. His glance dropped from mine. "Well," he faltered, "we're sons of Adam. We can sin like everybody else. I admit I was furious when you pulled that . . . that trick on us . . . on those innocents—"

My blade gleamed through an arc. "Stow the crap, Marmiadon. The solitary innocent in this whole miserable business is a three-year-old girl, and she's been snatched into hell."

His mouth fell wide. His eyes frogged.

"Start blabbing," I said.

For a while he couldn't get words out. Then, in complete horror: "No. Impossible. I would never, never—"

"How about your fellow priests? Which of them?"

"None. I swear it. Can't be." I pricked his throat with the knife point. He shuddered. "Please. Let me know what happened. Let me help."

I lowered the blade, shifted to a sitting position, rubbed my brow, and scowled. This wasn't according to formula. "See here," I accused him, "you did your best to disrupt my liveli-hood. When my life itself is busted apart, what am I supposed to think? If you're not responsible, you'd better give me a lot of convincing.''

The initiate gulped. ''I . . . yes, surely. I meant no harm. What you were doing, are doing—it's sinful. You're damning yourselves and aiding others to do likewise. The Church can't stand idle. More of its ministers volunteer to help than don't.''

''Skip the sermon,'' I ordered. Apart from everything else, I didn't want him working up enough zeal to stop being dominated by me. ''Stick to events. You were sent to abet that mob.''

''No. Not— Well, I was on the list of volunteers. When this occasion arose, I was the one allowed to go. But not to . . . do what you say . . . instead to give aid, counsel, spiritual guidance—and, well, yes, defend against possible spells— Nothing else! You were the ones who attacked.''

''Sure, sure. We began by picketing, and when that didn't work we started on trespass, vandalism, blockade, terrorizing— Uh-huh. And you were so strictly acting as a private citizen that when you failed, your superiors comforted you and you're back at your regular work already.''

''My penance is for the sin of anger,'' he said.

A tiny thrill ran along my spine. We'd reached a significant item. ''You aren't down here simply because you got irritated with us,'' I said. ''What'd you actually do?''

Fear seized him afresh. He raised strengthless hands. ''Please. I can't have— No.'' I brought my knife close again. He shut his eyes and said fast: ''In my wrath when you were so obdurate, I laid a curse on your group. The Curse of Mabon. My reverent superiors—I don't know how they knew what I'd done, but adepts have abilities— When I returned here, I was taxed with my sin. They told me the consequences could be grave. No more. I wasn't told there . . . there'd been any. Were there really?''

''Depends,'' I said. ''What is this curse?''

''No spell. You do understand the distinction, don't you? A spell brings paranatural forces to, to bear, by using the laws of goetics. Or it summons nonhuman beings or— It's the same principle as using a gun, any tool, or whistling up a dog, Mr. Matuchek. A prayer is different. It's an appeal to the Highest or His cohorts. A curse is nothing except a formula for asking Them to, well, punish somebody. They do it if They see fit—it's Them alone—''

''Recite it.''

''*Absit omen!* The danger!''

"You just got through saying it's harmless in itself."

"Don't you know? Johannine prayers are different from Petrine. We're the new dispensation, we've been given special knowledge and divine favor, the words we use have a potency of their own. I can't tell what would happen if I said them, even without intent, under uncontrolled conditions like these."

That was very possibly right, I thought. The essence of Gnosticism in the ancient world had been a search for power through hidden knowledge, ultimately power over God Himself. Doubtless Marmiadon was sincere in denying his church had revived that particular concept. But he hadn't progressed to adept status; the final secrets had not been revealed to him. I thought, reluctantly, that he wasn't likely to make it, either, being at heart not a bad little guy.

My mind leaped forward. Let's carry on that idea, I thought in the space of half a second. Let's assume the founders of modern Gnosticism did make some discoveries that gave them capabilities not known before, results that convinced them they were exerting direct influence on the Divine. Let's further suppose they were mistaken—deceived—because, hang it, the notion that mortals can budge Omnipotence *is* unreasonable. What conclusion do these premises lead us to? This: that whether they know it or not, the blessings and curses of the Johannines are in fact not prayers, but peculiarly subtle and powerful spells.

"I can show you the text," Marmiadon chattered. "You can read for yourself. It's not among the forbidden chapters."

"Okay," I agreed.

He lit his candle and opened the book. I'd glanced at Johannine Bibles but never gotten up the steam to get through one. They replaced the Old Testament with something that even a gentile like me considered blasphemous, and followed the standard parts of the New with a lot of the Apocrypha, plus other stuff whose source never has been identified by reputable scholars. Marmiadon's shaky finger touched a passage in that last section. I squinted, trying to make out the fine print. The Greek was paralleled with an English translation, and itself purported to render the meaning of a string of words like those in the canticles upstairs.

Holy, holy, holy. In the name of the seven thunders. O Mabon of righteousness, exceeding great, angel of the Spirit, who watcheth over the vials of wrath and the mystery of the bottomless pit, come thou to mine aid, wreak sorrow upon them that have done evil to me, that they may know contrition and afflict no longer the servants of the hidden truth and the Reign that is to come. By these words be thou summoned, Heliphomar Mabon Saruth Gefutha Enunnas Sacinos. Amen. Amen. Amen.

I closed the book. "I don't go for that kind of invocation," I said slowly.

"Oh, you could recite it aloud," Marmiadon blurted. "In fact, an ordinary communicant of the Church could, and get no response. But I'm a toller. A summoner, you'd call it. Not too high-ranking or skillful; nevertheless, certain masteries have been conferred."

"Ah, s-s-so!" The sickening explanation grew upon me. "You raise and control demons in your regular line of work—"

"Not demons. No, no, no. Ordinary paranatural beings for the most part. Occasionally a minor angel."

"You mean a thing that tells you it's an angel."

"But it is!"

"Never mind. Here's what happened. You say you got mad and spoke this curse, a black prayer, against us. I say that knowingly or not, you were casting a spell. Since nothing registered on detectors, it must've been a kind of spell unknown to science. A summons to something from out of this universe. Well, you Johnnies do seem to've acquired a pipeline to another world. You believe, most of you, that world is Heaven. I'm convinced you're fooled; it's actually hell."

"No," he groaned.

"I've got reason, remember. That's where my kid was taken."

"She couldn't have been."

"The demon answered your call. It happened that of the Nornwell people around, my wife and I had the one household exposed that night to his action. So the revenge was worked on us."

Marmiadon squared his puny shoulders. "Sir, I don't deny your child is missing. But if she was taken . . . as an unintended result of my action . . . well, you needn't fear."

"When she's in hell? Supposing I got her back this minute, what'll that place have done to her?"

"No, honestly, don't be afraid." Marmiadon ventured to pat my hand where it clenched white-knuckled around the knife. "If she were in the Low Continuum, retrieval operations would involve temporal phasing. Do you know what I mean? I'm not learned in such matters myself, but our adepts are, and a portion of their findings is taught to initiates, beginning at the fourth degree. The mathematics is beyond me. But as I recall, the hell universe has a peculiar, complex space-time geometry. It would be as easy to recover your daughter from the exact instant when she arrived there as from any other moment.''

The weapon clattered out of my grasp. A roar went through my head. "Is that the truth?"

"Yes. More than I'm canonically allowed to tell you—"

I covered my face. The tears ran out between my fingers.

"—but I want to help you, Mr. Matuchek. I repent my anger." Looking up, I saw him cry too.

After a while we were able to get to business. "Of course, I must not mislead you," he declared. "When I said it would be as easy to enter hell at one point of time as another, I did not mean it would not be difficult. Insuperably so, indeed, except for our highest adepts. No geometers are alive with the genius to find their way independently through those dimensions.

"Fortunately, however, the question doesn't arise. I just wanted to reassure you enough so you'd listen to the real case. It may be that your daughter was removed in answer to my curse. That would account for the displeasure of my superiors with me. But if so, she's under angelic care."

"Prove it," I challenged.

"I can try. Again, I'm breaking the rules, especially since I'm under penance and you're an unbeliever. Still, I can try to summon an angel." He smiled timidly at me. "Who knows? If you recant, your girl could be restored to you on the spot. A man of your gifts and energy would make a wonderful convert. Conceivably that's been God's purpose right along."

I didn't like the idea of a Calling. In fact, I was bloody well chilled by it. Marmiadon might think the creature that arrived was from Heaven. I didn't. But I was prepared to face worse than devils on this trip. "Go ahead."

He turned his Bible to another passage I didn't recognize. Kneeling, he started to chant, a high-pitched rise and fall which sawed at my nerves.

A wind blew down the tunnel. The lights didn't go out, but a dimness came over my eyes, deepening each second, as if I were dying, until I stood alone in a whistling dark. And the night was infinite and eternal; and the fear left me, but in its place there fell the suddenly remembered absolute despair. Yet never had I known a grief like this—not the three times before, not when Valeria was taken, not when my mother died—for now I had reached in the body the final end of every hope and looked upon the ultimate emptiness of all things; love, joy, honor were less than ash, they had never been, and I stood hollow as the only existence in hollow creation.

Far, far away a light was kindled. It moved toward me, a spark, a star, a sun. I looked upon the vast mask of a face, into the lifeless eyes; and the measured voice beat through me:

"The hour is here. Despite the afreet, the salamander, the incubus, and mortal man, your destiny has endured, Steven. It was not my will or my planning. I foresaw you would be among my keenest enemies in this cycle of the world, the danger that you would wreck my newest great enterprise. But I could not know what would bring you to confront my works: the thoughtless call of one fool, the rash obedience of another. Now you would seek to storm my inner keep.

"Be afraid, Steven. I may not touch you myself, but I have mightier agents to send than those you met before. If you go further against me, you go to your destruction. Return home; accept your loss as humbly as befits a son of Adam; beget other children, cease meddling in public matters, attend solely to what is your own. Then you shall have pleasure and wealth and success in abundance, and your days shall be long in the land. But this is if you make your peace with me. If not, you will be brought down, and likewise those you care for. Fear me."

The sight, the sound, the blindness ended. I sagged, wet and a-reek with sweat, looking stupidly at Marmiadon in the candlelight. He beamed and rubbed his hands. I could scarcely comprehend him:

"There! Wasn't I right? Aren't you glad? Wasn't he glorious? I'd be down on my knees if I were you, praising God for His mercy."

"Hu-u-uh?" dragged out of me.

"The angel, the angel!"

I shook myself, as if I'd come from wild waters that nearly drowned me. My heart was still drained. The world felt remote, fragile. But my brain functioned, in a mechanical fashion. It made my lips move. "I could have seen a different aspect of the being. What happened to you?"

"The crowned head, the shining wings," he crooned. "Your child is safe. She will be given back to you when your penitence is complete. And because of having been among the blessed in her mortal life, she will become a saint of the true Church."

Well, trickled through my head, this doubtless isn't the first time the Adversary's made an instrument of people who honestly believe they're serving God. What about Jonathan Edwards, back in old New England? "The floors of hell are paved with the skulls of unbaptized children." Who really was the Jehovah he called upon?

"What did you experience?" Marmiadon asked.

I might or might not have told him my revelation. Probably not; what good would that have done? A sound distracted us both—nearing footsteps, words.

"What if he hasn't been here?"

"We'll wait for some hours."

"In this thin garb?"

"The cause of the Lord, brother."

I stiffened. Two men coming: monks, from the noise of their sandals; big, from its volume on the stone. The adept I met upstairs must have grown suspicious; or Marmiadon's invocation and its effect had registered elsewhere; or both. If I got caught—I'd been warned. And my existence was beyond price, until I could get home the information that might help rescue Val.

I turned the flash on myself. Marmiadon whimpered as I changed shape. It's well I was in a hurry. Wolf, with wolf passions, I'd have torn his throat apart for what he'd done if there'd been time. Instead, I went out in a single gray streak.

The pair of monks didn't see me through the gloom until I was almost on them. They were beefy for sure. One carried a stick, the other a forty-five automatic. I darted between the legs of the latter, bowling him over. His buddy got a crack across my ribs with his cudgel. Pain slowed me for a moment. A bone may have been broken. It knitted with the speed of the were condition and I dashed on. The pistol barked. Slugs whanged nastily past. If they included argent rounds, a hit would stop me. I had to move!

Up the stairs I fled. The friars dropped from sight. But an alarm started ahead of me, bells crashing through the hymns. Did my pursuers have a walkie-talkie ball with them? Produced at Nornwell? I burst into the first-floor hallway. There must be other exits than the main door, but I didn't know them. A wolf can travel like bad news. I was through the curtain which screened off the choir vestry before any nightshifter had glanced out of an office or any sleepy monk arrived from another section.

The church was in a boil. I cracked the door to the aisle sufficiently for a look. The chant went on. But folk ran about in the nave, shouting. More to the point, a couple of them were closing doors to the vestibule. I couldn't get out.

Feet slapped floor in the corridor. The Johnnies weren't certain which way I'd skited, and were confused anyhow by this sudden unexplained emergency. Nevertheless, I'd scant time until someone thought to check here.

A possible tactic occurred to me. I didn't consider the wherefores of it, which a wolf isn't equipped to do. Trusting instinct, I slapped the switch on my flash with a forepaw. The blue entry-room lights didn't interfere with my reverting to human. Darting back to the vestry, I grabbed a surplice and threw it over my head. It fell nearly to my feet. They stayed bare, but maybe no one would notice.

Ascending to the choir loft in record time, I stopped in the archway entrance and studied the situation. Men and women stood grouped according to vocal range. They held hymnals. Spare books lay on a table. The view from here, down to the altar and up to the cupola, was breathtaking. But I'd no breath to spend. I picked my spot, helped myself to a book, and moved solemnly forward.

I wouldn't have gotten away with it under normal conditions. Conditions not being normal, the choir was agitated too, its attention continually pulled down to the excitement on the floor. The song kept wandering off key. I found a place on the edge of the baritones and opened my hymnal to the same page as my neighbor.

"*Mephnounos Chemiath Aroura Maridōn Elisōn,*" he chanted. I'd better make noises likewise. The trouble was, I'd not had the rehearsals they gave to laymen who wanted to participate. I couldn't even pronounce most of those words, let alone carry the tune.

My neighbor glanced at me. He was a portly, officious-looking priest. I oughtn't to stand around with my teeth in my mouth, he must be thinking. I gave him a weak smile. "*Thatis Etelelam Teheo abocia Rusar,*" he intoned in a marked manner.

I grabbed at the first melody I recalled which had some general resemblance to the one he was using. Mushing it up as much as I dared, I studied my book and commenced:

"*A sailor told me before he died—*
I don't know whether the bastard lied—"

In the general counterpoint, not to mention the uproar below, it passed. The cleric took his eyes off me. He continued with the canticle and I with *The Big Red Wheel.*

I trust I may be forgiven for some of the other expedients I found necessary in the hour that followed. An hour, I guessed, was an unsuspicious time for a lay singer to stay. Meanwhile, by eye and ear, I followed roughly the progress of the hunt for me. The size and complexity of the cathedral worked in my favor for once; I could be anywhere. Unquestionably, spells were being used in the search. But the wizards had little to go on except what Marmiadon could tell. And I had everything protective that Ginny, who's one of the best witches in the Guild, was able to give me before I left. Tracing me, identifying me, would be no simple matter, even for those beings that the most potent of the adepts might raise.

Not that I could hold out long. If I didn't scramble soon I was dead, or worse. A part of me actually rejoiced at that. You see, the danger, the calling up of every resource I had to meet it, wiped away the despair at the core of hell which I had met in the crypts. I was alive, and it mattered, and I'd do my best to kill whatever stood between me and my loves!

After a while the main entrance was reopened, though watched by monks. I'd figured out a plan to get around them. After leaving the choir and disrobing, I turned wolf. The north corridor was again deserted, which was lucky for any Johnnies I might have encountered. Having doubtless posted a guard at every door, they were cooling their chase. It went on, but quietly, systematically, no longer disruptive of religious atmosphere. Lupine senses helped me avoid patrols while I looked for a window.

On the lower levels, these were in rooms that were occupied or whose doors were locked. I had to go to the sixth floor—where the scent of wrongness was almost more than I could bear—before finding a window in the corridor wall. It took resolution, or desperation, to jump through. The pain as the glass broke and slashed me was as nothing to the pain when I hit the concrete beneath.

But I was lyco. My injuries were not fatal or permanently crippling. The red rag of me stirred, grew together, and became whole. Sufficient of my blood was smeared around, unrecoverable, that I felt a bit weak and dizzy; but a meal would fix that.

The stars still glittered overhead. Vision was uncertain. And I doubted the outer gatekeepers had been told much, if anything. The hierarchy would be anxious to hush up this trouble as far as might be. I stripped off what remained of my clothes with my teeth, leaving the wereflash fairly well covered by my ruff, and trotted off to the same place where I'd entered. ''Why, hullo, pooch,'' said my young friend. ''Where'd you come from?'' I submitted to having my ears rumpled before I left.

In Siloam's darkened downtown I committed a fresh crime, shoving through another window, this time in the rear of a grocery store. I could compensate the proprietor anonymously, later. Besides the several pounds of hamburger I found and ate, I needed transportation; and after humanizing I was more than penniless, I was naked. I phoned Barney. ''Come and get me,'' I said. ''I'll be wolf at one of these spots.'' I gave him half a dozen possibilities, in case the pursuit of me spilled beyond cathedral boundaries.

''What happened to my broom?'' he demanded.

''I had to leave it parked,'' I said. ''You can claim it tomorrow.''

''I'm eager to hear the story.''

''Well, it was quite a night, I can tell you.''

XXVIII

MY DETAILED RELATION I gave to Ginny after sneaking back into our house. I was numb with exhaustion, but she insisted on hearing everything at once, whispered as we lay side by side. Her questions drew each last detail from me, including a lot that had slipped my mind or that I hadn't especially noticed at the time. The sun was up before she fixed my breakfast and allowed me to rest. With a few pauses for nourishment and drowsy staring, I slept a full twenty-four hours.

Ginny explained this to our FBI man as the result of nervous prostration, which wasn't too mendacious. She also persuaded him and his immediate boss (Shining Knife had gone to Washington) that if they wanted to keep matters under wraps, they'd better not hold us incommunicado. Our neighbors already knew something was afoot. They could be stalled for but a short while, our close friends and business associates for a shorter while yet. If the latter got worried, they could bring more to bear in the way of sortileges than the average person.

The upshot was that we kept our guest. When Mrs. Delacorte dropped around to borrow a gill of brimstone, we introduced him as my cousin Louis and mentioned that we'd sent Val on an out-of-town visit while our burglary was being investigated. It didn't rate more than a paragraph on an inside page of the daily paper. However, I was allowed to work again, Ginny to go shopping. We were told what number to call if we received any demands. Nothing was said about the men who shadowed us. They were good; without our special skills, we'd never have known about them.

On the third morning, therefore, I showed at Nornwell. Barney Sturlason was primed. He found a do-not-disturb job for me to do in my office—rather, to fake doing while I paced, chain-smoked my tongue to leather, drank coffee till it gurgled in my ears—until time for an after-lunch conference with some outside businessmen. I knew what that conference was really to be

about. When the intercom asked me to go there, I damn near
snapped my head off accelerating before I remembered to walk
the distance and say hello to those I passed.

The meeting room was upstairs. Its hex against industrial
espionage operated equally well against official surveillance.
Barney bulked at the end of the table, collar open, cigar fuming.
The assembled team comprised eleven, to help assure we'd
harbor no Judas. I knew three well besides Barney and myself—
Griswold, Hardy, Janice Wenzel—and another slightly, Dr.
Nobu, a metaphysicist whom we had sometimes consulted. The
rest were strangers to me. One turned out to be a retired admiral,
Hugh Charles, who'd specialized in Intelligence operations;
another was a mathematician named Falkenberg; a third was
Pastor Karlslund from Barney's church. All of these looked
weary. They'd worked like galley slaves, practically up to this
minute. The last pair seemed fresh, and totally undistinguished
except that one had a large sample case which he'd put on the
table.

Before he got to their names, Barney made a pass and spoke a
phrase. "Okay," he said, "the security field is back at full
strength. Come on out and join the coven." He grinned at me.
"Steve, I'd like you to meet Mr. Smith and Mr. Brown, repre-
senting the company whose proposal we're to discuss today."

Their outlines blurred, went smoky, and firmed again as the
Seeming passed. Ginny's hair gleamed copper in the sunlight
from the windows. Dr. Ashman opened his case. Svartalf
poured out, restored to health, big, black, and arrogant as ever.
He stretched cramped muscles. "Mee-owr-r-r," he scolded us.
The pastor offered the cat a soothing hand. I didn't have time to
warn him. Luckily, Ashman was in the habit of carrying Band-
Aids. Svartalf sat down by Ginny and washed himself.

"How'd you manage it?" the admiral asked with professional
interest.

Ginny shrugged. "Simple. Barney'd been in contact with Dr.
Ashman, you know, and arranged a time when he'd've can-
celled his appointments. He went to the animal hospital and
fetched Svartalf, who can lie quiet in a box if he must. We'd
already verified there was no tail on the doctor." Svartalf
switched his in a smug fashion. "Meanwhile I'd gone downtown. They're having a sale at Perlman's. Easiest crowd in the
world to disappear into, and who'll notice a bit of sorcery there?
Having changed my looks, I rendezvoused with Dr. Ashman and
altered him." Svartalf threw the man a speculative look. "We

proceeded here. Barney knew exactly when we'd arrive, and had the field low enough that it didn't whiff our disguises."

She opened her purse, which hadn't needed much work to resemble a briefcase, got out her vanity, and inspected her appearance. In demure make-up and demure little dress, she hardly suggested a top-flight witch, till you noticed what else she was packing along.

"To business," Barney said. "We informed this team at once of what you'd discovered, Steve. From the strictly scientific angle, your hints, added to what'd already been assembled, were a jolt. Working together, certain of our people have developed some insights that should prove revolutionary." He paused. "But let's begin with the political mess we're in."

"Or the religious," Janice Wenzel said.

"In this case," Pastor Karlslund said, "I doubt if there's any clear distinction." He was a large, blond, scholarly-looking man.

"If the Johannine Church is indeed of diabolic origin—" Griswold grimaced. "I hate to believe that. I don't agree with its tenets, but to say they come not from error but from evil does go rather far. Are you sure, Mr. Matuchek, that you really encountered the Adversary?"

"One of his higher-ups, anyway," I said. "Or lower-downs, if you prefer. Not for the first time, either. Those earlier visions and experiences of mine fall into a pattern now."

"I mean, well, you were under considerable stress. A hallucination would be very reasonable . . . expectable, I mean."

"If the Johnnies are legit," my wife clipped, "why are they keeping quiet? They have Steve's identity. They've had ample time to get in touch with him, or to file an official complaint. But never a peep. Barney's man, sent to fetch his broomstick, took it from where it was parked with no questions asked. I say they can't risk an investigation."

"They might be trying to get your daughter returned to you through their paranatural contacts," Hardy suggested without conviction.

Admiral Charles snorted. "Big chance! I don't doubt the Adversary would like to cancel the whole episode. But how? He can return her with zero time-lapse in hell, you say, Mr. Matuchek—quite astounding, that. Nevertheless, I don't imagine he can change the past: the days we've lived without her, the things we've learned as a consequence."

"Our silence could be her ransom," Hardy said.

"What man would feel bound by that kind of bargain?" the admiral replied.

Karlslund added: "No contracts can be made with the Low Ones anyhow. Contract implies a meeting of minds, an intent to abide by the terms reached. Being incapable of probity, a devil is unable to believe humans won't try to cheat him in turn."

"So," Charles said, "he'd gain nothing by releasing her, and lose whatever hostage value she has."

Ashman said painfully: "He's already succeeded in dividing the forces of good. I get the impression this meeting is in defiance of the government, an actual conspiracy. Is that wise?"

"I suppose you mean we should make a clean breast to Uncle Sam and trust him to set everything right." The hurt in me powered my sneer.

"What resources have we in comparison?" Ashman asked. "What right have we to withhold the information you've gathered? It's vital to the common weal."

"Let me handle that question," Barney said. "I've got connections in Washington, and Admiral Charles, who has more, confirms my guess as to what's going on there. The key datum is this: that the facts of the kidnaping are being officially suppressed. Our local FBI head is a sharp boy. He saw at once that that's what policy would be, and acted in anticipation of a directive he knew he'd get.

"The reasons for such a policy are complicated, but boil down to two items. First, hardly anything is known about the hell universe. This is one of the few cases, maybe unique, that looks like a direct, physical assault from demon territory. Nobody can be sure what it portends. In those circumstances, caution is inevitable. They'll argue in the State Department that the truth could be altogether different from the semblance. They'll argue in Defense that we'd better not commit ourselves to anything before we have more data and especially a bigger military appropriation. The President, the Cabinet, the top men in Congress, will agree on sitting tight. That involves sitting on the news, to forestall an inconvenient public furore.

"Second, maybe less critical at the moment but definitely to be considered, the Johannine Church. This is a democratic country. A lot of perfectly sincere voters are either Johnnies or believe Johanninism is just another creed. A fair number of important people fall into the same classes. Remember what a stink went up when the House committee tried to probe a little. The present affair does suggest the faction is right which says the

Johannine Church was instigated by the Lowest as a means of discrediting religion, undermining society, and turning man against man. The last thing the Administration will want—at this ticklish juncture—is to go through that 'subversion' versus 'suppression' shouting match again. Secrecy buys peace, quiet, and time.''

Barney halted to rekindle his cigar. The room had become very still as we listened. Smoke filled the sunbeams with blue strata and our nostrils with staleness. Ginny and I exchanged a forlorn look across the table. Yesterday I'd gone into the basement to replace a blown fuse. She'd come along, because these days we stayed together when we could. Some things of Valeria's stood on a shelf, lately outgrown and not yet discarded. The everfilled bottle, the Ouroboros teething ring, the winged training spoon, the little pot with a rainbow at the end— We went upstairs and asked our guard to change the fuse.

Her fists clenched before her. Svartalf rubbed his head on her arm, slowly, demanding no attention in return.

''The conclusion,'' Barney said, ''is that, resources or no, the government isn't likely to use them for quite a while, if ever. As of today, we, this bunch of us, have the right and duty to take what action we can.

''You see, Doctor, we've done nothing technically illegal. Steve was not under arrest. He was free to go in and out of his home, in a Tarnkappe via the window if he chose, accountable to nobody. I was free to lend him my broom. The cathedral is open to the public. If Steve went into other parts of the building, looking for someone who might have information helpful in his hour of need, at most he committed a civil tort. Let the hierarchy sue him for damages if it wants. He can charge felonious assault, remember. One does not have the privilege of using lethal weapons in defense of mere privacy, and he was clubbed and shot at.

''Accordingly, no crime having been committed, none of us are accessories after the fact. No crime being contemplated, none of us are engaging in conspiracy. I grant you, soon the National Defense Act, and anything else the President finds handy, will be invoked. Then we would be in trouble if we behaved as we're doing. But no legally binding prohibition has been laid on us to date; and the Constitution forbids ex post facto proceedings.''

''Hm.'' Ashman reflected.

''As for the withholding of essential information,'' Barney

continued, "don't worry, we aren't about to do that either. We are sifting what we've been told, as responsible citizens who don't want to make accusations that may be unfounded. But we will see that whatever is sound gets into the right hands."

"Must we act so fast?" Ashman demurred. "If the child can be recovered from the same instant as she arrived . . . yonder . . . isn't it best for her too that we let the government operate on her behalf at a slow, careful pace, rather than going off ourselves ill-prepared and underequipped?"

Admiral Charles' lean features darkened. "Frankly," he said, "if no further incidents occur, I don't expect this Administration will act. It's let unfriendly countries rob, imprison, or kill American nationals—some in uniform—without doing more than protest. What do you imagine they'll say in Foggy Bottom at the thought of taking on hell itself for one small girl? I'm sorry, Mrs. Matuchek, but that's the way matters are."

"Be that as it may," said Falkenberg in haste, for the look on Ginny's face had become terrifying, "as I understand the situation, the, ah, enemy are off balance at present. Mr. Matuchek took them by surprise. Evidently the, ah, Adversary is debarred from giving them direct help, counsel, or information. Or else he considers it inadvisable, as it might provoke intervention by the Highest. The, ah, Johannine Mages can do extraordinary things, no doubt. But they are not omniscient or omnipotent. They can't be sure what we have learned and what we will attempt. Give them time, however, in this universe, and they will, ah, recover their equilibrium, mend their fences, possibly make some countermove."

Ginny said out of her Medusa mask: "Whatever the rest of you decide, Steve and I won't sit waiting."

"Blazes, no!" exploded from me. Svartalf laid back his ears, fangs gleamed amidst his whiskers and the fur stood up on him.

"You see?" Barney said to the group. "I know these people. You can't stop them short of throwing them in jail for life; and I'm not convinced any jail would hold them. They might have to be killed. Do we let that happen, or do we help them while we still can?"

Voices rumbled around the table, hands went aloft, Janice Wenzel cried loudest: "I've got kids of my own, Virginia!" Eyes turned from us to Ashman. He flushed and said:

"I'm not going henhouse on you. Remember, all this has just been sprung on me without warning. I'm bound to raise the arguments that occur to me. I don't believe that encouraging

Valeria's parents to commit suicide will do her any good.''

"What do you mean?'' Barney asked.

"Do I misunderstand? Isn't your intention to send Steven and Virginia—my patients—into the hell universe?''

That brought me up cold. I'd been ready and raging for action; but this was as if a leap had fetched me to the rim of Ginnungagap. The heart slammed in me. I stared at Ginny. She nodded.

The whole group registered various degrees of consternation. I scarely noticed the babble that lifted or Barney's quelling of it. Finally we all sat in a taut-strung silence.

"I must apologize to this committee,'' Barney said. His tone was deep and measured as a vesper bell's. "The problem that I set most of you was to collect and collate available information on the Low Continuum with a view to rescue operations. You did magnificently. When you were informed of Steve's findings, you used them to make a conceptual breakthrough that may give us the method we want. But you were too busy to think beyond the assignment, or to imagine that it was more than a long-range, rather hypothetical study: something that might eventually give us capabilities against further troubles of this nature. Likewise, those of you I discussed the political or religious aspects with didn't know how close we might be to facing them in reality.

"I saw no alternative to handling it that way. But Mrs. Matuchek reached me meanwhile, surreptitiously. I gave her the whole picture, we discussed it at length and evolved a plan of campaign.'' He bowed slightly toward Ashman. "Congratulations on your astuteness, Doctor.''

She knew, I thought in the shards of thinking, and yet no one could have told it on her, not even me—not till this instant, and then solely because she chose. A part of me wondered if other husbands experienced corresponding surprises.

She raised her hand. "The case is this,'' she said with the same military crispness as when first I'd met her. "A small, skilled group has a chance of success. A large, unskilled group has none. It'd doubtless suffer more than the Army or the Faustus teams did, since they retreated quickly.''

"Death, insanity, or imprisonment in hell with everything that that implies—'' Ashman whispered. "You assume Steven will go.''

"I know better than to try stopping him,'' she said.

That gave me a measure of self-control again. I was not unconscious of admiring glances. But mainly I listened to her:

"He and I and Svartalf are as good a squad as you'll find. If anybody has a hope of pulling the stunt off, we do. The rest of you can help with preparations and with recovering us. If we don't make it back, you'll be the repositories of what has already been learned. Because this is a public matter. It goes far beyond our girl . . . agreed. That's your main reason for assisting us. To try and make sure your children and grandchildren will inherit a world worth having.''

She reached in her purse. "Damn," she said, "I'm out of cigarets."

She got a lot of offers, but accepted mine. Our hands clung for a second. Ashman sat staring at his intertwined fingers. Abruptly he straightened and said, with a kind of smile:

"All right, I apologize. You must admit my reaction was natural. But you're an able group. If you think you've found a way to enter hell and return unharmed, you could be right and you have my support. May I ask what your scheme is?"

Barney relaxed a trifle. "You may," he said. "Especially since we've got to explain it to some of the others."

He stubbed out his cigar and began on a fresh one. "Let me put the proposition in nickel words first," he said, "then the experts can correct and amplify according to their specialties. Our universe has a straightforward space-time geometry, except in odd places like the cores of white dwarf stars. Demons can move around in it without trouble—in fact, they can play tricks with distance and chronology that gave them the reputation of being supernatural in olden days—because their home universe is wildly complicated and variable. Modern researchers have discovered how to get there, but not how to travel around or remain whole of body and mind.

"Well, Steve's information that we could reach any point in hell time, if we knew the method, opened a door or broke a logjam or something. Suddenly there was a definite basic fact to go on, a relationship between the Low Continuum and ours that could be mathematically described. Dr. Falkenberg set up the equations and started solving them for different conditions. Dr. Griswold helped by suggesting ways in which the results would affect the laws of physics; Bill Hardy did likewise for chemistry and atomistics; et cetera. Oh, they've barely begun, and their conclusions haven't been subjected to experimental test. But at least they've enabled Dr. Nobu, as a metaphysicist, and me, as a practical engineer, to design some spells. We completed them this morning. They should project the expedition, give it some guardianship when it arrives, and haul it back fast. That's more than anybody previous had going for them.''

''Insufficient.'' Charles was the new objector. ''You can't have a full description of the hell universe—why, we don't have that even for this cosmos—and you absolutely can't predict what crazy ways the metric there varies from point to point.''

''True,'' Barney said.

''So protection which is adequate at one place will be useless elsewhere.''

''Not if the space-time configuration can be described mathematically as one travels. Then the spells can be adjusted accordingly.''

''What? But that's an impossible job. No mortal man—''

''Right,'' Ginny said.

We gaped at her.

''A passing thing Steve heard, down in the crypts, was the clue,'' Ginny said. ''Same as your remark, actually, Admiral. No mortal man could do it. But the greatest geometers are dead.''

A gasp went around the table.

XXIX

WITH APPROPRIATE SEEMINGS laid on, and Svartalf indignantly back in the sample case, our committee left the plant on a company carpet. It was now close to four. If my FBI shadow didn't see me start home around five or six o'clock, he'd get suspicious. But there wasn't a lot I could do about that.

We landed first at St. Olaf's while Pastor Karlslund went in to fetch some articles. Janice Wenzel, seated behind us, leaned forward and murmured: "I guess I'm ignorant, but isn't this appealing to the saints a Catholic rather than a Lutheran thing?"

The question hadn't been raised at the conference. Karlslund was satisfied with making clear the distinction between a prayer—a petition to the Highest, with any spells we cast intended merely to ease the way for whoever might freely respond—and necromancy, an attempt to force our will on departed spirits. (While the latter is illegal, that's mainly a concession to public taste. There's no reliable record of its ever having succeeded; it's just another superstition.)

"I doubt if the sect makes any odds," Ginny said. "What is the soul? Nobody knows. The observations that prove it exists are valid, but scattered and not repeatable under controlled conditions. As tends to be the case for many paranatural phenomena."

"Which, however," Dr. Nobu put in, "is the reason in turn why practical progress in goetics is so rapid once a correct insight is available. Unlike the force-fields of physics—gravitation, electromagnetism, and so on—the force-fields of paraphysics—such as similarity and ergody—are not limited by the speed of light. Hence they can, in principle, shift energy from any part of the plenum to any other. That is why a vanishingly small input can give an indefinitely large output. Because of this, qualitative understanding is more important to control than quantitative. And so, a mere three days after learning about the time variability of hell, we feel some confidence that our new spells will work. . . . But as for the soul, I incline to the belief that its character is supernatural rather than paranatural.''

"Not me," Ginny said. "I'd call it an energy structure within those parafields. It's formed by the body but outlives that matrix. Once free, it can easily move between universes. If it hangs around here for some reason, disembodied, isn't that a ghost? If it enters a newly fertilized ovum, isn't that reincarnation? If the Highest allows it to come nearer His presence, isn't that salvation? If the Lowest has more attraction for it, isn't that damnation?''

"Dear me," Janice said. Ginny uttered a brittle laugh.

Barney turned around in the pilot's seat. "About your question that started this seminar, Janice," he said, "it's true we Lutherans don't make a habit of calling on the saints. But neither do we deny they sometimes intervene. Maybe a Catholic priest or a Neo-Chassidic rabbi would know better how to pray for help. But I couldn't get any on short notice that I dared co-opt, while I've known Jim Karlslund for years. . . . Speak of the, er, pastor—'' Everybody chuckled in a strained way as our man boarded with an armful of ecclesiastical gear.

We took off again and proceeded to Trismegistus University. Sunlight slanted gold across remembered lawns, groves, buildings. Few persons were about in this pause between spring and summer sessions; a hush lay over the campus, distantly backgrounded by the city's whirr. It seemed epochs ago that Ginny and I had been students here, a different cycle of creation. I glanced at her, but her countenance was unreadable.

Wings rustled near, a raven that paced us. An omen? Of what? It banked as we landed and flapped out of sight.

We entered the Physical Sciences building. Corridors and stairwells reached gloomy, full of echoes. Desertion was one reason we'd chosen it, another being Griswold's keys to each lab and stockroom. Karlslund would have preferred the chapel, but we were too likely to be noticed there. Besides, Ginny and Barney had decided in their plan-laying that the religious part of our undertaking was secondary.

We needed someone whose appeal would be unselfish and devout, or no saint was apt to respond. However, they seldom do anyway, compared to the number of prayers that must arise daily. The Highest expects us to solve our own problems. What we relied on—what gave us a degree of confidence we would get some kind of reaction—was the progress we'd made, the direct access we believed we had to the Adversary's realm and our stiff resolve to use it. The implications were too enormous for Heaven to ignore . . . we hoped.

I thought, in the floating lightheadedness to which stress had brought me: Perhaps we'll be forbidden to try.

We picked the Berkeley Philosophical Laboratory for our calling. It was a new, large, splendidly outfitted wing tacked onto the shabby old structure that housed Griswold's department before the salamander episode. Here senior and graduate physical-science students learned how to apply paranatural forces to natural research. So it had every kind of apparatus we could imagine needing. The main chamber was wide and high, uncluttered by more than a few shelves and workbenches along the walls. Light fell cool through gray-green glass in the Gothic windows. Zodiacal symbols on the deep-blue ceiling encircled a golden Bohr atom. You'd never find a place further in spirit from that cathedral at Siloam. My kind of people had raised this. I felt some measure of its sanity enter me to strengthen.

Griswold locked the door. Ginny took off the Seemings and let Svartalf out. He padded into a corner, tail going like a metronome. Karlslund laid an altar cloth on a bench, arranged on it cross, bell, chalice, sacred bread, and wine. The rest of us worked under Barney. We established a shieldfield and an antispy hex around the area in the usual way. Next we prepared to open the gates between universes.

So the popular phrase has it, altogether inaccurately. In truth there are no gates, there are means of transmitting influences from one continuum to another, and fundamentally it does not depend on apparatus but on knowing how. The physical things we set out—Bible and Poimanderes opened to the appropriate passages, menorah with seven tall candles lit by flint and steel, vial of pure air, chest of consecrated earth, horn of Jordan water, Pythagorean harp—were symbolic more than they were sympathetic.

I want to emphasize that, because it isn't as well known as it should be: one reason why Gnosticism caught on. The Petrine tenet goes along with the higher non-Christian faiths and the findings of modern science. You *can't* compel Heaven. It's too great. You can exert an influence, yes, but it won't have effect unless the Highest allows, any more than a baby's tug on your trouser cuff can turn you from your path by itself.

Our prayer was an earnest of our appeal, which God had already read in our hearts. In a way, its purpose was to convince us that we really meant what we said we wanted. Likewise, our spells would help any spirit that chose to come here. But he or she didn't really need assistance. What would matter was that we were doing our best.

Hell is another case entirely. In physical terms, it's on a lower energy level than our universe. In spiritual terms, the Adversary and his minions aren't interested in assisting us to anything except our destruction. We could definitely force our way in and lay compulsions on the demons by sheer power of wizardry—if we swung enough power!—and we would definitely have to if Val was to be rescued.

The formulas for trying to summon Heavenly aid aren't common knowledge, but they aren't hidden either. You can find them in the right reference works. Our hell spells were something else. I will never describe them. Since you may well guess they involve an inversion of the prayer ritual, I'll state that we employed these articles: a certain one of the Apocrypha, a Liber Veneficarum, a torch, a globe of wind from a hurricane, some mummy dust, thirteen drops of blood, and a sword. I don't swear to the truthfulness of my list.

We didn't expect we'd require that stuff right away, but it was another demonstration of intent. Besides, Ginny needed a chance to study it and use her trained intuition to optimize the layout.

Karlslund's bell called us. He was ready. We assembled before the improvised altar. "I must first consecrate this and hold as full a service as possible," he announced. I looked at my watch—damn near five—but dared not object. His feeling of respect for due process was vital.

He handed out prayer books and we commenced. The effect on me was curious. As said, I don't believe any set of dogmas is preferable to any other or to an upright agnosticism. On the rare occasions I've been in church, I've found that the high Episcopalians put on the best show, and that's it. Now, at first, I wanted to whisper to Ginny, "Hey, this is a secret service." But soon the wish for a joke slipped from me together with the racked emotions that generated it. Out of that simple rite grew peace and a wordless wonder. That's what religion is about, I suppose, a turning toward God. Not that I became a convert; but on this one occasion it felt as if some aspect of Him might be turning toward *us*.

"Let us pray."

"Our Father, Who art in Heaven—"

There was a knock on the door.

I didn't notice at first. But it came again, and again, and a voice trickled through the heavy panels: "Dr. Griswold! Are you in there? Phone call for you. A Mr. Knife from the FBI. Says it's urgent."

That rocked me. My mood went smash. Ginny's nostrils dilated and she clutched her book as if it were a weapon. Karlslund's tones faltered.

Griswold pattered to the door and said to the janitor or whoever our Porlockian was: "Tell him I've a delicate experiment under way. It can't be interrupted. Get his number, and I'll call back in an hour or so."

Good for you! half of me wanted to shout. The rest was tangled in cold coils of wondering about God's mercy. Thy will be done . . . but what is Thy will? Can't be everything that happens, or men would be mere puppets in a cruel charade.

God won't frustrate us. He won't let a little girl stay in hell. He's done it on occasion. Read police records.

But death finally released those victims, and they were given comfort. Or so the churches claim. How do the churches know? Maybe nothing exists but a blind interplay of forces; or maybe the Lowest and Highest are identical; or— No, that's the despair of hell, which you have met before. Carry on, Matuchek. Don't give up the crypt. "Onward, Christian sô-oldiers" in your irregular baritone. If this doesn't work out, we'll try something else.

And at last we had struggled through the service to the benediction. Then Karlslund said, troubled: "I'm not sure we're going to get anywhere now. The proper reverence is lost."

Hardy replied unexpectedly, "Your church puts its prime emphasis on faith, Pastor. But to us Catholics, works count too."

Karlslund yielded. "Well—all right. We can make the attempt. What exact help do you wish?"

Barney, Ginny, and the rest exchanged blank looks. I realized that in the rush, they'd forgotten to get specific about that. It probably hadn't seemed urgent, since Heaven is not as narrowly literal-minded as hell. Our formula could be anything reasonable . . . presumably.

Barney cleared his throat. "Uh, the idea is," he said, "that a first-rank mathematician would go on learning, improving, gaining knowledge and power we can't guess at, after passing on. We want a man who pioneered in non-Euclidean geometry."

"Riemann is considered definitive," Falkenberg told us, "but he did build on the work of others, like Hamilton, and had successors of his own. We don't know how far the incomparable Gauss went, since he published only a fraction of his thought. On the whole, I'd favor Lobachevsky. He was the first to prove a geometry can be self-consistent that denies the axiom of parallels. Around 1830 or 1840 as I recall, though the history of mathematics isn't my long suit. Everything in that branch of it stems from him."

"That'll do," Barney decided, "considering we don't know if we can get any particular soul for an ally. Any whatsoever, for that matter," he added raggedly. To Falkenberg: "You and the pastor work out the words while we establish the spell."

That took time also, but kept us busy enough that it wasn't as maddening as the service had been after the distraction. We made the motions, spoke the phrases, directed the will, felt the indescribable stress of energies build toward breaking point. This was no everyday hex, it was heap big medicine.

Shadows thickened out of nowhere until the windows shone like pale lamps at night. The seven candle flames burned unnaturally tall without casting a glow. The symbols overhead glowed with their own radiance, a mythic heaven, and began slowly turning. St. Elmo's fire crawled blue over our upraised hands and Ginny's wand, crackled from Svartalf's fur where he stood on her shoulders and from her unbound hair. The harp played itself, strings plangent with the music of the spheres. Weaving my way back and forth across the floor I couldn't see for darkness, hand in hand as one of the seven who trod the slow measures of the *bransle grave,* I heard a voice cry: "Aleph!" and long afterward: "Zain."

At that we halted, the harp ceased, the eternal silence of the infinite spaces fell upon us, and the zodiac spun faster and faster until its figures blurred together and were time's wheel. What light remained lay wholly on the pastor. He stood, arms lifted, before the altar. "Hear us, O God, from Heaven Thy dwelling place," he called. "Thou knowest our desire; make it pure, we pray Thee, In Thy sight stand this man Steven and this woman Virginia, who are prepared to harrow hell as best as is granted them to do, that they may confound Thine enemies and rescue an unstained child from the dungeons of the worm. Without Thine aid they have no hope. We beg Thee to allow them a guide and counselor through the wilderness of hell. If we are not worthy of an angel, we ask that Thou commend them unto Thy departed servant Nikolai Ivanovitch Lobachevsky, or whomever else may be knowledgeable in these matters as having been on earth a discoverer of them. This do we pray in the name of the Father, and of the Son, and of the Holy Ghost. Amen.''

There was another stillness.

Then the cross on the altar shone forth, momentarily sunbright, and we heard one piercing, exquisite note, and I felt within me a rush of joy I can only vaguely compare to the first winning of first love. But another noise followed, as of a huge wind. The candles went out, the panes went black, we staggered when the floor shook beneath us. Svartalf screamed.

"Ginny!" I heard myself yell. Simultaneously I was whirled down a vortex of images, memories, a bulbous-towered church on an illimitable plain, a dirt track between rows of low thatch-roofed cottages and a horseman squeaking and jingling along it with saber at belt, an iron winter that ended in thaw and watery gleams and returning bird-flocks and shy breath of green across the beechwoods, a disordered stack of books, faces, faces, hands, a woman who was my wife, a son who died too young, half of Kazan in one red blaze, the year of the cholera, the letter from Göttingen, loves, failures, blindness closing in day by slow day *and none of it was me.*

A thunderclap rattled our teeth. The wind stopped, the light came back, the sense of poised forces was no more. We stood bewildered in our ordinary lives. Ginny cast herself into my arms.

"Lyubimyets," I croaked to her, "no, darling— *Gospodny pomiluie—"* while the kaleidoscope gyred within me. Svartalf stood on a workbench, back arched, tail bottled, not in rage but in panic. His lips, throat, tongue writhed through a ghastly fight with sounds no cat can make. He was trying to talk.

"What's gone wrong?" Barney roared.

XXX

GINNY TOOK OVER. She beckoned to the closest men. "Karlslund, Hardy, help Steve," she rapped. "Check him, Doc." I heard her fragmentarily through the chaos. My friends supported me. I reached a chair, collapsed, and fought for breath.

My derangement was short. The recollections of another land, another time, stopped rocketing forth at random. They had been terrifying because they were strange and out of my control. *Poko'y* sounded in my awareness, together with *Peace,* and I knew they meant the same. Courage lifted. I sensed myself thinking, with overtones of both formalism and compassion:

—I beg your pardon, sir. This re-embodiment confused me likewise. I had not paused to reflect what a difference would be made by more than a hundred years in the far realms where I have been. A few minutes will suffice, I believe, for preliminary studies providing the informational basis for a modus vivendi that shall be tolerable to you. Rest assured that I regret any intrusion and will minimize the same. I may add, with due respect, that what I chance to learn about your private affairs will doubtless be of no special significance to one who has left the flesh behind him.

Lobachevsky! I realized.

—Your servant, sir. Ah, yes, Steven Anton Matuchek. Will you graciously excuse me for the necessary brief interval?

This, and the indescribable stirring of two memory sets that followed, went on at the back of my consciousness. The rest of me was again alert: uncannily so. I waved Ashman aside with an "I'm okay" and scanned the scene before me.

In Svartalf's hysterical condition, he was dangerous to approach. Ginny tapped a basin of water at a workbench sink and threw it over him. He squalled, sprang to the floor, dashed to a corner, crouched and glowered. "Poor puss," she consoled. "I had to do that." She found a towel. "Come here to mama and

175

we'll dry you off.'' He made her come to him. She squatted and rubbed his fur.

"What got into him?" Charles asked.

Ginny looked up. Against the red hair her face was doubly pale. "Good phrase, Admiral," she said. "Something did. I shocked his body with a drenching. The natural cat reflexes took over, and the invading spirit lost its dominance. But it's still there. As soon as it learns its psychosomatic way around, it'll try to assume control and do what it's come for.''

"Which is?"

"I don't know. We'd better secure him.''

I rose. "No, wait," I said. "I can find out." Their eyes swiveled toward me. "You see, uh, I've got Lobachevsky."

"What?" Karlslund protested. "His soul in your— Can't be! The saints never—''

I brushed past, knelt by Ginny, took Svartalf's head between my hands, and said, "Relax. Nobody wants to hurt you. My guest thinks he understands what's happened. Savvy? Nikolai Ivanovitch Lobachevsky is his name. Who are you?''

The muscles bunched, the fangs appeared, a growing ululation swept the room. Svartalf was about to have another fit.

—Sir, by your leave, the thought went in me. He is not hostile. I would know if he were. He is disconcerted at what has occurred, and has merely a feline brain to think with. Evidently he is unacquainted with your language. May I endeavor to calm him?

Russian purled and fizzled from my lips. Svartalf started, then I felt him ease a bit in my grasp. He looked and listened as intently as if I were a mousehole. When I stopped, he shook his head and mewed.

—So he was not of my nationality either. But he appears to have grasped our intent.

Look, I thought, you can follow English, using my knowledge. Svartalf knows it too. Why can't his . . . inhabitant . . . do like you?

—I told you, sir, the feline brain is inadequate. It has nothing like a human speech-handling structure. The visiting soul must use every available cortical cell to maintain bare reason. But it can freely draw upon its terrestrial experience, thanks to the immense data storage capacity of even a diminutive mammalian body. Hence we can use what languages it knew before.

I thought: I see. Don't underrate Svartalf. He's pure-bred from a long line of witch familiars, more intelligent than an ordinary cat. And the spells that've surrounded him through his life must've had effects.

—Excellent. *"Sprechen Sie Deutsch?"*

Svartalf nodded eagerly. "Mee-öh," he said with an umlaut.

"Guten Tag, gnädiger Herr. Ich bin der Mathematiker Nikolai Iwanowitsch Lobatschewski, quondam Oberpfarrer zu der Kasans Universität in Russland. Je suis votre très humble serviteur, Monsieur." That last was in French, as politeness called for in the earlier nineteenth century.

"W-r-r-rar-r." Claws gestured across the floor.

Ginny said, wide-eyed with awe: "He wants to write. . . . Svartalf, listen. Don't be angry. Don't be afraid. Let him do what he will. Don't fight, help him. When this is over, you'll have more cream and sardines than you can eat. I promise. There's a good cat." She rubbed him under the chin. It didn't seem quite the proper treatment for a visiting savant, but it worked, because at last he purred.

While she and Griswold made preparations, I concentrated on meshing with Lobachevsky. The rest stood around, shaken by what had happened and the sudden complete unknownness of the next hour. A fraction of me hearkened to their low voices.

Charles: "Damnedest apparition of saints I ever heard of."

Karlslund: "Admiral, please!"

Janice: "Well, it's true. They shouldn't have intruded in bodies like, like demons taking possession."

Griswold: "Maybe they had to. We did neglect to provide counter-transferral mass for inter-continuum crossing."

Karlslund: "They aren't devils. They never required it in the past."

Barney: "Whoa. Let's think about that. A spirit or a thought can travel free between universes. Maybe that's what returned saints always were—visions, not solid bodies."

Karlslund: "Some were positively substantial."

Nobu: "I would guess that a saint can utilize any mass to form a body. Air, for instance, and a few pounds of dust for minerals, would provide the necessary atoms. Don't forget what he or she is, as far as we know: a soul in Heaven, which is to say one near God. How can he fail to gain remarkable abilities as well as spiritual eminence—from the Source of power and creativity?"

Charles: "What ails these characters, then?"

"Messieurs," my body said, stepping toward them, "I beg your indulgence. As yet I have not entirely accustomed myself to thinking in this corporeal manifold. Do me the honor to remem-

ber that it is unlike the one I originally inhabited. Nor have I
assimilated the details of the problem which led to your request
for help. Finally, while confined to human form, I have no better means than you for discovering the identity of the gentleman
in the cat. I do believe I know his purpose, but let us wait, if
you will, for more exact knowledge before drawing conclusions.''

"Wow," Barney breathed. "How's it feel, Steve?"

"Not bad," I said. "Better by the minute." That was an
ultimate understatement. As Lobachevsky and I got acquainted,
I felt in myself, coexistent with my own thoughts and emotions,
those of a being grown good and wise beyond imagining.

Of course, I couldn't share his afterlife, nor the holiness
thereof. My mortal brain and grimy soul didn't reach to it. At
most, there sang at the edge of perception a peace and joy which
were not static but a high eternal adventure. I did, though, have
the presence of Lobachevsky the man to savor. Think of your
oldest and best friend and you'll have a rough idea what that was
like.

"We should be ready now," Ginny said.

She and Griswold had set a Ouija board on a bench, the easiest
implement for a paw to operate. She perched herself on the edge,
swinging legs whose shapeliness my associate noticed too,
though mainly he worked out in my head the equation describing
them. Svartalf took position at the gadget while I leaned across
the opposite side to interrogate.

The planchette moved in a silence broken only by breathing. It
was sympathetic with a piece of chalk under a broomstick spell,
that wrote large on a blackboard where everyone could see.

ICH BIN JANOS BOLYAI VON UNGARN

"Bolyai!" gasped Falkenberg. "God, I forgot about him! No
wonder he—but how—"

"Enchanté, Monsieur," Lobachevsky said with a low bow.
*"Dies ist für mich eine grosse Ehre. Ihrer Werke sint eine
Inspiration für alles."* He meant it.

Neither Bolyai nor Svartalf were to be outdone in courtliness.
They stood up on his hind legs, made a reverence with paw on
heart, followed with a military salute, took the planchette again
and launched into a string of flowery French compliments.

"Who is he, anyhow?" Charles hissed behind me.

"I . . . I don't know his biography," Falkenberg answered
likewise. "But I recall now, he was the morning star of the new
geometry."

"I'll check the library," Griswold offered. "These courtesies look as if they'll go on for some time."

"Yes," Ginny said in my ear, "can't you hurry things along a bit? We're way overdue at home, you and I. And that phone call could be trouble."

I put it to Lobachevsky, who put it to Bolyai, who wrote ABER NATÜERLICH for the lack of an umlaut and gave us his assurances—at considerable length—that as an Imperial officer he had learned how to act with the decisiveness that became a soldier when need existed, as it clearly did in the present instance, especially when two such charming young ladies in distress laid claim upon his honor, which honor he would maintain upon any field without flinching, as he trusted he had done in life. . . .

I don't intend to mock a great man. Among us, he was a soul trying to think with the brain and feel with the nerves and glands of a tomcat. It magnified human failings and made well-nigh impossible the expression of his intellect and knightliness. We found these hinted at in the notes on him that Griswold located in encyclopedias and mathematical histories, which we read while he did his gallant best to communicate with Lobachevsky.

János Bolyai was born in Hungary in 1802, when it was hardly more than a province of the Austrian Empire. His father, a noted mathematician who was a close friend of Gauss, taught him calculus and analytical mechanics before he was thirteen and enrolled him in the Royal Engineering College in Vienna at fifteen. Twenty years old, he became an officer of engineers, well-known as a violinist and a swordsman dangerous to meet in a duel. In 1823 he sent to his father a draft of his *Absolute Science of Space*. While Gauss had anticipated some of its ideas in a general, philosophical way—unknown at the time to Bolyai—the young Hungarian had here done the first rigorous treatment of a non-Euclidean geometry, the first solid proof that space doesn't logically need to obey axioms like the one about parallel lines.

Unfortunately, it wasn't published till 1833, and just as an appendix to a two-volume work of his father's which, being in Latin, bore the gorgeous title *Tentatem juventutem studiosam in elementa matheseos purae introducendi.* By then Lobachevsky had independently announced similar results. Bolyai remained obscure.

It seemed to have discouraged him. He settled down in the same place as his father, who taught at the Reformed College of

Maros-Vásárhely, and died there in 1860. His lifetime covered a
rising Hungarian nationalism, Kossuth's rebellion in 1848, its
failure and the reactionary oppression that followed; but the
articles said nothing about his conduct or opinions. He did see
the end of martial law in 1857 and the increasing liberalization
afterward: though his land did not achieve full national status
under the dual monarchy till seven years past his death. I wondered if his ghost had hung around that long, waiting, before it
departed for wider universes.

We found more on Lobachevsky. He was born in 1793, in
Nizhni Novgorod. His mother was widowed when he was seven.
She moved to Kazan and raised her boys in genteel but often
desperate poverty. They won scholarships to the Gymnasium,
Nikolai at the age of eight. He entered the local university at
fourteen, got his master's degree at eighteen, was appointed
assistant professor at twenty-one and full professor at twenty-
three. Presently he had charge of the library and the museum. It
was a tough distinction—both were neglected, disordered, so
short of funds that he had to do most of the sheer physical labor
himself—but over the years he made them a pride of Russia. In
addition, while Czar Alexander lived, he was supposed to keep
tabs on student politics. He managed to satisfy the government
without finking; the kids adored him.

In 1827 he became rector, head of the university. He built it up
in every way, including literally; he learned architecture so he
could design proper structures. In 1830, when cholera struck, he
pulled the academic community through with scant mortality, by
enforcing sanitation as opposed to the medieval measures taken
elsewhere in Kazan. Another time a fire totalled half the town.
His new observatory, his best buildings went. But he rescued the
instruments and books, and two years later had restored what
was lost.

As early as 1826, he'd discussed non-Euclidean geometry. He
might as well have done it in Kansas as Kazan. Word spread to
western Europe with a slowness that would have driven a less
patient, unegotistical man up the wall. But it did travel. When
Gauss heard, he was impressed enough to get Lobachevsky
elected to the Royal Society of Göttingen in 1842.

Maybe that—xenophobia, or simple spiteful jealousy—was
what prompted the Czarist regime in 1846 to bounce him as
rector. They let him keep his study at the university, but scant
else. Heartbroken, he withdrew to his mathematical work. His
eyesight failed. His son died. He thought on, dictating the

Pangeometry that crowned his life. In 1856, shortly after he finished the book, that life ended.

Of course he was a saint!

—No, Steven Pavlovitch, you should not raise me above my worth. I stumbled and sinned more than most, I am sure. But the mercy of God has no bounds. I have been . . . it is impossible to explain. Let us say I have been allowed to progress.

The blackboard filled. Janice wielded an eraser and the chalk squeaked on. To those who knew French—which the Russian and the Hungarian had switched to as being more elegant than German—it gradually became clear what had happened. But I alone shared Lobachevsky's degree of comprehension. As this grew, I fretted over ways to convey it in American. Time was shrinking on us fast.

—Indeed, Lobachevsky answered. Brusque though contemporary manners have become *(pardonnez-moi, je vous en prie),* haste is needed, for I agree that the hour is late and the peril dire.

Therefore I called the group to me when at last the questioning was done. Except for Ginny, who couldn't help being spectacular, and Svartalf, who sat at her feet with a human soul in his eyes, they were an unimpressive lot to see, tired, sweaty, haggard, neckties loosened or discarded, hair unkempt, cigarets in most hands. I was probably less glamorous, perched on a stool facing them. My voice grated and I'd developed a tic in one cheek. The fact that a blessed spirit had joint tenancy of my body didn't much affect plain, scared, fallible me.

"Things have got straightened out," I said. "We made a mistake. God doesn't issue personal orders to His angels and saints, at least not on our behalf. It appears, Pastor, from the form of your invocation, you understood that. But consciously or not, the rest of us assumed we're more important than we are." Lobachevsky corrected me. "No, everybody's important to Him. But there must be freedom, even for evil. And furthermore, there are considerations of—well, I guess you can't say *Realpolitik.* I don't know if it has earthly analogues. Roughly speaking, though, neither God nor the Adversary want to provoke an early Armageddon. For two thousand years, they've avoided direct incursions into each other's, uh, home territories, Heaven or hell. That policy's not about to be changed.

"Our appeal was heard. Lobachevsky's a full-fledged saint. He couldn't resist coming down, and he wasn't forbidden to. But he's not allowed to aid us in hell. If he goes along, it has to be strictly as an observer, inside a mortal frame. He's sorry, but that's the way the elixir elides. If we get scragged there, he can't help our souls escape. Every spirit has to make its own way— No matter. The result was, he entered this continuum, with me as his logical target.

"Bolyai's different. He heard too, especially since the prayer was so loosely phrased it could well have referred to him. Now, he hasn't made sainthood. He says he's been in Purgatory. I suspect most of us'd think of it as a condition where you haven't got what it takes to know God directly but you can improve yourself. At any rate, while he wasn't in Heaven, he wasn't damned either. And so he's under no prohibition as regards taking an active part in a fight. This looked like a chance to do a good deed. He assessed the content of our appeal, including the parts we didn't speak, and likewise chose me. Lobachevsky, who's more powerful by virtue of sanctity, and wasn't aware of his intent, arrived a split second ahead of him."

I stopped to bum a cigaret. What I really wanted was a gallon of hard cider. My throat felt like a washboard road in summer. "Evidently these cases are governed by rules," I said. "Don't ask me why; I'm sure the reasons are valid if we could know them; in part, I guess, it's to protect mortal flesh from undue shock and strain. Only one extra identity per customer. Bolyai hasn't the capability of a saint, to create a temporary real body out of whatever's handy, as you suggested a while back, Dr. Nobu. In fact, he probably couldn't have used organized material if we'd prepared some. His way to manifest himself was to enter a live corpus. Another rule: the returned soul can't switch from person to person. It must stay with whom it's at for the duration of the affair.

"Bolyai had to make a snap decision. I was pre-empted. His sense of propriety wouldn't let him, uh, enter a woman. It wouldn't do a lot of good if he hooked up with one of you others, who aren't going. Though our prayer hadn't mentioned it, he'd gathered from the overtones that the expedition did have a third member who was male. He willed himself there. He always was rash. Too late, he discovered he'd landed in Svartalf."

Barney's brick-house shoulders drooped. "Our project's gone for nothing?"

"No," I said. "With Ginny's witchcraft to help—boost his feline brain power—Bolyai thinks he can operate. He's spent a sizable chunk of afterlife studying the geometry of the continua, exploring planes of existence too weird for him to hint at. He loves the idea of a filibuster into hell.''

Svartalf's tail swung, his ears stood erect, his whiskers dithered.

"Then it worked!" Ginny shouted. "Whoopee!"

"So far and to this extent, yeah.'' My determination was unchanged but my enthusiasm less. Lobachevsky's knowledge darkened me: —I sense a crisis. The Adversary can ill afford to let you succeed. His mightiest and subtlest forces will be arrayed against you.

"Well,'' Karlslund said blankly. "Well, well.''

Ginny stopped her war dance when I said: "Maybe you better make that phone call, Dr. Griswold.''

The little scientist nodded. "I'll do it from my office. We can plug in an extension here, audio-visual reception.'' We were far too groggy to give a curse about the lawfulness of that, though I do believe it's permissble, not being an actual scryertap.

We had a few minutes' wait. I held Ginny close by my side. Our troops muttered aimlessly or slumped exhausted. Bolyai was alone in his cheerfulness. He used Svartalf to tour the lab with eager curiosity. By now he knew more math and science than living men will acquire before world's end; but it intrigued him to see how we were going about things. He was ecstatic when Janice found him a copy of the *National Geographic*.

The phone awoke. We saw what Griswold did. The breath sucked in between my teeth. Shining Knife was indeed back.

"I'm sorry to keep you waiting,'' the professor said. "It was impossible for me to come earlier. What can I do for you?''

The G-man identified himself and showed his sigil. "I'm trying to get in touch with Mr. and Mrs. Steven Matuchek. You know them, don't you?''

"Well, ah, yes . . . haven't seen them lately—'' Griswold was a lousy liar.

Shining Knife's countenance hardened. "Please listen, sir. I returned this afternoon from a trip to Washington on their account. The matter they're involved in is that big. I checked with my subordinates. Mrs. Matuchek had disappeared. Her husband had spent time in a spyproof conference room. He'd not been seen to leave his place of work at quitting time. I sent a man in to ask for him, and he wasn't to be found. Our people had taken pictures of those who went into the plant. A crime lab worker here recognized you among the members of the conference. Are you sure the Matucheks aren't with you?''

"Y-yes. Yes. What do you want with them? Not a criminal charge?''

"No, unless they misbehave. I've a special order enjoining them from certain actions they may undertake. Whoever abetted them would be equally subject to arrest.''

Griswold was game. He overcame his shyness and sputtered: "Frankly, sir, I resent your implication. And in any event, the writ must be served to have force. Until such time, they are not bound by it, nor are their associates.''

"True. Mind if I come look around your place? They might happen to be there . . . without your knowledge.''

"Yes, sir, I do mind. You may not.''

"Be reasonable, Dr. Griswold. Among other things, the purpose is to protect them from themselves.''

"That attitude is a major part of what I dislike about the present Administration. Good day to you, sir.''

"Uh, hold.'' Shining Knife's tone remained soft, but nobody could mistake his expression. "You don't own the building you're in.''

"I'm responsible for it. Trismegistus is a private foundation. I can exercise discretionary authority and forbid access to your . . . your myrmidons.''

"Not when they arrive with a warrant, Professor.''

"Then I suggest you obtain one.'' Griswold broke the spell.

In the lab, we regarded each other. "How long?'' I asked. Barney shrugged. "Under thirty minutes. The FBI has ways.''

"Can we scram out of here?'' Ginny inquired of him.

"I wouldn't try it. The area probably went under surveillance before Shining Knife tried to call. I expect he stayed his hand simply because he doesn't know what we're doing and his orders are to proceed with extreme caution.''

She straightened. "Okay. Then we go to hell.'' Her mouth twitched faintly upward. "Go directly to hell. Do not pass Go. Do not collect two hundred dollars.''

"Huh?'' Barney grunted, as if he'd been kicked in the stomach. "No! You're as crazy as the Feds think you are! No preparation, no proper equipment—''

"We can cobble together a lot with what's around here,'' Ginny said. "Bolyai can advise us, and Lobachevsky till we leave. We'll win an advantage of surprise. The demonic forces won't have had time to organize against our foray. Once we're out of American jurisdiction, can Shining Knife legally recall us? And he won't keep you from operating our lifeline. That'd be murder. Besides, I suspect he's on our side, not glad of his duty. He may well offer you help.'' She went to Barney, took one of his hands between both of hers, and looked up into his craggy face. ''Don't hinder us, old friend,'' she pleaded. ''We've got to have you on our side.''

His torment was hurtful to see. But he started ripping out commands. Our team plunged into work.

Griswold entered. ''Did you— Oh. You can't leave now.''

''We can't not,'' I said.

''But you haven't . . . haven't had dinner! You'll be weak and— Well, I know I can't stop you. We keep a fridge with food in the research lab, for when a project runs late. I'll see what it holds.''

So that's how we went to storm the fastness of hell: Janice's borrowed shoulder purse on Ginny, and the pockets of Barney's outsize jacket (sleeves haggled short) on me, abulge with peanut butter sandwiches, tinned kipper for Svartalf-Bolyai, and four cans of beer.

XXXI

WE HAD SOME equipment, notably Ginny's kit. This included Valeria's primary birth certificate, which Ashman had brought. The directions he could give her for using it were the main reason he'd been recruited. She put in in her own bag, clipped to her waist, for the time being.

Nobody, including our geometers, knew exactly what would and would not work in hell. Lobachevsky was able to tell us that high-religious symbols had no power there as they do here. Their virtue comes from their orientation to the Highest, and the fundamental thing about hell is that no dweller in it can love. However, we might gain something from paganism. Its element of honor and justice meant nothing where we were bound, but its element of power and propitiation did, and although centuries have passed since anyone served those gods, the mana has not wholly vanished from their emblems.

Ginny habitually wore on her dress the owl pin that showed she was a licensed witch. Griswold found a miniature jade plaque, Aztec, carved with a grotesque grinning feathered serpent, that could be secured to the wereflash beneath my shirt. A bit sheepish under Pastor Karlslund's eye, Barney fished out a silver hammer pendant, copy of a Viking era original. It belonged to his wife, but he'd carried it himself "for a rabbit's foot" since this trouble broke, and now passed the chain around Svartalf's neck.

Projectile weapons weren't apt to be worth lugging. Ginny and I are pretty good shots in the nearly Euclidean space of this plenum. But when the trajectory is through unpredictable distortions that affect the very gravity, forget it, chum. We buckled on swords. She had a slender modern Solingen blade, meant for ritual use but whetted to a sharp point and edge. Mine was heavier and older, likewise kept for its goetic potency, but that stemmed from its being a cutlass which had once sailed with Decatur.

Air might be a problem. Hell was notoriously foul. Scuba rigs were in stock, being used for underwater investigations. When this gets you involved with nixies or other tricky creatures, you need a wizard or witch along, whose familiar won't be a convenient beast like a seal unless you have the luck to engage one of the few specialists. Accordingly there are miniature oxygen bottles and adjustable masks for a wide variety of animals. We could outfit Svartalf, and I tied another pint-size unit to the tank on my back—for Val, in case.

That completed the list. Given time, we could have done better. We could have ridden a dragon instead of two brooms, with an extra beast packing several tons of stuff against every contingency that a strategic analysis team might propose. Still, the Army had used that approach and failed. We had fresh knowledge and a unique scout. Maybe those would serve.

While we busked ourselves with several helpers, Barney and Nobu made the final preparations to transmit us. Or almost final. At the last minute I asked them to do an additional job as soon as might be.

At the center of the Nexus drawn on the floor, whose shape I won't reveal, they'd put a regular confining pentacle set about with blessed candles. A giant bell jar hung from a block and tackle above, ready to be lowered. This was for the counter-mass from the hell universe, which might be alive, gaseous, or otherwise troublesome. "After we've gone," I said, "lay a few hundred extra pounds of material in there, if the area's not too dangerous to enter."

"What?" Barney said, astonished. "But that'd allow, uh, anything—a pursuer—to make the transition with no difficulty."

"Having arrived here, it can't leave the diagram," I pointed out. "We can and will, in a mighty quick jump. Have spells ready to prevent its return home. Thing is, I don't know what we'll find. Could be an item, oh, of scientific value; and the race needs more data about hell. Probably we won't collect any loot. But let's keep the option."

"Okay. Sound thinking, for a lunatic." Barney wiped his eyes. "Damn, I must be allergic to something here."

Janice didn't weep alone when we bade good-bye. And within me paced the grave thought:

—No more may I aid you, Steven Pavlovitch, Virginia Williamovna, Janos Fárkasovitch, and cat who surely has a soul of his own. Now must I become a mere watcher and recorder, for the sake of nothing except my curiosity. I will not burden you with the grief this causes me. You will not be further aware of my presence. May you fare with God's blessing.

I felt him depart from the conscious part of my mind like a dream that fades as you wake and try to remember. Soon he was only something good that had happened to me for a couple of hours. Or no, not entirely. I suspect what calm I kept in the time that followed was due to his unsensed companionship. He couldn't help being what he was.

Holding our brooms, Ginny and I walked hand in hand to the Nexus. Svartalf paced ahead. At the midpoint of the figure, we halted for a kiss and a whisper before we slipped the masks on. Our people cast the spell. Again the chamber filled with night. Energies gathered. Thunder and earthquake brawled. I hung onto my fellows lest we get separated. Through the rising racket, I heard my witch read from the parchment whereon stood the name Victrix, urging us toward her through diabolic space-time.

The room, the world, the stars, and universes began to rotate about the storm's eye where we stood. Swifter and swifter they turned until they were sheer spinning, the Grotte quern itself. Then was only a roar as of great waters. We were drawn down the maelstrom. The final glimpse of light dwindled with horrible speed; and when we reached infinity, it was snuffed out. Afterward came such twistings and terrors that nothing would have sent us through them except our Valeria Victrix.

XXXII

I MUST HAVE blanked out for a minute or a millennium. At least, I became aware with ax-chop abruptness that the passage was over and we had arrived.

Wherever it was.

I clutched Ginny to me. We searched each other with a touch that quivered and found no injuries. Svartalf was hale too. He didn't insist on attention as he normally would. Bolyai made him pad in widening spirals, feeling out our environment.

With caution I slipped off my mask and tried the air. It was bitterly cold, driving in a wind that sought to the bones, but seemed clean—sterile, in fact.

Sterility. That was the whole of this place. The sky was absolute and endless black, though in some fashion we could see stars and ugly cindered planets, visibly moving in chaotic paths; they were pieces of still deeper darkness, not an absence but a negation of light. We stood on a bare plain, hard and gray and flat as concrete, relieved by nothing except scattered boulders whose shapes were never alike and always hideous. The illumination came from the ground, wan, shadowless, colorless. Vision faded at last into utter distance. For that plain had no horizon, no interruptions; it went on. The sole direction, sound, movement, came from the drearily whistling wind.

I've seen some abominations in my time, I thought, but none to beat this. . . . No. The worst is forever a changeling in my daughter's crib.

Ginny removed her mask too, letting it hang over the closed bottle like mine. She shuddered and hugged herself. The dress whipped around her. "I w-w-was ready to guard against flames," she said. It was as appropriate a remark as most that are made on historic occasions.

"Dante described the seventh circle of the Inferno as frozen," I answered slowly. "There's reason to believe he knew something. Where are we?"

"I can't tell. If the name spell worked, along with the rest, we're on the same planet—if 'planet' means a lot here—as Val will be, and not too far away." We'd naturally tried for a beforehand arrival.

"This isn't like what the previous expeditions reported."

"No. Nor was our transition. We used different rituals, and slanted across time to boot. Return should be easier."

Svartalf disappeared behind a rock. I didn't approve of that. *"Kommen Sie zurück!"* I shouted into the wind. *"Retournez-vous!"* I realized that, without making a fuss about it, Lobachevsky had prior to our departure impressed on me fluent French and German. By golly, Russian too!

"Mneowr-r," blew back. I turned. The cat was headed our way from opposite to where he'd been. "What the dickens?" I exclaimed.

"Warped space," Ginny said. "Look." While he trotted steadily, Svartalf's path wove as if he were drunk. "A line where he is must answer to a curve elsewhere. And he's within a few yards. What about miles off?"

I squinted around. "Everything appears straight."

"It would, while you're stationary. Br-r-r! We've got to get warmer."

She drew the telescoping wand from her purse. The star at its tip didn't coruscate here; it was an ember. But it made a lighted match held under our signatures and Svartalf's pawprint generate welcome heat in our bodies. A bit too much, to be frank; we started sweating. I decided the hell universe was at such high entropy—so deep into thermodynamic decay—that a little potential went very far.

Svartalf arrived. Staring uneasily over the plain, I muttered, "We haven't met enough troubles. What're we being set up for?"

"We've two items in our favor," Ginny said. "First, a really effective transfer spell. Its influence is still perceptible here, warding us, tending to smooth out fluctuations and similarize nature to home. Second, the demons must have known well in advance where and when the earlier expeditions would come through. They'd ample time to fix up some nasty tricks. We, though, we've stolen a march." She brushed an elflock from her brow and added starkly: "I expect we'll get our fill of problems as we travel."

"We have to?"

"Yes. Why should the kidnaper make re-entry at this desert

spot? We can't have landed at the exact point we want. Be quiet while I get a bearing."

Held over the Victrix parchment, the proper words sung, her dowser pointed out an unequivocal direction. The scryer globe remained cloudy, giving us no hint of distance or look at what lay ahead. Space-time in between was too alien.

We ate, drank, rested what minutes we dared, and took off. Ginny had the lead with Svartalf on her saddlebow, I flew on her right in echelon. The sticks were cranky and sluggish, the screenfields kaput, leaving us exposed to the wind from starboard. But we did loft and level off before the going got tough.

At first it was visual distortion. What I saw—my grasp on the controls, Svartalf, Ginny's splendid figure, the stones underneath—rippled, wavered, widened, narrowed, flowed from one obscene caricature of itself to a worse. Gobs of flesh seemed to slough off, hang in drops, stretch thin, break free and disappear. Sound altered too; the skirl turned into a cacophony of yells, buzzes, drones, fleetingly like words almost understandable and threatening, pulses too deep to hear except with the body's automatic terror reaction. "Don't pay heed!" I called. "Optical effects, Doppler—" but no message could get through that gibbering.

Suddenly my love receded. She whirled from me like a blown leaf. I tried to follow, straight into the blast that lashed tears from my eyes. The more rudder I gave the broom, the faster our courses split apart. "Bolyai, help!" I cried into the aloneness. It swallowed me.

I slid down a long wild curve. The stick would not pull out of it. Well, flashed through my fear, I'm not in a crash dive, it'll flatten a short ways above—

And the line of rocks athwart my path were not rocks, they were a mountain range toward which I catapulted. The gale laughed in my skull and shivered the broom beneath me. I hauled on controls, I bellowed the spells, but any change I could make would dash me on the ground before I hit those cliffs.

Somehow I'd traveled thousands of miles—had to be that much, or I'd have seen these peaks on the limitless plain, wouldn't I have?—and Ginny was lost, Val was lost, I could brace myself for death but not for the end of hope.

"Yeee-ow-w-w!" cut through the clamor. I twisted in my seat. And there came Ginny. Her hair blew in fire. The star on her wand burned anew like Sirius. Bolyai was using Svartalf's paws to steer; yellow eyes and white fangs flared in the panther countenance.

They pulled alongside. Ginny leaned over till our fingers met. Her sensations ran down the circuit to me. I saw with her what the cat was doing. I imitated. It would have wrecked us at home. But here we slewed sideways and started gaining altitude.

How to explain? Suppose you were a Flatlander, a mythical creature (if any creature is mythical) of two space dimensions, no more. You live in a surface. That's right, *in*. If this is a plane, its geometry obeys the Euclidean rules we learn in high school: parallel lines don't meet, the shortest distance between two points is a straight line, the angles of a triangle total 180 degrees, et cetera. But now imagine that some three-dimensional giant plucks you out and drops you into a surface of different shape. It might be a sphere, for example. You'll find space fantastically changed. In a sphere, you must think of lines in terms of meridians and parallels, which means they have finite length; in general, distance between points is minimized by following a great circle; triangles have a variable number of degrees, but always more than 180— You might well go mad. Now imagine cones, hyperboloids, rotated trigonometric and logarithmic curves, Möbius bands, whatever you can.

And now imagine a planet which is all water, churned by storms and not constrained by the ordinary laws of physics. At any point its surface can have any form, which won't even stay constant in time. Expand the two dimensions into three; make it four for the temporal axis, unless this requires more than one, as many philosophers believe; add the hyperspace in which paranatural forces act; put it under the rule of chaos and hatred: and you've got some analogy to the hell universe.

We'd hit a saddle point back yonder, Ginny passing to one side of it, I to the other. Our courses diverged because the curvatures of space did. My attempt to intercept her was worse than useless; in the region where I found myself, a line aimed her way quickly bent in a different direction. I blundered from geometry to geometry, through a tuck in space that bypassed enormous reaches, toward my doom.

No mortal could have avoided it. But Bolyai was mortal no longer. To his genius had been added the knowledge and skill of more than a century's liberation from the dear but confining flesh. Svartalf's body had changed from a trap to a tool, once his rapport with Ginny enabled the mathematician to draw on her resources also. He could make lightning-quick observations of a domain, mentally write and solve the equations that described it, calculate what its properties would be, get an excellent notion of what the contour would shade into next—in fractional seconds. He wove through the dimensional storms of hell like a quarter-back bound for a touchdown.

He gloried. For lack of other voice, he sang the songs of a black tomcat out after fornication and battle. We clawed over the mountains and streaked toward our goal.

It was no milk run. We must keep aware and reacting each instant. Often we made an error that well-nigh brought us to grief. I'd lose contact with Ginny and wander off again; or a lurch would nearly make us collide; or the intense gravitational field where space was sharply warped hurled our sticks ground-ward and tried to yank out guts and eyeballs; or a quick drop in weight sent us spinning; or we shot through folds in space instead of going around and were immediately elsewhere; or we passed into volumes where hyperspace was so flat that our broomspells didn't work and we must get through on momentum and aerodynamics—I don't recall every incident. I was too busy to notice a lot of them.

We traveled, though, and faster than we'd hoped, once Bolyai discovered what tricks we could play when the time dimension was buckled. The deafening racket and disgusting illusions plagued us less as we got the hang of passing smoothly from metric to metric. Moreover, the world around us grew steadier. Somebody or something wanted to lair in a region where distur-bances tended to cancel out.

At last we could study the landscape. Hitherto we'd simply kept flying. We'd noted the plain had given way to crags, to miles of jumbled bones, to a pit that seemed without bottom, to a lava sea across which sleeted flames and from which rose fumes that made us don our masks before the lungs were corroded within us. But such glimpses were remote, things to stay well above while we fought to make distance. Now progress was, by comparison, easy. We could spare a little attention. And we'd better. When Ginny lifted out her globe, a pale but waxing glow from inside it showed we were approaching the goal.

I released her hand, not because I wanted to but because our arms ached from straining across the gap. We flew quietly for a while, observing.

Quietly. . . . The wind had fallen behind; nothing blew around us but a murmur of cloven air. It bore a graveyard stench, we gasped in its warmth and slimy humidity, but it could be breathed. The sky remained black, with its more-than-black crawling orbs. Sometimes a huge pitted meteoroid passed close overhead, hardly faster than we, following a track above shallow atmosphere to vanishment over the horizonless world. Sometimes corposants blossomed and bobbed in the nether gloom.

The mournful phosphorescence of the ground remained our chief illumination. We were on the fringes of a swamp as vast as every other piece of country we'd seen here. Pools, bayous, lakes stretched beyond sight, dimly glimmering where they were not scummed with decayed matter. Trees stood thick and gnarled, branches tangled together, cypress knees thrust above water and floating logs; but not one of them was alive. Reeds choked the shorelines, dense and dead. Yellow mists stole through the murk between boles: tendrils of a fogbank that hid the inner reaches of marsh in a slow dirty seething.

Immensely far ahead, light reflected ruddy and restless off low clouds. Without warning, a slip or convulsion in space brought us on top of it.

Sound assailed us, drums, pipings, screeches. At the middle of a cleared island, a fire burned, high as a steeple, heat striking from it like a flayer's knife. Past its white heart, where things writhed and screamed that were not clear to the eye, I glimpsed the shapes that danced around it, black, naked, thin as mantises. When they saw us, their shrieks pierced the surf roar of the flames, and the tom-toms went *Boom-ba-da-boom, boom-ba-da-boom.* A dozen birds labored from the leafless trees. They were the size and color of vultures, but with no flesh on their skulls and cruel claws.

Svartalf spat defiance. Our sticks accelerated and left the flock behind. I don't think it was alive either. From miles in front we heard new drums commence, and after them, a whisper across the leagues, again *Boom-ba-da-boom, boom-ba-da-boom.*

Ginny beckoned me and I edged close. She looked grim. "If I don't miss my guess," she said, "we're over Diddy-Wah-Diddy and the word's being passed on."

My left hand dropped to my cutlass hilt. "What should we do?"

"Veer. Try for a different approach. But fast."

The wind of our speed felt nearly good after that blistering calor; and presently it cooled and lost its stench. When we'd passed a line of dolmens, the air was again wintry for a while. Beneath us lay a barren moor. Two armies fought. They must have been doing it for centuries, because many wore chain mail and peaked helmets, the rest were in skins and rough cloth, the weapons were sword, spear, ax. We heard the iron clamor, the shuffling, slipping feet, the butcher sound of blows driven home: but no cries, no trumpets, no rasp of breath. Wearily, hopelessly, the dead men fought their war that had no end.

Beyond them we turned and made once more for our destination. We crossed a forest of gallows and a river that flowed with a noise like sobbing and whose spray, cast up by a gust, tasted warm and salt. We suffered the heat and poisonous vapors from a system of roads where motor vehicles of some kind crawled nose to tail, a network miles wide and I know not how long, nor can I guess its purpose. We traversed hills gouged with trenches and the craters of explosions, rusted cannon the last sign of life except for one flag, raised as in victory, whose colors had faded to gray. The hills climbed till we met another range so high we needed our masks; flitting through its canyons, we dodged stones that fell upward.

But past those mountains the land swooped down anew. Another plain of boulders reached beyond sight. Far off upon it, toylike at their remove, we spied gaunt black towers. The globe flared brilliant, the wand leaped to point in Ginny's fingers. "By Hecate," she cried, "that's it!"

XXXIII

I DREW ALONGSIDE. The air was still cold and blowing, a wail in our ears, a streaming past our ribs, a smell akin to burning sulfur and wet iron. At hover, the broomsticks rocked and pitched. Her foot against mine was a very precious contact.

We peered into the globe she held. Svartalf-Bolyai craned around her arm to see. This close, the intervening space not too different from home geometry, the scrying functioned well. Ginny zoomed in on the castle. It was sable in hue, monstrous in size and shape. Or had it a shape? It sprawled, it soared, it burrowed with no unity except ugliness. Here a thin spire lifted crookedly from a cubical donjon, there a dome swelled pustular, yonder a stone beard overhung a misproportioned gate . . . square miles of planless deformity, aswarm with the maggoty traffic of devils.

We tried to look through the walls, but didn't penetrate far. Behind and beneath the cavernous chambers and twisted labyrinths that we discerned, too much evil force roiled. It was as well, considering what we did vaguely make out. At the limit, a thought came from just beyond, for an instant—no, not a thought, a wave of such agony that Ginny cried aloud and I bit blood out of my lip. We blanked the globe and embraced till we could stop shuddering.

"Can't afford this," she said, drawing free. "Time's gotten in short supply."

She reactivated the scryer, with a foreseer spell. Those rarely work in our universe, but Lobachevsky had theorized the fluid dimensions of the Low Continuum might give us a better chance. The view in the globe panned, steadied on one spot, and moved close. Slablike buildings and contorted towers enclosed a certain courtyard in an irregular septagon. At the middle of this was a small, lumpy stone house, windowless and with a single doorway. A steeple climbed from it, suggestive of a malformed ebon toadstool, that overtopped the surrounding structures and over-shadowed the pavement.

We couldn't view the inside of this either, for the same reason as before. It seemed to be untenanted, though. I had the creepy feeling that it corresponded in some perverted way to a chapel.

"Unambiguous and sharp," Ginny said. "That means she'll arrive there, and soon. We'll have to lay our plans fast."

"And move fast, too," I said. "Give me an overall scan, will you, with spot close-ups?"

She nodded. The scene changed to one from on high. I noted afresh how it pullulated in the crowds. Were they always this frantic? Not quite, surely. We focused on a single band of demons. No two looked alike; vanity runs high in hell. A body covered with spines, a tentacled dinosaur, a fat slattern whose nipples were tiny grinning heads, a flying swine, a changeable blob, a nude man with a snake for a phallus, a face in a belly, a dwarf on ten-foot pencil-thin legs, and less describable sights— What held my attention was that most of them were armed. They didn't go for projectiles either, evidently. However, those medievalish weapons would be bad to encounter.

Sweeping around, our vision caught similar groups. The confusion was unbelievable. There was no discipline, no consideration, everybody dashed about like a decapitated chicken yelling at everybody else, they jostled and snarled and broke into fights. But more arms were being fetched each minute from inside, more grotesque flyers lumbered into the air and circled.

"They've been alerted, all right," I said. "The drums—"

"I don't suppose they know what to expect," Ginny said in a low tight voice. "They aren't especially guarding the site we're after. Didn't the Adversary pass word about us?"

"He seems to be debarred from taking a personal hand in this matter, same as Lobachevsky and for analogous reasons, I guess. At most, he may've tipped his underlings to watch out for trouble from us. But they can't know we've acquired the capability to do what we did. Especially since we've made an end run in time."

"And the diabolic forces are stupid," Ginny said. "Evil is never intelligent or creative. They receive word a raid is possible, and look at that mess!"

"Don't underrate them. An idiot can kill you just as dead." I pondered. "Here's what we'll do, if you agree. Rush straight in. We can't prevent them seeing us, so we have to be quick. Good thing our sticks function close to normal in this neighborhood.

We won't make directly for the yard or they might block us off. See that palace, I assume it is, over to the left—the one with the columns in front that look like bowels? Must belong to the big cheese, which makes it a logical spot for enemies to drop a bomb on. At the last moment we'll swerve toward our real mark. You get inside, establish our paranatural defenses, and ready the return spell. I'll keep the door. The instant Val appears, you skewer the kidnaper and grab her. Got it?"

"Yes. Oh, Steve." The tears ran silently from her eyes. "I love you."

We kissed a final time, there in the sky of hell. Then we attacked.

The wind of our passage shouted around us. The drear landscape reeled away beneath. I heard Svartalf's challenge and answered with my own whoop. Fear blew out of me. Gangway, you legions of darkness, we're coming to fetch our girl!

They began to see us. Croaks and yammers reached our ears, answered by shrieks from below. The flying devils milled in the air. Others joined them till several hundred wings beat in a swarm across the sooty stars. They couldn't make up the minds they scarcely had what to do about us. Nearer we came and nearer. The castle rose in our vision like the ranges we had crossed.

Ginny must spend her entire force warding off sorceries. Lightning bolts spattered blue on the shieldfield, yards off, followed by thunder and ozone. Lethal clouds boiled from smokestacks, englobed our volume of air and dissipated. I had no doubt that, unperceived by us, curses, hoodoos, illusions, temptations, and screaming meemies rained upward and rebounded.

The effort was draining her. I glimpsed the white, strained countenance, hair plastered to brow and cheeks by sweat, wand darting while the free hand gestured and the lips talked spells. Svartalf snarled in front of her; Bolyai piloted the broom. None of them could keep it up for many minutes.

But that conjure wave made it impossible for anything to get at us physically. The creature in charge must have realized this at the end, for the assault stopped. An eagle the size of a horse, wearing a crocodile's head, stooped upon us.

My cutlass was drawn. I rose in the stirrups. "Not one cent for tribute!" I bayed, and struck. The old power awoke in the blade. It smote home with a force I felt through my bones. Blood spurted from a sheared-off wing. The devil bawled and dropped.

A batsnake threw a loop around my right arm. I grabbed its neck with my left hand before it could sink fangs in me. Human, I remain wolf; I bit its head off. Barely in time, I cut at a twin-tailed manta coming for Ginny. It fell aft, spilling guts. An aerial hound sought to intercept us. I held my weapon straight and got him with the point.

Horns hooted their discord. The flapping, cawing, stinking flock retreated in its regular disorder. Our stratagem had worked. Their entire outfit, infantry, air corps, and all, was being summoned to defend the palace.

We pursued to within a hundred yards. The manor was no longer visible for wings and feculent bodies. I lifted my blade as signal. We swung right and whizzed downward. Babel erupted behind us.

We landed jarringly hard. Surrounded by walls, brooded over by the cap of its tower, the building huddled in twilight. I bounced from my seat to the door and tried its ill-feeling handle. It creaked open and we ran in.

A single room, dank jagged stone, lay before us. It wasn't large in area, but opened above on the measureless dark of the tower. The room was bare except for an altar where a Glory Hand cast dull blue light. The arrangement of objects and the pattern on the floor were similar to those we'd employed for transit.

The heart cracked in me. "Val!" I sobbed. Ginny wrestled me to a halt. She couldn't have done so without Svartalf getting between my ankles.

"Hold it," she gasped. "Don't move. That's the changeling."

I drew a lungful of air and regained my sanity. Of course, of course. But it was more than I could endure to look at that chubby shape before the altar, gold curls and empty, empty eyes. Strange, also, to see next to the half-alive thing the mass already exchanged from our house: dust, sandbox contents, coffee grounds, soggy paper towels, a Campbell's Soup can—

The devil garrison was boiling over the walls and through the portals into this courtyard. I slammed the door and dropped the bolt. It was good and heavy: might buy us a few minutes.

How many did we need? I tried to reconstruct events. The kidnaper was doubtless moronic even by hell's standards. He'd heard Marmiadon's curse. A lot of them must have, but didn't see anything they could do to fulfill it. This one noticed our vulnerability. "Duh," he said, and flashed off to collect some kudos, without consulting any of the few demons that are able to think. Such a higher-up could have told him to lay off. His action would give a clue to the link between hell and the Johannine Church, and thus imperil the whole scheme for the sabotage of religion and society that the Adversary had been working on since he deluded the first of the neo-Gnostics.

Being the dimbulb he was, this creature could not solve the momentum problem of transferring a body other than his own between universes, unless the exchange mass was nearly identical in configuration. His plan would have been to appear in our home, scan Valeria as she slept, return here, 'chant a hunk of meat into her semblance, and go back after her. The first part would only have taken seconds, though it got the wind up Svartalf. The snatch ought to have gone quickly too, but the cat was waiting and attacked.

At this moment, if simultaneity had meaning between universes, the fight ramped and Svartalf's blood was riven from him. My throat tightened. I stooped over him. "We'd've arrived too late here except for you," I whispered. "They don't make thanks for that sort of help." Infinitely gently, I stroked the sleek head. He twitched his ears, annoyed. In these surroundings, he'd no patience with fine sentiments. Besides, currently they were János Bolyai's ears too.

Ginny was chalking a diagram around the room for a passive defense against demonurgy. It took care, because she mustn't disturb altar, emblem, or objects elsewhere. They were the fiend's return ticket. Given them, he need simply cast the appropriate spell in our cosmos, just as we'd use the things and symbols in Griswold's lab for a lifeline. If the kidnaper found himself unable to make it back with his victim, God alone knew what would happen. They'd certainly both leave our home and a changeling replace them. But we'd have no inkling of how this came about or where they'd gone. It might provide the exact chance the enemy needed to get his project back on the rails.

Outside, noise swelled—stamp, hop, clang, howl, whistle, grunt, gibber, bubble, hiss, yelp, whine, squawk, moan, bellow. The door reverberated under fists, feet, hoofs. I might well have to transform. I dropped the scuba gear and my outer garments, except for wrapping Barney's jacket around my left forearm.

A mouth, six feet wide and full of clashing teeth, floated through a wall. I yelled, Svartalf spat. Ginny grabbed her wand

and cried dismissal. The thing vanished. But thereafter she was continally interrupted to fight off such attacks.

She had to erect fortifications against them before she could begin the spell that would send us home. The latter ritual must not be broken off till at least a weak field had been established between this point and the lab on earth, or it became worthless. Having made initial contact, Ginny could feel out at leisure what balance of forces was required, and bring them up to the strength necessary for carrying us. Now she wasn't getting leisure. In consequence, her defensive construction went jaggedly and slowly.

The hullabaloo outside dwindled somewhat. I heard orders barked. Thuds and yammers suggested they were enforced with clubs. A galloping grew. The door rocked under a battering ram.

I stood aside. At the third blow, the door splintered and its hinges tore loose. The lead devil on the log stumbled through. He was rather like a man-sized cockroach. I cut him apart with a brisk sweep. The halves threshed and clawed for a while after they fell. They entangled the stag-horned being that came next, enabling me to take him with ease.

The others hauled back the log, which blocked the narrow entrance. But my kills remained as a partial barrier in front of me. The murk outside turned most of the garrison into shadows, though their noise stayed deafening and their odors revolting.

One trod forward in the shape of a gorilla on man's legs. He wielded an ax in proportion to his size. It hewed. Poised in karate stance, I shifted to let it go by. Chips sleeted where it hit stone. My cutlass sang. Fingers came off him. He dropped the ax. Bawling his pain, he cuffed at me. I did the fastest squat on record. While that skull-cracker of a hand boomed above, I got an Achilles tendon. He fell. I didn't try for a death, because he barred access while he dragged himself away. My pulse seethed in my ears.

A thing with sword and shield was next. We traded blows for a couple of minutes. He was good. I parried, except for slashes that the jacket absorbed; but I could not get past that shield. Metal clashed above the bedlam, sparks showered in twilight. My breath started coming hard. He pressed close. A notion flashed in me. As he cut over the top of his shield, I dropped down again. My weapon turned his, barely. My left hand grabbed the ax, stuck the helve between his legs, and shoved. He toppled, exposing his neck. I smote.

Rising, I threw the ax at the monster behind, who reeled back. A spear wielder poked at me. I got hold of the shaft and chopped it over.

No further candidates advanced right away. The mass churned around, arguing with itself. Through the hammering of my heart, I realized I couldn't hold out much longer. As human, that is. Here was a chance to assume the less vulnerable lyco state. I tossed my blade aside and turned the flash on myself.

At once I discovered that transformation was slow and agonizing amidst these influences. For a space I writhed helpless between shapes. A rooster-headed fiend cackled his glee and rushed forward, snickersnee on high. Were or no, I couldn't survive bisection. Svartalf bolted past me, walked up the enemy's abdomen, and clawed his eyes out.

Wolf, I resumed my post. The cat went back inside. We were just in time. The garrison finally got the idea of throwing stuff. Space grew thick with rocks, weapons, and assorted impedimenta. Most missed. Hell is no place to develop your throwing arm. Those that hit knocked me about, briefly in pain, but couldn't do any real damage.

The barrage ended when, in sheer hysteria, they tried to storm us. That was turmoil, slice, hack, rip, tumbling about in their vile welter. They might have overrun me by numbers had Ginny not finished her paranatural defenses and come to my aid. Her weapon disposed of the demons that crawled over the pile of struggling bodies.

When at last they withdrew, their dead and wounded were heaped high. I sat down amidst the ichor, the fragments, the lamentations, unreeled my tongue and gulped air. Ginny rumpled my fur, half laughing, half crying. Some claws had reached her; blood trickled from scratches and her dress was tattered into battle banners. Svartalf's aid had prevented her opponents from inflicting serious wounds, though. I glanced within and saw him playing mousey with a devil's tail.

More important was the soft luminosity from the lines woven across the floor. We were accessible as ever to physical force, but goetics couldn't touch us now. To break down her impalpable walls would take longer than we'd possibly stay.

"Steve, Steve, Steve—" Ginny straightened. "I'd better prepare for our return."

"Halt!" called a voice from the dusk. It was hoarse, with an eerie hypnotic rhythm, not calming, but, rather, invoking wrath

and blind energy. *"Waffenstillstand. Parlamentieren Sie mit uns."*

The devils, even the strewn wounded, fell quiet. Their noise sibilated away until the silence was nearly total, and those who could, withdrew until they merged in vision with the blackness behind them. I knew their master had spoken, the lord of this castle . . . who stood high in the Adversary's councils, if he commanded obedience from these mad creatures.

Boots clacked over flagstones. The demon chief came before us. The shape he had adopted startled me. Like his voice, it was human; but it was completely unmemorable. He was of medium height or less, narrow-shouldered, face homely and a bit puffy, ornamented with nothing but a small toothbrush mustache and a lock of dark hair slanting across the brow. He wore some kind of plain brown military uniform. But why did he add a red armband with the ancient and honorable sign of the fylfot?

Svartalf quit his game and bristled. Through diabolic stench, I caught the smell of Ginny's fear. When you looked into the eyes in that face, it stopped being ordinary. She braced herself, made a point of staring down along the couple of inches she overtopped him, and said in her haughtiest tone, *"Was willst du?"*

It was the *du* of insult. Her personal German was limited, but while Bolyai was in Svartalf she could tap his fluency by rapport with her familiar. (Why did the devil prince insist on German? There's a mystery here that I've never solved.) I retained sufficient human-type capabilities to follow along.

"I ask you the same," the enemy replied. Though he kept to the formal pronoun, his manner was peremptory. "You have encroached on our fatherland. You have flouted our laws. You have killed and maimed our gallant warriors when they sought to defend themselves. You desecrate our House of Sendings with your odious presence. What is your excuse?"

"We have come to gain back what is ours."

"Well? Say on."

I growled a warning, which Ginny didn't need. "If I told you, you might find ways to thwart us," she said. "Be assured, however, we don't intend to stay. We'll soon have completed our mission." Sweat glistened forth on her brow. "I . . . I suggest it will be to the advantage of both parties if you let us alone meanwhile."

He stamped a boot. "I must know! I demand to know! It is my right!"

"Diseases have no rights," Ginny said. "Think. You cannot pierce our spell-wall nor break through by violence in the time that is left. You can only lose troops. I do not believe your ultimate master would be pleased at such squandering of resources."

He waved his arms. His tone loudened. "I do not admit defeat. For me, defeat has no existence. If I suffer a reverse, it is because I have been stabbed in the back by traitors." He was heading off into half a trance. His words became a harsh, compelling chant. "We shall break the iron ring. We shall crush the vermin that infest the universes. We shall go on to victory. No surrender! No compromise! Destiny calls us onward!"

The mob of monsters picked up a cue and cried hail to him. Ginny said: "If you want to make an offer, make it. Otherwise go away. I've work to do."

His features writhed, but he got back the self-control to say: "I prefer not to demolish the building. Much effort and wizardry is in these stones. Yield yourselves and I promise fair treatment."

"What are your promises worth?"

"We might discuss, for example, the worldly gains rewarding those who serve the cause of the rightful—"

Svartalf mewed. Ginny spun about. I threw a look behind, as a new odor came to me. The kidnaper had materialized. Valeria lay in his grasp.

She was just coming awake, lashes aflutter, head turning, one fist to her lips. "Daddy?" the sleepy little voice murmured. "Mothuh?"

The thing that held her was actually of less weight. It wore an armor-plated spiky-backed body on two clawed feet, a pair of gibbon-like arms ending in similarly murderous talons, and a tiny head with blob features. Blood dripped off it here and there. The loose lips bubbled with an imbecilic grin, till it saw what was waiting.

It yowled an English, "Boss, help!" as it let Val go and tried to scuttle aside. Svartalf blocked the way. It raked at him. He dodged. Ginny got there. She stamped down. I heard a crunch. The demon ululated.

I'd stuck at my post. The lord of the castle tried to get past me. I removed a chunk of his calf. It tasted human, too, sort of. He retreated, into the shadow chaos of his appalled followers. Through their din I followed his screams: "I shall have revenge for this! I shall unleash a secret weapon! Let the House be destroyed! Our pride demands satisfaction! *My patience is exhausted!''*

I braced myself for a fresh combat. For a minute, I almost got one. But the baron managed to control his horde; the haranguing voice overrode theirs. As Ginny said, he couldn't afford more futile casualties.

I thought, as well as a wolf can: Good thing he doesn't know they might not have been futile this time.

For Ginny could not have aided me. After the briefest possible enfolding of her daughter, she'd given the kid to Svartalf. The familiar—and no doubt the mathematician—busied himself with dances, pounces, patty-cake and wurrawurra, to keep her out of her mother's hair. I heard the delighted laughter, like silver bells and springtime rain. But I heard, likewise, Ginny's incantation.

She must have about five unbroken minutes to establish initial contact with home, before she could stop and rest. Then she'd need an additional period to determine the precise configuration of vectors and gather the required paranatural energies. And then we'd go!

It clamored in the dark. An occasional missile flew at me, for no reason except hatred. I stood in the door and wondered if we had time.

A rumbling went through the air. The ground shuddered underfoot. The devils keened among shadows. I heard them retreating. Fear gripped me by the gullet. I have never done anything harder than to keep that guardian post.

The castle groaned at its foundations. Dislodged blocks slid from the battlements and crashed. Flamelight flickered out of cracks opened in gates and shutters. Smoke tried to strangle me. It passed, and was followed by the smell of ancient mold.

". . . *in nomine Potestatis, fiat janua . . . ,''* the witch's hurried verses ran at my back.

The giant upheaved himself.

Higher he stood than the highest spire of this stronghold beside which he had lain buried. The blackness of him blotted out the stars of hell. His tottering feet knocked a curtain wall down in a grinding roar; dust whirled up, earthquake ran. Nearly as loud was the rain of dirt, mud, gravel from the wrinkled skin. Fungi grew there, pallidly phosphorescent, and worms dripped from his eye sockets. The corruption of him seized the breath. The heat of his decay smoldered and radiated. He was dead; but the power of the demon was in him.

". . . *saeculi aeternitatis.*" Ginny had kept going till she could pause without danger to the spell. She was that kind of girl. But now she came to kneel by me. "Oh, darling," she wept, "we almost won through!"

I fumbled at my flash. The giant wove his head from side to side as if he still had vision. The faceless visage came to a stop, pointed our way. I shoved the switch and underwent the Skinturning back to human. The giant raised a foot. He who operated him was trying to minimize damage to the castle. Slowly, carefully, he set it down inside the fortifications.

I held my girl to me. My other girl laughed and romped with the cat. Why trouble them? "We've no chance?"

"I . . . no time . . . first-stage field ready, b-b-but flesh can't cross before I . . . complete— I love you, I love you."

I reached for Decatur's sword where it gleamed in the Handlight. We've come to the end of creation, I thought, and we'll die here. Let's go out fighting. Maybe our souls can escape.

Souls!

I grabbed Ginny by the shoulder and thrust her back to look at. "We can send for help," burst from me. "Not mortals, and angels're forbidden, but, but you do have contact established and . . . the energy state of this universe—it doesn't take a lot to— There's bound to be many c-creatures, not of Heaven but still no friends of hell—"

Her eyes kindled. She sprang erect, seized wand and sword, swung them aloft and shouted.

The giant stepped into our courtyard. The crippled devils gibbered their terror, those he did not crush underfoot. His fingers closed around the tower.

I couldn't tell what language Ginny's formula was in, but she ended her cry in English: "Ye who knew man and were enemies of Chaos, by the mana of the signs we bear I call on you and tell you that the way from earth stands open!"

The chapel rocked. Stones fell, inside and outside. The tower came off. It broke apart in the giant's clutch, a torrent that buried the last of hell's wounded. We looked into lightless constellations. The giant groped to scoop us out.

Our rescuers arrived.

I don't know who or what they were. Perhaps their looks were illusion. I'll admit that the quarters of the compass were from which they came, because these are nonsense in hell. Perhaps what answered Ginny's call was simply a group of beings, from our universe or yet another, who were glad of a chance to raid the realm of the Adversary that is theirs too. She had built a bridge that was, as yet, too frail to bear mortal bodies. However, as I'd guessed, the entropy of the Low Continuum made paranatural forces able to accomplish what was impossible elsewhere.

Explain it as you like. This is what I saw:

From the west, the figure of a woman, queenly in blue-bordered white robe. Her eyes were gray, her features of icicle beauty. The dark tresses bore a crested helmet. Her right hand carried a spear whose head shimmered midnight azure with glitters as of earthly stars; and upon that shoulder sat an owl. On her left arm was a long shield, which for boss had the agonized face of another woman whose locks were serpents.

From the south, the greatest serpent of them all. His orbs were like suns, his teeth like white knives. Plumes of rainbow color grew on his head, nodding in the wind he brought with him, shining with droplets of the rain that walked beneath. More feathers made a glory down his back. His scales were coral, the scutes upon his belly shone golden. The coils of him lashed about as does the lightning.

From the north, a man in a chariot drawn by two goats. He stood burly, red-bearded, clad in helmet and ringmail, iron gloves and an iron belt. Driving with his left hand, he gripped a short-handled hammer in his right. The cloak blew behind him on mighty gales. The rumble of his car wheels went down and down the sky. He laughed, swung the hammer and threw it. Where it struck, fire blasted and the air roared; it returned to him.

Each of these loomed so tall that the firmament would hardly contain them. Hell trembled at their passage. The devils fled in a cloud. When his master left, the giant's animation ceased. He fell with an impact that knocked me off my feet. It demolished a large part of the castle. The newcomers didn't stop to level the rest right away, but took off after the fiends. I don't imagine that many escaped.

We didn't watch. Ginny completed the transfer spell and seized Valeria in both her arms. I tucked Decatur's sword under one of mine—damn if it'd be left here!—and offered Svartalf the crook of that elbow. From the floor I plucked up the kidnaper demon. It had a broken leg. "Boss, don't hurt me, I'll be good, I'll talk, I'll tell ya ever't'ing ya want," it kept whining. Evil has no honor.

Ginny spoke the final word, made the final pass. We crossed.

XXXIV

THAT WAS NOTHING like the outbound trip. We were headed back where we belonged. The cosmic forces didn't buck us, they worked for us. We knew a moment of whirling, and were there.

Barney's gang waited in the lab. They sprang back with a cry, a sob, a prayer of thanks as we whoofed into sight under the bell jar. It turned out that we'd only been absent a couple of hours from this continuum. And maybe no more in hell? We couldn't be sure, our watches having stopped during the first transition. It felt like centuries. I looked upon Valeria and Ginny, and it felt like no time.

The child was blinking those big heaven-colored eyes around in astonishment. It struck me that the terrible things she'd witnessed might have scarred her for life. Shakily, I bent over her. "Are you okay, sweetheart?"

"Ooh, Daddy," she beamed. " 'At was fun. Do it again?"

Ginny set her down. I bent and swept the little one to me. She was restless. "I'm hungry," she complained.

I'd let the prisoner go. After the bell jar was raised, it tried to creep off. But it couldn't leave the pentacle, and Barney had laid the spell I asked for that prevented it from returning to the Low Continuum without our leave. Shining Knife had gotten his warrant. He waited too, with a number of his men. He strode in among us and lifted the demon by its sound leg. The grotesque figure sprattled in his grasp. "Boss, gimme a break, boss," it begged. "I'll squeal."

We found out later that the diabolic mass exchanged for us was a heap of rocks, dirt, and similar material. It happened to include a considerable amount of elemental sulfur, pitch, and light hydrocarbons. Hardy and Griswold had passed some time rearranging this into an explosive-incendiary configuration. Following my request, they mixed in some earthly stuff as well. It had to be safe for us, in case little or none of it got swapped (and in fact, as you see, only a few pounds did). The team scurried around collecting bottles of strong acid, shotgun shells, razor blades, and whatnot. Barney then rigged a photocell-controlled gizmo that would ignite the whole mess the exact instant that it left our universe. I don't suppose that whatever part of hell it materialized in was done any good.

The changeling, of course, vanished from the juvenile home when Valeria was restored. Poor flesh, I hope it was allowed to die.

I didn't think of these matters immediately. Being sure our daughter was well, Ginny and I sought each other. What broke our kiss was a joy greater yet, a happiness whose echo will never stop chiming in us: *"Free! O Father!"* And when we could look at this world again, Svartalf was only Svartalf.

The gracious presence within me said: —Yes, for this deed János Bolyai is made a saint and admitted to the nearness of God. How glad I am. And how glad you won your cause, dear friends, and Valeria Stevenovna is safe and the enemies of the Highest confounded! (Shyly) I have a selfish reason for additional pleasure, be it confessed. What I observed on this journey has given me some fascinating new ideas. A rigorous theoretical treatment—

I sensed the wish that Lobachevsky could not bring himself to think overtly, and uttered it for him: You'd like to stick around awhile?

—Frankly, yes. A few days, after which I must indeed return. It would be marvelous to explore these discoveries, not as a soul, but once again as a mortal. It is like a game, Steven Pavlovitch. One would like to see how far it is possible to go within the constraints of humanity. (In haste) But I beg you, esteemed friend, do not consider this a request. Your lady and yourself have endured perils, hardships, and fear of losing more than your lives. You wish to celebrate your triumph. Believe me, I would never be so indelicate as to—

I looked fondly, a trifle wistfully at Ginny and thought back: I know what you mean, Nick, and I've every intention of celebrating with her, at frequent intervals, till we reach an implausibly ripe old age. But you've forgotten that the flesh has physical as well as mental limits. She needs a good rest. I need a better one. You might as well stay for a bit. Besides, I want to see that what you write goes to the proper journals. It'll be quite a boost for our side.

And this is how it happened that, although Bolyai led our expedition, Lobachevsky published first.

XXXV

THERE'S NO SUCH thing as living happily ever after.

You'd like to be famous? You can have it, buster: every last reporter, crystal interview, daily ton of mail, pitch for Worthy Causes, autograph hound, belligerent drunk, crank phone call, uninvited visitor, sycophant, and you name it. Luckily, we followed sound advice and played loose. I ended up with a better position than I probably rate, Ginny with the free-lance studio she'd always wanted, and we're no longer especially newsworthy. Meanwhile Valeria's gotten to the boy-friend stage, and none of them seem worthy of her. They tell me every father of a girl goes through that. The other children keep me too busy to fret much.

It *was* quite a story. The demon's public confession brought the Johannine Church down in spectacular style. We've got its diehards around yet, but they're harmless. Then there's the reformed sect of it—where my old sparring partner Marmiadon is prominent—that tries to promulgate the Gospel of Love as merely another creed. Since the Gnosticism and the secret diabolism are out, I don't expect that either St. Peter or gentle St. John greatly mind.

Before he left me for Heaven, Lobachevsky proved some theorems I don't understand. I'm told they've doubled the effectiveness of the spells that Barney's people worked out in those long-ago terrible hours. Our buddy Bob Shining Knife had a lot to do with arranging sensible dissemination of the new knowledge. It has to be classified; you can't trust any old nut with the capabilities conferred. However, the United States government is not the only one that knows how to invade hell if provoked. The armies of Earth couldn't hope to conquer it, but they could make big trouble, and Heaven would probably intervene. As a result, we've no cause to fear other direct assaults from the Adversary's dominion. From men, yes—because he still tempts, corrupts, seduces, tricks, and betrays. But I think

PORTLAND / OR Legacy Good Sam XN series   tech

Position:
Doctor: 02/03/2022 19:21:18 BF
Birth:
Nickname: XN-2000-1-R
            Sex:

WDF   WNR

if we keep our honor clean and our powder dry we won't suffer more than we can bear.

Looking back, I often can't believe it happened: that this was done by a red-haired witch, a bobtailed werewolf, and a snooty black tomcat. Then I remember it's the Adversary who is humorless. I'm sure God likes to laugh.

SCIENCE FICTION BESTSELLERS
FROM BERKLEY

Frank Herbert

DUNE   (03698-7—$2.25)

DUNE MESSIAH   (03585-9—$1.75)

CHILDREN OF DUNE   (03310-4—$1.95)

Philip José Farmer

THE FABULOUS RIVERBOAT   (03378-3—$1.50)

NIGHT OF LIGHT   (03366-X—$1.50)

TO YOUR SCATTERED
BODIES GO   (03175-6—$1.75)

*   *   *   *   *   *   *

STRANGER IN
A STRANGE LAND   (03782-7—$2.25)
  by Robert A. Heinlein

TAU ZERO   (03909-9—$1.75)
  by Poul Anderson

THE WORD FOR
WORLD IS FOREST   (03466-6—$1.75)
  by Ursula K. Le Guin

Send for a list of all our books in print.

These books are available at your local bookstore, or send price indicated plus 30¢ for postage and handling. If more than four books are ordered, only $1.00 is necessary for postage. Allow three weeks for delivery. Send orders to:

Berkley Book Mailing Service
P.O. Box 690
Rockville Centre, New York 11570

FANTASY FROM BERKLEY

Robert E. Howard

JOURNEY THROUGH TIME AND SPACE

IN 1942 THE U.S. RATIONED GASOLINE

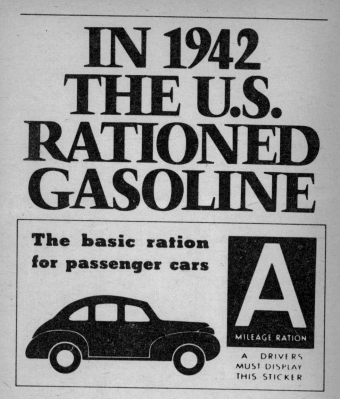

The basic ration for passenger cars

A

MILEAGE RATION

A DRIVERS MUST DISPLAY THIS STICKER

That was wartime and the spirit of sacrifice was in the air. No one liked it, but everyone went along. Today we need a wartime spirit to solve our energy problems. A spirit of thrift in our use of all fuels, especially gasoline. We Americans pump over 200 million gallons of gasoline into our automobiles each day. That is nearly one-third the nation's total daily oil consumption and more than half of the oil we import every day . . . at a cost of some $40 billion a year. So con serving gasoline is more than a way to save money at the pump and help solve the nation's balance of payments, it also can tackle a major portion of the nation's energy problem. And that is something we all have a stake in doing . . . with the wartime spirit, but without the devastation of war or the incon venience of rationing.

ENERGY CONSERVATION - IT'S YOUR CHANCE TO SAVE, AMERICA

Department of Energy, Washington, D.C.